T[...] SEVEN FABU[...] [...]NDERS OF THE ANCIENT WORLD

THE GREAT PYRAMID OF GIZA

THE HANGING GARDENS OF BABYLON

THE TEMPLE OF ARTEMIS AT EPHESOS

THE MAUSOLEUM AT HALICARNASSOS

THE STATUE OF ZEUS AT OLYMPIA

THE COLOSSUS OF RHODES

THE PHAROS AT ALEXANDRIA

For Sue, who played the first game.

For more information about Katherine Roberts, visit
www.katherineroberts.com

First published in Great Britain by Collins Voyager 2002
HarperCollins *Children's Books* is a division of HarperCollins*Publishers* Ltd
77-85 Fulham Palace Road, Hammersmith
London W6 8JB

The HarperCollins *Children's Books* website address is:
www.harpercollinschildrensbooks.co.uk

3

Translations from *Prayers of the Lifting of the Hand*,
translated by Leonard W. King
Illustrations by Fiona Land

ISBN 0 00 711279 3

Printed and bound in England by
Clays Ltd, St Ives plc

Katherine Roberts

THE BABYLON GAME

HarperCollins *Children's Books*

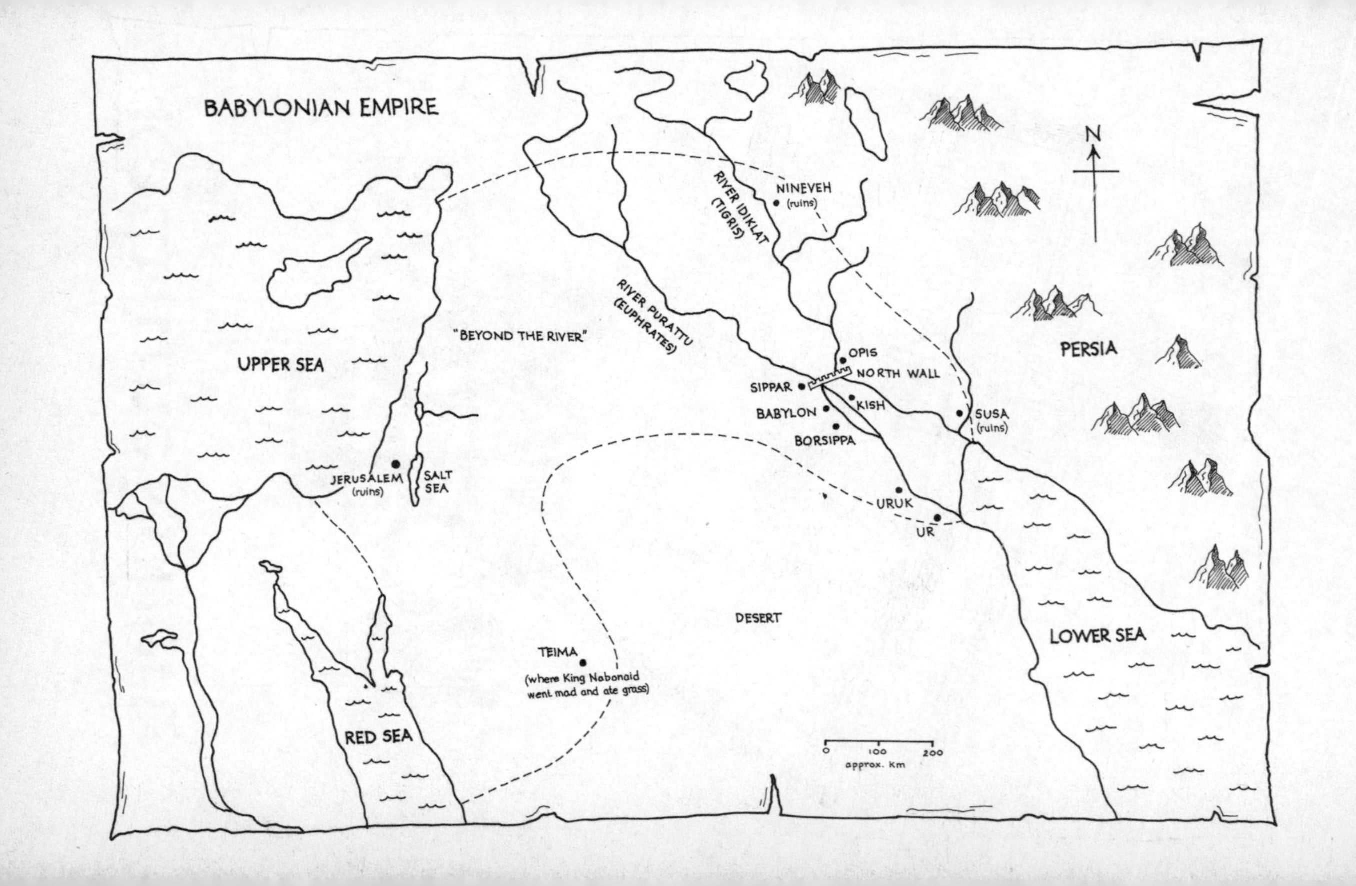
BABYLONIAN EMPIRE
N
UPPER SEA
"BEYOND THE RIVER"
RIVER IDIKLAT (TIGRIS)
NINEVEH (ruins)
RIVER PURATTU (EUPHRATES)
OPIS
NORTH WALL
SIPPAR
KISH
BABYLON
BORSIPPA
SUSA (ruins)
PERSIA
JERUSALEM (ruins)
SALT SEA
URUK
UR
DESERT
LOWER SEA
TEIMA
(where King Nabonaid went mad and ate grass)
RED SEA
0 100 200
approx. Km

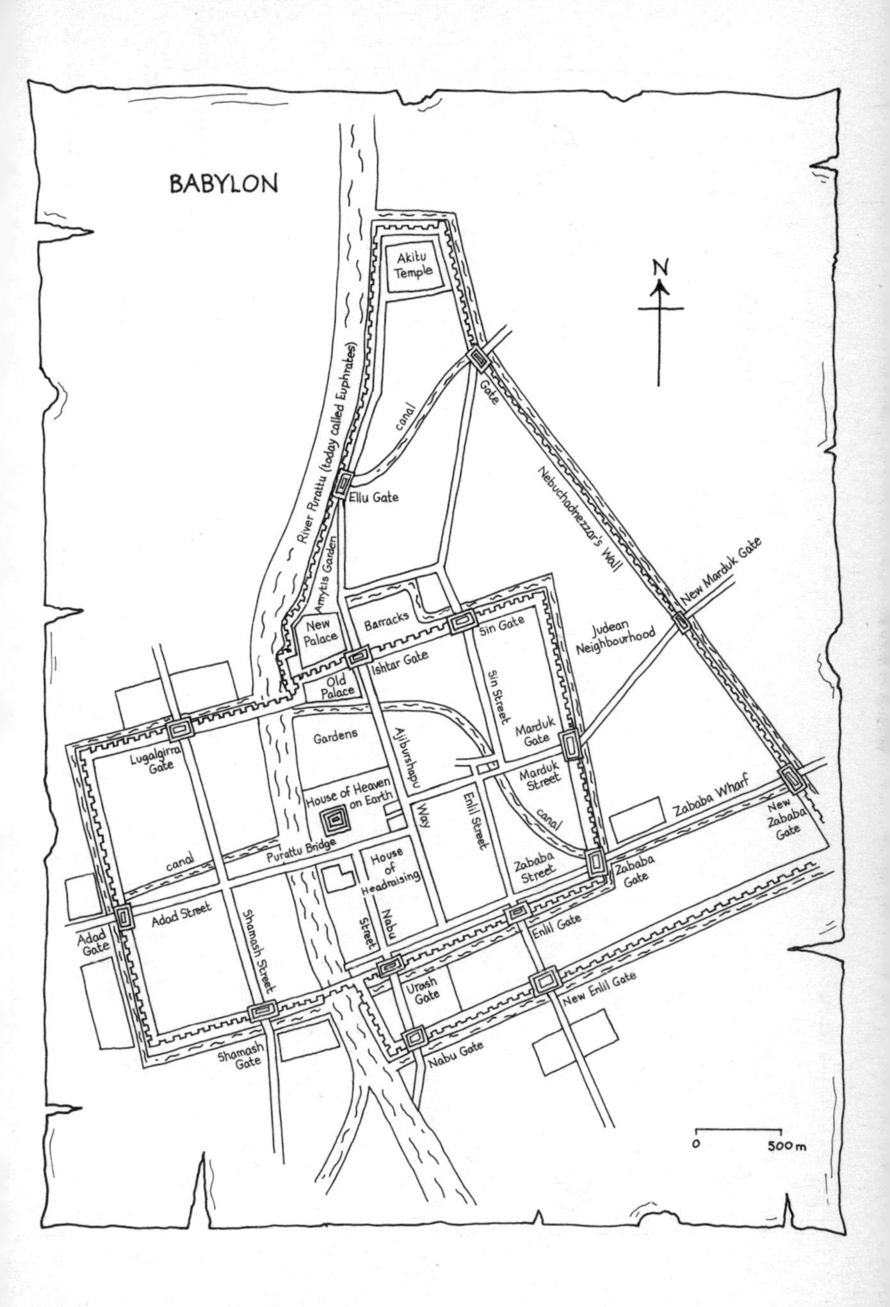

BABYLON
N
Akitu Temple
Gate
canal
River Purattu (today called Euphrates)
Ellu Gate
Nebuchadnezzar's Wall
New Marduk Gate
Amytis Garden
New Palace
Barracks
Sin Gate
Judean Neighbourhood
Ishtar Gate
Old Palace
Sin Street
Gardens
Ajiburshapu Way
Marduk Gate
Lugalgirra Gate
Marduk Street
House of Heaven on Earth
Enlil Street
canal
Zababa Wharf
New Zababa Gate
canal
Purattu Bridge
House of Headraising
Zababa Street
Zababa Gate
Adad Street
Shamash Street
Nabu Street
Enlil Gate
Adad Gate
Urash Gate
New Enlil Gate
Shamash Gate
Nabu Gate
0
500 m

RIDDLE OF PRINCESS AMYTIS' SEAL

A garden with a foundation like heaven,
A stairway where Shamash and Sin stroll hand in hand,
A gate which like a copper drum has been covered with skin,
Blessed of Marduk has opened it,
Ishtar's Gift comes out of it.

EGIBI TWENTY SQUARES TEAM

26th Ululu

Gamesmaster

ANDULLI	Egibi Family of Babylon

Team

ENKI	Master Andulli's son, Enlil Street, inner city
SIMEON	Jacob's son, Judean Neighbourhood, outer city
HILLALUM	farmer's son, country
MUNA	astrologer's daughter, outer city
IKUPPI	Zerim's son, inner city

Reserve

LABINSIN	Ikuppi's best friend, inner city

Chapter 1

SIRRUSH

When I plan, let me attain my purpose!

TAKING HER FRIEND halfway across Babylon in the middle of the night was stupid, Tiamat knew. If they were caught, they'd both be in big trouble. But she had to get into the Twenty Squares Team, and before Simeon would agree to help her, he wanted to know why someone who showed so little talent for the game should care about such things. Telling Simeon was never enough. He had to see with his own eyes.

She'd waited until a luck-night to bring him, though she wasn't sure the luck would hold if only one of them believed in it. Shrugging her pouch into a more comfortable position, she wiped her sweaty hands on her dress and glanced back to make sure her friend was still following. In the starlit streets, with their towering battlements, Simeon moved like a small, dark ghost.

He flashed her a smile as he caught up. "Where's this

great secret of yours, then?"

Tiamat frowned. "In the princess's garden, I told you. Shh! Sentry."

Simeon froze, his thin face raised to the double wall that separated the inner and outer cities. They were close to Sin Gate. As usual at this time of night, the massive bronze-barred gates were firmly shut. The moat outside was oily and choked with waste that the people of the outer city had thrown into it. Holding their noses, they waited in the shadows until the slap of a soldier's sandals patrolling the battlements had passed. Then Tiamat took Simeon's hand and dragged him across torchlit Sin Street into the unlit alleys beyond.

She let out her breath. Her heart was hammering far more than it did when she made this journey alone. She experienced a flicker of guilt at putting her friend in danger. "You sure you still want to come?" she whispered.

The boy grinned, more relaxed now that they were safely across the lighted street. "I can't wait to see what's so important that you'd risk Master Andulli's wrath."

Her determination returned. "I'm not asking you to get me into the Team so I can *play*," she said, leading the way confidently through the maze of alleys. "Only as Reserve. Just so I can get into the Palace with you."

He gave her a quizzical look. "And what happens if someone's ill and we need our Reserve player?"

"You won't. No one's going to be ill."

"How do you know?"

Tiamat sighed. "Please, Simeon. All I'm asking is for you to lose a few times when you're playing me so Master Andulli thinks I'm good enough to be Reserve. The others won't think you're useless or anything. You can still beat them like you normally do."

Simeon grimaced. "Not all of them."

"You know what I mean!" she said. "If you're not going to help me, there's no point you coming any further. I'll think of another way to get in."

Except she couldn't. There were four thick, high walls and several moats between the outer city and the Palace, each lookout tower manned by a patrol of King Nabonaid's soldiers, more paranoid than ever after the current rumour that the Persian army had taken Opis and breached the North Wall. And even if she did manage to get in on her own, what then? The whole point was to get out again.

Simeon touched her arm. His fingers were cold. "I'll help you all I can, you know that. I just want to see why you're so determined to get in the Team. There might be a better way."

Tiamat gave him a wry smile. Same old Simeon. In the Club, they teased him because he always thought out every possible consequence before he moved.

"There isn't a better way," she said. "You'll understand when you see what I found."

"What you found?" Simeon raised an eyebrow.

"What I found," she said firmly, grasping his hand again. "C'mon!"

As they neared the Ajiburshapu Way, Simeon went quiet again. This street, being the ancient approach to Babylon, was bordered by high, blue walls that closed it off from the rest of the city. It separated the gardens and New Palace complex on the river bank from the common neighbourhoods of the outer city where Tiamat and Simeon lived. If they were caught here, they had some explaining to do. Simeon kept watch while Tiamat quietly opened the little access gate in the wall.

She glanced up and down the starlit street, her heart thudding again. The life-sized lions that paraded along the blue walls almost seemed alive. They waited until another patrolling sentry had passed before scrambling up the steps on to the paved surface of the Way and making a dash for the other side. Tiamat fumbled the second gate in the shadows and Simeon, racing down the steps behind her, knocked her into a thicket growing inside.

"Steady!" She fought her way out of the bushes with a giggle. "They're not real lions, you know."

He blinked back up at the Ajiburshapu Way. "I know. It's just that I've heard people talk about them, but I never thought they'd be so... realistic."

Tiamat closed the street gate and gave Simeon a disbelieving look. "Don't tell me you've never sneaked a look at them before now?"

He flushed. "Judeans aren't allowed on the Ajiburshapu Way."

"Oh, Simeon!" She giggled again. "If people stopped

doing things just because they weren't allowed, they'd never see anything interesting at all! You're not allowed in the princess's garden either, remember?"

The boy looked round at the lush vegetation, his eyes searching the shadows. "It's different for you. So where's this secret of yours?"

"This way."

Star-silvered leaves and wonderful scents surrounded them as they climbed the overgrown terraces. Water dripped endlessly from the neglected irrigation system. Interlaced branches formed tunnels overhead, creating secret paths where the noise of thc city was muted and the crowds never came.

Tiamat took the next flight of steps two at a time, pausing at the top to let Simeon catch up. "Wait here." She pushed through a tangle of sweetly-scented jasmine into the shadows beyond.

Simeon peered after her as she felt around the cracked stone basin, into the little recess at the back of the broken fountain. Her heart gave a leap of relief when her fingers brushed the small cylinder hidden within. Although no one ever came up here, she always expected to find it gone.

"Tia?" Simeon's voice was tense. "You still in there?"

She teased the cylinder out of its hiding place and pushed back through the vines, making Simeon jump.

He looked curiously at her hand. "Is that it? Show me, then."

Tiamat exposed the cylinder to the starlight. It filled

her palm, blue and mysterious. The stone had been engraved with a grid of tiny, wedge-shaped characters beside a picture that included trees growing over sun, moon and star symbols. Beneath these was a stepped triangle, and inside the triangle was a robed figure holding out its hand to a strange creature. She turned the cylinder and showed it to Simeon. "What does that look like to you?"

Simeon looked a bit disappointed. "It's just someone's old seal."

"I know that! It's what's on it that's interesting." She pointed to the picture again.

"It looks like the ziqqurat with trees growing on it. So what? Maybe Marduk's priests are going to take up gardening."

Tiamat controlled an urge to thump him. "Underneath the ziqqurat. That creature – do you recognize it?"

"Looks like some sort of dragon." Simeon frowned. "I don't get it. Why do you need to get into the Palace if your secret is right here in the garden? You're allowed to come here whenever you like. Where did you find it, anyway?"

Tiamat sucked her lower lip and touched the engraving. "In the fountain, ages ago. I thought it was just a picture like the mouldings on the Ishtar Gate, but last week I saw..." She looked up, to where the terraces climbed to the height of Nebuchadnezzar's city wall, and took a deep breath. "Them."

Simeon looked blank.

"Real ones," Tiamat added, pointing to the creature engraved on the cylinder.

"Real what?"

"Real sirrush – real dragons."

He stared at her as if she were as mad as the old King. Then he grinned. "Now you're having me on."

"No, I'm not. I've seen them! They run between the double walls of the inner city – and they're half starved, Simeon! They're only let out at night. I've been bringing them food, but they never eat it. That's why I have to get into the Palace. I have to find out where the sirrush are being kept and what they eat, so I can help them."

Simeon shook his head. "You and your animals! Feeding stray dogs and pigs is one thing, Tia, but whatever's between those walls belongs to the King." His dark eyes were serious. "Are you sure you didn't see a goat or something?"

"I know a goat when I see one! These are definitely sirrush. They're supposed to be Marduk's creatures, aren't they? The sentries must've let them out because the Persians are coming."

Simeon was still shaking his head. Tiamat sighed. She might have known he wouldn't believe her.

"All right," she said. "I'll prove it to you."

She dropped the seal into her pouch on top of the scraps she'd brought for the sirrush and led the way up more flights of steps. Simeon followed in silence, saving his breath for the climb. When they broke through the canopy under a sky blazing with stars, they were both panting. They had bits of twig caught in their hair and their tunics were damp with sweat. Tiamat's head spun with the height and the sudden view. Beside her, Simeon whistled softly. They had emerged level with the battlements of Nebuchadnezzar's Wall. The plain stretched away beneath them, glittering with the silver ribbons of canals. The narrow gap between the highest terrace and the wall was filled with ropes and equipment to lift water from the river.

Simeon peered down at it with interest.

Tiamat pulled him back and pointed at the battlements between the two lookout towers opposite. "The sentries never bother to do the last bit from here to the corner," she whispered. "If we time it right, we can get across before anyone sees us. That branch reaches right over to the wall. It's a long drop, so don't look down. I'll go first and wave when it's clear. All right?"

Simeon eyed the branch doubtfully as she started across. For a moment, hanging upside-down over the dizzy gap with her legs wrapped around the branch and her pouch dragging at her shoulder, Tiamat wondered if he was going to follow. But when she dropped safely on the broad battlements and waved, the boy wriggled across like a little dark snake. She put a finger to her lips. They ran, crouched double to keep their heads below the parapet, round the corner of the new palace to the junction where Nebuchadnezzar's Wall met the double inner city wall. They crouched in the shadows, breathing hard and listening for the tell-tale slap of soldiers' sandals.

When she was certain no sentries were in sight, Tiamat wormed on her stomach between two of the crenellations and pointed down at the strip of dust that ran between the double wall. "There!"

Simeon lay beside her and peered down. "I can't see anything."

The gap between the walls was in shadow, but the sirrush's unique smell – part lion, part snake – was strong.

"They're probably round the other side of the city," Tiamat said, disappointed. "We'll have to wait."

Simeon smiled. "Come on, Tia. Admit it. You made the dragons up. You just didn't think I'd come this far." He wriggled back to safety and gave her a measuring look. "Tell you what. If you want to be in the Team that much, why don't you let me give you some lessons in strategy? It'd improve your game no end, and maybe Master Andulli will consider you for next year."

"Next year will be too late!" Tiamat swung a leg over the parapet.

Simeon's eyes widened in alarm. "What are you doing?"

"What does it look like I'm doing? I'm going down to fetch them."

"Down *there*?" His voice was full of fear for her. "But you can't! If the sentries see you, they'll think you're a Persian and put an arrow in you!"

Tiamat's heart was thudding and her palms were sweaty again. But now she'd started, she couldn't go back without losing face. She'd seen the rough steps cut into the join of the walls before tonight, but without Simeon's goading she'd never have had the courage to venture down them.

Simeon was trying to talk her out of it, promising to help her get in the Team anyway, dragons or no dragons. Ignoring him, she felt for the first step with her toes. It was uneven and smaller than she'd thought, but the next one wasn't far beneath it and the two great walls enclosing her in their corner made her feel safer. She braced her hands against the bricks and slowly made her way down into the shadows.

"Don't be so stupid, Tia! I believe you. Come back!"

There was real panic in Simeon's voice. She paused. His head was outlined against the stars, his hair hanging round his thin cheeks as he peered down at her. She waved, forcing a grin. "Don't worry. It's perfectly safe."

"If you don't come back up here right now, I'll call the guard!"

She stopped. The way he glanced over his shoulder told her he'd do it, in spite of the trouble they'd be in.

"I won't be long," she called. "You keep watch for the sentries."

As she descended, the smell grew stronger. The battlements loomed overhead, seeming a lot higher and thicker than they did from the streets of the outer city. The lower layers of bricks were crumbling. About three quarters of the way down, her foot slipped and Simeon hissed, "Look out!" She dug her nails into the steps, her heart hammering and her breath shallow. When she raised her head, Simeon was pointing urgently past her. She found a firmer foothold and twisted her head.

A draught stirred the dust between the walls. The smell increased. Then the creatures rounded the corner, running swift and low on their taloned hind feet with a peculiar, lizard-like gait, scaly necks extended and long tails stretched behind for balance. Six sirrush, the size of large camels, closer than she'd ever seen them before.

Tiamat's heart pounded with excitement. Holding on with her right hand, she felt in her pouch with her left and slowly extracted a bruised pomegranate.

The leader's horn gleamed as the creature raised itself on its hind legs. A forked tongue flickered out, tasting the air. Its forelegs, lion-pawed, hung motionless. Tiamat was close enough to see every rib of its half-starved body and every fiery spine along its neck. As she stared into its eyes, she forgot the danger she was in, forgot Simeon waiting for her on the wall, forgot everything except the creatures trapped below.

She felt her way down two more steps and leant backwards, hand with the pomegranate outstretched, aching to touch the leader's soft muzzle. She still wasn't quite low enough. But as she was trying to pluck up the courage to descend another step, the creature raised its head a little and its tongue flickered out to lay a cool, shivery kiss across her fingertips.

She held her breath. It was as if she were on the edge of something wonderful and exciting, like the night before a big festival. The sirrush's tongue quested around the pomegranate. Very slowly, its lips closed on the bruised fruit—

A shout from the top of the wall broke the spell. Just as the sirrush was about to take the fruit from her hand, feet pounded above and rough voices split the night. Helmets and spears glittered in the starlight as a row of heads peered over the parapet.

"Is it the Persians?" they shouted. "Get 'em, boys! Gore the barbarians to death!"

Simeon's head had disappeared. The patrol on Nebuchadnezzar's Wall, alerted by all the shouting, had arrived at the junction, and the two sets of sentries shouted questions across the gap. This spooked the sirrush still further. The creature below Tiamat spat out the pomegranate and gave an angry hiss, clawing the air with its forefeet. She hastily scrambled further up the steps as a large paw raked crumbling brick from the wall where her leg had been only moments before. The rest of the herd flung themselves at the walls as well, trying in vain to reach the men at the top.

Tiamat glared up at the sentries, too angry to be afraid. "Go away!" she yelled. "Can't you see you're scaring them?"

At the sound of her voice, the men peered down in alarm and raised their spears, searching the shadows for a target. One of them cursed. "Marduk's Teeth! There's a child down there!"

The other sentries stared down at Tiamat in disbelief. "How did she get down there?" … "Did she fall?" … "Is she hurt?" They sounded more amazed than angry. Then a trained voice boomed, "GET BACK UP HERE THIS DOUBLE-MINUTE, YOU STUPID GIRL!" and reality kicked in.

Tiamat looked down, wondering if she could make a run for it. But the sirrush, crazed by the scent of the men, were still hissing and clawing at the walls. They might hurt her without meaning to. Besides, there was Simeon.

Resigned, she climbed back up the crumbling steps. It was easier than going down. But by the time she reached the top of the wall, her tunic was stuck to her back and she was trembling with delayed reaction.

Strong hands helped her over the parapet. The men shook their heads. She pushed back her hair and stood straighter. One of the soldiers kept hold of her arm with a firm grip. Nearby, Simeon was similarly held. He looked pale but gave her a little smile of relief when he saw she was in one piece. Some of the sentries smiled, too.

"This is no laughing matter!" snapped the man who had shouted for Tiamat to come up. Hands on hips, he frowned at the two children. His beard and hair were curled and oiled and he wore the long, blue cloak of an officer. His stern gaze settled on Tiamat. "What in Marduk's Name were you doing down there? You're very lucky to be alive, Green-Eyes."

Tiamat scowled. People were always picking on her eyes, as if they'd never seen anyone with green eyes before. Her trembling eased, replaced by fear for her friend. "Let Simeon go," she said. "He didn't do anything. It was my fault. I made him come."

"She didn't— " Simeon began, but the officer cut him off with a raised hand.

"Trespassing on the walls of the inner city is a serious offence," he said, still frowning. "I could have you both arrested as Persian spies – your parents, too."

Simeon went paler still.

But one of the sentries, who had been peering closely at Tiamat, said, "I know this girl, sir! She's the perfume-maker's daughter. She often comes to the princess's old garden to collect plants and things. Is that what you were doing, girl?"

Tiamat breathed a little easier, seeing a way out. "Yes! Lady Nanname sent me to pick some herbs that have to be gathered on a moonless night, and Simeon had to come along to... to... help me carry them. Because they're so heavy," she finished lamely.

The officer turned his frown back on her. "And you were going to take so long gathering these heavy herbs that you brought a picnic?" He eyed the contents of her pouch, which she hadn't had a chance to throw down to the sirrush. Too late, she remembered the seal. She quickly jiggled it to the bottom. But the officer didn't seem interested in searching through the overripe fruit and soiled vegetables she'd collected earlier that day from the rubbish heaps of the outer city. "Lies will not help your case, Green-Eyes," he said. "What were you doing on the wall?"

Tiamat decided to tell the truth. "I only brought the sirrush some food. They're so hungry! It's cruel keeping them down there in the dark."

The officer's lips twitched. "Is that so? You know better than the King's advisors, do you? Sirrush are dangerous creatures. There's a good reason they're kept in the dark."

"They're not dangerous! You scared them. I almost—"

"Almost got yourself poisoned, and me in a whole lot of trouble for letting a child get killed on my patrol." The officer's smile vanished as he addressed his men. "Escort these two home and make sure their parents know exactly where they were caught. Warn the Lady Nanname that should she or her daughter abuse their privileges in future, she will no longer be permitted to use plants from the Amytis Garden. Tell the Judeans that should their son be found on the walls again, they will be turned out of their home, have their possessions confiscated, and be banished from the city to cut reeds in the marshes. Take a scribe with you. I want both their names entered on the List of First Offenders as an example to their friends. This sort of prank stops right here!"

He jabbed a finger at the wall beneath their feet and turned back to Tiamat and Simeon. "What if the Persians had attacked the city while we were wasting time rescuing you two? The King and that lazy, spoilt son of his might think we can rely on our walls to keep the enemy out, but it'll take more than bricks and bitumen this time. You mark my words."

The men shuffled their feet and avoided their officer's gaze, as if they'd heard all this before. Tiamat and Simeon stared at each other in dismay as the sentries straightened their helmets. Neither of them spoke as they were marched down one of the access stairways and through the dark streets of the outer city. Tiamat was worrying about her hand, which was tingling strangely where the sirrush had licked it, while Simeon walked with his head down and his hair shadowing his face.

Why had she been so stupid as to take him up on the wall? He'd never agree to help her now.

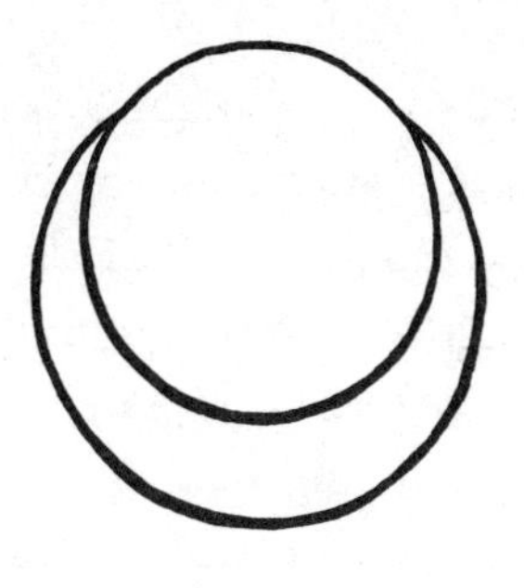

Chapter 2

ROYAL SEAL

May thine angry heart have rest!

TIAMAT HAD EXPECTED to be punished. Nanname was often stricter with her adopted daughter than the other outer city mothers were with their children. But a whole week had passed since the sentries had thumped on the perfume-maker's door in the middle of the night and handed over their tangle-haired charge.

That night, there had been simply a hard look and bed without supper. In the morning, Tiamat endured the expected lecture. Then it was straight downstairs to the laboratory, where Nanname had kept her busy ever since. Not once had she been allowed outside the house, not even to replenish their stocks of herbs and petals from the princess's garden. When Simeon came round to see why she hadn't turned up for Twenty Squares Club, she wasn't allowed to talk to him.

The steamy ground floor room with its single, clay-grille window and vats of boiling greenery was starting to feel like a prison. Nanname sat on her usual high stool with her crutch leaning against the bench. She plucked the petals off a heap of white roses in silence, glancing up only to tell Tiamat to stir faster or to watch she didn't break an irreplaceable glass tube. Tiamat could hardly bear it. Several times she opened her mouth, only to close it again when Nanname's expression warned her excuses would do no good. She dropped another handful of rose petals into the vat and stirred vigorously. The steam made her eyes water.

Outside, the sun was shining and the sky was an unbroken blue. Laughter and the cries of traders carried from the market down at Zababa Wharf. Tiamat clenched her fist on the stirring rod. The end that went in the vat was glass but the handle was of cedar. She wasn't supposed to let the handle touch the liquid in case impurities got into the perfume, but right now she didn't care. She stared longingly at the open door, her imagination creating sirrush out of the shadows cast by the steam. A frustrated tear trickled down her cheek and the fingers of her left hand gave another of their strange tingles. Before she could prevent it, the rod slipped through them.

"Careful!" Nanname's hand shot across the bench and caught the rod before it could disappear into the hot liquid. "What's got into you today? You haven't been concentrating since you came downstairs."

Tiamat surreptitiously rubbed her fingers. Sweaty

curls escaped Nanname's hairband, their black streaked with silver. The perfume-maker wasn't young, yet her figure remained slender because she'd never married and borne children of her own. Sometimes Tiamat thought of her as an older sister rather than a mother. Not today.

"What's wrong?" Nanname pressed.

Tiamat clenched her jaw. "You know what's wrong!"

Nanname wiped her forehead on her sleeve and sighed. "I'm not letting you go to the garden, if that's what you mean."

"You can't keep me in here for ever! I'm not your wardum to order about like you please."

"No, you're my legally adopted daughter. And you'll stay indoors until you give me the respect due to a mother and tell me the truth." The sharpness of Nanname's tone matched her own.

Tiamat bit her lip. "I told you. I went on the wall to feed the sirrush. I said I was sorry. It's been a week..."

"You had no business to be up on that wall! I'm surprised Simeon went with you. I thought you both had more sense. And at a time like this, with the Persians virtually knocking on our gates!" She shook her head. "But that's not all, is it, Tia? Why don't you tell me the rest?"

Tears pricked Tiamat's eyes. "I only wanted to show him the sirrush. He didn't believe they were real."

"Sirrush belong to the King. They're not pets. They're dangerous creatures, only hatched in time of great need. It's a miracle you weren't poisoned. But they're not the reason I'm keeping you in. I think you know that."

Tiamat blinked. "I don't understand."

Ever since the sirrush had licked her, she'd hardly stopped thinking about the creature's beautiful, sad eyes. *Trapped. Hungry.* But Nanname didn't know that.

"Oh, I think you do."

"I told you everything that happened."

Nanname sighed and carefully laid the stirring rod on the bench. "I was going to wait until you owned up of your own accord, but I can't have you ruining my perfumes much longer. It's time we had this out."

She bent stiffly, groped under the bench and emerged with the pouch Tiamat had used that night. The scraps had gone, no doubt returned to the rubbish heaps she'd collected them from in the first place. But the pouch wasn't quite empty.

"Recognize this?"

The question was deceptively soft. Lady Nanname limped around the bench. She stood over Tiamat, leaning on her crutch to support her bad leg, a small, blue cylinder in her hand.

"Yes!" Tiamat smiled in relief. With all the worry over whether she'd been poisoned and whether Simeon was going to agree to help her, she'd quite forgotten the seal. "It proves the sirrush aren't dangerous. Look, it shows one licking someone—"

Lady Nanname slapped her.

Tiamat staggered backwards in shock, a hand raised to

her stinging cheek. Outside, small children laughed and screamed in the alley as before. A cart rumbled along Marduk Street on its way to the inner city. Down at the wharf, a donkey brayed. But in the laboratory, time had stopped. Nanname had never hit her before.

They stared at each other, breathing hard.

"How much good do you think you'll be to me in my old age without your hands, Tia?" Nanname said quietly.

Tiamat was trying desperately not to cry. "Wh–what?"

"That's the penalty for stealing, according to the Laws of Khammurabi. They chop off your right hand. Then, if you do it again, they chop off your left."

Tiamat curled her left hand, which was throbbing again. "But I didn't steal anything."

Nanname shook her head. "Oh, Tia... I didn't rescue you from the dogs and bring you up as my own daughter, only to lose you because you can't resist taking things that aren't yours. I realize it must have been the picture on the seal that attracted you, rather than its value, but that's no excuse. I'm deeply ashamed of you."

Tiamat bit her lip. She'd heard the story of how Lady Nanname had rescued her from the dogs when she was a baby. How there had been a large pack around her, and Nanname had rushed in with only a glass rod to drive them away. The dogs, cheated of their meal, had turned on the perfume-maker and bitten her in the leg – or that was how the other mothers told it. They said Tiamat was a very lucky girl and Nanname was a very brave lady, which was true. But she hated the way Nanname brought it up at times like this, as if it were Tiamat's fault the bite had become infected and crippled the perfume-maker for life.

"But I didn't steal it," she protested again.

Nanname sighed. "It'd be bad enough if it was just some craftsman's seal, but this blue stone is lapis lazuli. Do you know what that means?"

Tiamat shook her head.

"It means this seal belongs to a member of the King's own household. Only royalty have lapis lazuli seals."

Tiamat stared at the seal in surprise, then turned cold when she thought of her narrow escape. What if they'd searched her?

Nanname looked hard at her. "You didn't know that, obviously. Maybe you realize now how much trouble you'll be in – we'll be in – if anyone finds it here. Quite apart from the question of theft, a royal seal can be made good use of by spies, and the last thing we want is the city guard snooping around here thinking we support the Persians. Now then, I've got to think what to do. Maybe we can get rid of it with the waste from the lab. That would be safest—"

"No!" Tiamat lunged for the seal. Catching Nanname off balance, she managed to get it away from her. She hugged it tightly. "I *didn't* steal it. I found it. It's mine."

Lady Nanname's face hardened. "Tiamat! Give that back this instant. Don't make things worse by lying to me."

Tiamat was losing the battle with the tears. "I did find it, honestly I did! I found it in the princess's garden. I didn't think it might belong to someone... I kept it there, right where I found it, and no one ever came back for it. I never meant to bring it home. I only took it out to show Simeon that the creatures between the walls were the same as the sirrush on the seal. But then the sentries caught us, and there wasn't a chance to put it back."

Nanname must have seen she wasn't lying. She frowned at her. "How long ago did you find it?"

"Ages ago… when you first started sending me to the garden for herbs and things. It was hidden in a fountain on one of the high terraces. It's old, you can see that."

The strength seemed to flow out of Nanname. "You're lucky the sentries on the wall didn't search you before they brought you home."

Tiamat held her tongue. Little prickles were going up and down her spine. What if they had found the seal? Would they really have arrested her as a spy and chopped off her hands?

Nanname sighed and touched her cheek where she'd struck her earlier. "All right. If it really was that long ago, then I think we can assume the owner has stopped looking for it. But I want you to put it back anyway, exactly where you found it, just in case. Then I want you to promise me you'll never touch it again."

Tiamat squeezed the seal. "I promise," she whispered. Nanname needn't know if she looked at it now and then, so long as she didn't make the mistake of bringing it out of the garden again.

Unexpectedly, the perfume-maker hugged her. "Oh, Tia… There I was, waiting for you to admit your crime, and you've been hating me because you didn't understand why I was keeping you indoors. I'm sorry I jumped to conclusions. But I love you, don't you see? I don't want anything bad to happen to you. The old Laws aren't usually followed to the letter these days, but with the King's Demon in charge of law and order and this stupid war as an excuse for arresting anyone who doesn't have pure Black Head blood, I'm not so sure... Those soldiers scared me when they brought you home like that."

Tiamat wriggled free, embarrassed. "Can I go and put the seal back in the garden now? I've got to see Simeon, and I ought to apologize to Master Andulli for missing Twenty Squares Club." Her heart sank. She'd never get in the Team now, no matter how many games Simeon might let her "win".

But Nanname surprised her. "Don't worry about missing your Club. The Gamesmaster thinks you've had a touch of fever. He doesn't know about your little escapade on the wall – Simeon's been warned not to say anything."

"You lied to the *Egibi Family*?"

Tiamat stared at Nanname with a mixture of disbelief and admiration. The Egibi Family owned half of Zababa Wharf, as well as many other warehouses and properties in both outer and inner cities and across the river. They also owned property in the neighbouring cities of Borsippa, Kish, Uruk, and the sea port of Ur. They didn't make anything like Nanname's perfumes or the reed mats of the marsh people, nor did they farm their own land. Yet somehow they made small amounts of silver into large amounts of silver. Tiamat didn't pretend to understand how. But she was glad they did because their wealth made it possible for the Twenty Squares Club to exist, and without the Club she'd have no friends.

Nanname frowned. "That doesn't mean it's good to tell lies, Tia! But in this case, it seemed the best for everyone concerned. There are children from all neighbourhoods of the city in that Club. We don't want things like this spreading to the wrong ears."

Tiamat thought she could guess who the "wrong ears" belonged to. She smiled. And for the first time in a week, Lady Nanname smiled back.

Chapter 3

TABLET HOUSE

I have sought thee; I have turned to thee.

WHAT TIAMAT SHOULD have done was return the seal to its hiding place straight away. But she had more important matters to take care of first. As soon as Nanname let her go out, she went looking for Simeon.

After being indoors so long, even the narrow streets and shabby houses of the Judean Neighbourhood seemed like freedom. She raced through the familiar alleys, trailed by an excited dog who thought the luck-beads she wore around her ankles were something to chase. By the time she reached Simeon's house, the dog was barking wildly. A pig which had been scavenging through rubbish at the end of the alley bolted, while behind the mudbrick walls tightly-swaddled Judean babies woke up and started to cry. Tiamat shooed the dog away. It was a chunky mastiff with a patchy coat and normally she'd have made a fuss of it. But today, all it did was remind her of the sirrush. The dog gave her a hurt look as it sloped off.

Simeon wasn't home, but his grandfather peered down from the roof garden and told her how wicked she was to lead his grandson astray. Tiamat escaped before he could start telling her about the "good old days" back in Jerusalem, and made her way down to the wharf to try the Egibi Tablet House.

The door of the Tablet House was of cedar, bound with bronze, and the step had been intricately carved to look like a carpet. Tiamat self-consciously scraped some dung off the bottom of her foot before standing on it to knock.

An Egibi wardum, immaculately robed in the family's blue and yellow colours, answered her second knock. He frowned down his nose at her. "It's not Club day," he said.

"I know. I've... er... a message for Simeon, Jacob's son. Is he here?" She tried to see past the man. "He has lessons sometimes."

"The outer city boys are doing their mathematics, yes," said the servant. "They're not to be disturbed."

"It's very important I speak to him." Again, she tried to see into the hall.

The wardum folded his arms. "I'm sure whatever it is will wait until the lesson's over," he said with a note of finality.

Tiamat chewed her lip in frustration. "Can't I go in and wait? I'll be very quiet, I promise."

This earned her a condescending smile. "Girls don't learn numbers. What's the point?"

She raised her chin. "I'm in the Twenty Squares Club! I know enough to keep score. You just ask Master Andulli."

Again, the servant's lips curled into that little smile. "Everybody knows the only reason he let you join is because his wife likes your mother's perfume. Go home, Green-Eyes."

Tiamat had been about to give in and wait outside for the lesson to finish. But the servant's attitude made her blood rise, exactly as it had when Simeon had challenged her word on the wall. What the servant said was probably true, but he didn't have to rub it in.

With an effort, she unclenched her fists. "I've an important message from Simeon's father and he said I was to deliver it personally. You'll be in trouble if you don't let me see him right away."

She stared the wardum in the eye, her heart thudding. But if Nanname had lied to the Egibi Family and got away with it, then so could she.

After giving her a hard look, the wardum sighed and stood aside. "He's in the school room at the end of the east hall. Go straight there. No lingering and poking your nose where you shouldn't."

Tiamat was already halfway down the passage. She couldn't resist a peek into the room where they played Twenty Squares. It was empty today, the familiar clay boards lit by beams of dusty sunshine that streamed through the window grilles. She glanced back. The servant was watching her suspiciously. She turned into the east hall. The door at the end was closed. A long bench ran down one side of the hall, bearing several round clay tablets still soft from the storage tank. It seemed not as many boys had turned up for their lesson as anticipated.

The temptation was just too great. Tiamat glanced all round. Heart thudding wildly, she snatched a tablet off the top of the pile and slipped it beneath her dress. Gripping her prize firmly under her left armpit, she knocked on the door, opened it, and raised the fingers of her right hand to her nose in respectful greeting to the Egibi tutor. She repeated what she'd said to the wardum, only a lot more politely and with her eyes suitably lowered.

Simeon was perched on a stool at the end of a row of silent boys, pressing neat, wedge-shaped numbers into his tablet with a reed pen. He flashed her a look of surprise mingled with relief. The tutor sighed and signalled for him to hand in his tablet. "The rest of you get on with your work!" he snapped as the other boys nudged one another and winked at Tiamat. "Your fathers aren't paying for you to waste your time in here."

At last, they were alone in the hall. Tiamat grinned in triumph, while Simeon frowned at her. "What's wrong?" he hissed. "Why has Father sent for me?"

"What?" Tiamat shifted the stolen tablet into a more comfortable position. "Oh, that... he didn't send for you, silly. I just made it up to get you out of there. We need to talk. Have you decided if you're going to help me yet?"

Simeon's frown deepened. "I got in a lot of trouble over that night on the wall, you know." He glanced over his shoulder and lowered his voice. "I admit your dragons are real, and I'm sorry I didn't believe you, but some things just aren't worth the bother, Tia. I ought to go back and finish my lesson if Father doesn't want me."

Tiamat scowled. "I got in a lot more trouble than you! I was grounded for a whole week. Besides, there's something else..." She curled her left hand. "I can't tell you here. Come on, before someone comes."

Too late. The servant must have got suspicious, after all, and reported her. One of the junior masters who helped at Twenty Squares Club came round the corner. Seeing the two of them together, he smiled. "Ah, so there you are! We've missed you, Tiamat. Are you feeling better?"

Tiamat, desperately aware of the tablet sticking to her armpit, couldn't think for a moment what he meant. "Er... oh, yes! I mean yes, sir! Much better, thank you." Only just in time, she remembered to give him the formal greeting, her flustered hand-to-nose gesture several heartbeats behind Simeon's.

The junior master smiled again. "Good. Then you'll be at the Club tomorrow evening?"

"Oh, yes, sir!" she said in relief. "Of course."

Another nod. "I'm glad to hear it. Master Andulli

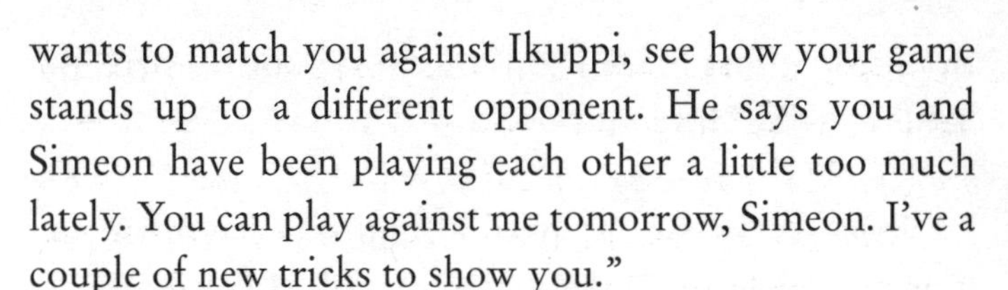

wants to match you against Ikuppi, see how your game stands up to a different opponent. He says you and Simeon have been playing each other a little too much lately. You can play against me tomorrow, Simeon. I've a couple of new tricks to show you."

Simeon's confusion turned to a glow of pride that matched Tiamat's despair. "Thank you, sir!" he said.

The junior master frowned at Tiamat. "Are you sure you're feeling all right? You look a little flushed."

"I'm fine, sir," she said quickly, glancing at Simeon. "But we really must go now. Simeon's father's waiting."

To her relief, the junior master dismissed them, though she could feel his eyes on her back all the way down the passage. The tablet under her arm was slipping. She pushed past the servant and ran, expecting to be called back at any moment and hauled before the Egibi Family as a thief, thrown out of Twenty Squares Club in disgrace, dragged away by the Demon's men to have her hands chopped off before Lady Nanname's tearful gaze...

"What's *wrong*, Tia?" Simeon puffed, grabbing her elbow. "I'm glad you got me out of maths and I'm glad Lady Nanname's let you come out at last, but what's so important that it couldn't wait till later?"

He stared in surprise as the tablet that had been wedged under her arm thudded into the dust between them. Two dogs bounded up, looking for a game. Tiamat massaged her arm and shooed them away.

Simeon frowned at the tablet. "Where did you get

that? You didn't... Oh, Tia! You didn't steal it from the Tablet House, did you?"

They'd run through the market by this time and were near the water gate in Nebuchadnezzar's Wall, where canal traffic had to stop and be searched before it was allowed into the city. A couple of bored sentries were poking their spears into a pile of reed mats, looking for concealed Persians.

Simeon snatched up the tablet and dusted it off, examining the stamp on the back. "You're crazy, Tia! If the Egibi Family find out, they'll report you to the Demon!"

Tiamat closed her eyes. It was nearly midday. The sun was blisteringly hot and the glare hurt her head. The cries of the traders made her ears ring. The wharf stank of too many sweaty people and animals crowded together in too small a space. She was hungry and thirsty and couldn't cope with yet another person telling her she'd get her hands chopped off.

"So they shouldn't have left it lying around, should they?" she snapped, snatching it back. "It's not as if anything's written on it. Calm down, Simeon. The Egibi Family's so rich, they're hardly going to miss a single blank student tablet, are they? Who's going to tell them? You?"

Simeon shook his head. "Course not. But they keep careful records, you know."

"I'll risk it." Tiamat led him round the corner to a small courtyard shaded by palm trees. She sat on the rim of the fountain, glanced round to make sure they were alone, then balanced the tablet across her knees and pulled out the blue seal.

Simeon looked more interested. "That's the seal you showed me in the garden, isn't it?"

She nodded. "Apparently, it belonged to someone from the royal family. It's made of lapis lazuli and it's supposed to be quite valuable. Nanname says I've got to put it back where I found it in case someone comes looking for it, but I want to get a picture of the sirrush to keep first – hold this still for me, will you?"

The clay had dried out slightly, but was still soft enough to take an impression. While Simeon steadied the tablet on her knee, she rolled the cylinder firmly across the middle. "There!"

Simeon ran his finger over the neat grid of wedge-shaped characters beside the picture. "Strange, these look like Sumerian letters. It must be really old. No one writes in Sumerian any more. I wonder what it says."

Tiamat pushed his hand away. "Never mind the writing. Do you think the sirrush is supposed to be licking that person's hand? It looks quite tame to me. They can't really be poisonous, can they? I expect the sentries just made that up to scare us, don't you?"

Simeon shook his head. "Not that again, Tia! It doesn't matter if they're poisonous or not, after seeing them attack those walls! You were quite crazy going down there. I don't know how you think you're going to help them, even if you do manage to get inside the Palace during the Championships – which isn't likely, if Master Andulli keeps pairing you with Ikuppi."

This was all too true. Ikuppi was the best player in the Club. Even Simeon lost when he played him.

Tiamat set her jaw. "He won't make me play Ikuppi for long. You will help me get into the Team, won't you, Simeon? As soon as we can play each other again?"

He gave her an exasperated look. But after a moment he sighed and touched her arm. "If it'll stop you climbing any more walls, I'll do what I can. Only don't get your hopes up too high. I doubt Master Andulli will change the Team at this late stage."

She grinned and jumped to her feet. "He did last year! He's always changing it. Thanks, Simeon! Let's go and see if any of the merchants are throwing stale goods out. I'm starving!"

"You go." Simeon brushed himself off. "I'd better find Father. If the Egibi Family check up on me, I want to be where I'm supposed to be. I don't want to get thrown out of Twenty Squares Club, even if you do. With the northern cities not sending teams because of the war, we've a good chance in the Championships this year." As Tiamat stared at him in disgust, he nodded to the tablet and added, "Better hide that."

"I'm not stupid."

She watched him disappear into the crowds, her elation fading now she was alone. *My hand hurts*, she'd meant to tell him. *I'm scared I've been poisoned.*

Then her stomach rumbled, reminding her of more

immediate concerns. Trying not to think of tomorrow night's match with Ikuppi, she slipped the tablet back under her dress and went in search of food to give her the energy for the long climb up the terraces of the princess's garden. Simeon's words had brought back the chill she'd felt when Nanname had told her why she was being punished. The sooner the seal was back in the fountain, the better.

Chapter 4

TWENTY SQUARES CLUB

That which is on thy right hand increase good fortune; that which is on thy left hand attain favour!

THE EGIBI TWENTY Squares Club met once a week at sunset in the Tablet House on Zababa Wharf. There were no formal entrance requirements, but Master Andulli was strict about attendance. Anyone arriving late, or missing more than two sessions without a valid excuse, was thrown out of the Club no matter who their parents were. This didn't go down too well with the children from the inner city, who usually left of their own accord once they discovered they wouldn't be allowed to win just because their families were rich. But the serious ones stayed. It was the best club in the city with the best masters. Many of the top champions of the past few years had been Egibi players. And if that meant occasionally sitting at a board opposite a Judean or a girl, then the boys from the inner city had learnt to hold their tongues – with one notable exception.

Tiamat knew she was in for a hard time the moment she walked through the door and saw Ikuppi seated with his back to her at the board furthest from the lamps. His long legs were folded under his stool and he'd draped his cloak over his knees. He was fiddling with the Black counters, making them spin on the edge of the table, flattening his hand over them whenever one of the masters walked past.

As Tiamat slid on to the stool opposite, his lips twitched into a sneer. "So you came, then?" he said. "I thought you'd pretend to be sick again when you heard you'd have to play a real opponent." He straightened the counters and yawned. "Let's get this stupid match over with. Then maybe I can get a proper game with somebody tonight."

Tiamat scowled. "I didn't ask to play you."

"That makes two of us."

"I'm usually Black."

"Hard luck."

"You're supposed to let the—let me choose."

She'd been going to say "the weaker player", until she realized this was exactly what Ikuppi had meant her to say. His sneer spread to the other side of his mouth.

Tiamat settled herself more comfortably on the stool, scooped up the seven White counters and laid the first one on White's starting square. She reached for the die. But of course Ikuppi had been waiting for her to do just that and got there first. His eye contained a challenge as he threw. She bit her lip, not really surprised when he moved his first counter without waiting for a "six" as he was supposed to. He was going to win, anyway. What did it matter if he cheated? She had more important things to worry about.

Ikuppi hunched over the board as he played. The room was lit by lamps suspended from the ceiling by bronze chains, but there was always a problem with shadows on this particular table. She couldn't see what Ikuppi was doing. Over the boy's immaculately oiled curls, she watched Simeon take his place opposite the junior master who had spoken to them yesterday. Simeon looked serious and determined and missed her wink. He obviously wanted a good report when Master Andulli looked in later to see how they were all doing. The room quietened as the others paired off and settled at their boards. Soon the rattle of dice, the click of counters, and the occasional groan when someone's counter got knocked off the board and returned to the start, were all that could be heard above the soft tread of the masters patrolling the room and the hiss of the lamps.

At first Tiamat didn't concentrate on the game. Her head was too full of the poor sirrush and how she was going to get into the Palace to help them if she couldn't get into the Team. Also, her hand was bothering her again, made worse by the fact that Ikuppi wouldn't let her get away with right-handed throws. She wondered if she should have admitted to Nanname that the sirrush had licked her. But after she'd moved four or five times, she realized in amazement that she was winning. Not only that, but Black was in severe trouble.

Ikuppi hunched lower still as he snatched the die for his next throw. "Think it's funny, do you?" he hissed, squinting suspiciously at the little cube with its wedge-shaped numbers pressed into the sides. "You and your little Judean friend fixed the die, didn't you? Planning on a good giggle afterwards, huh? Well it won't work with me, Green-Eyes!"

Tiamat stared at him. "But—"

Ikuppi raised his fist. "We need a referee!" he called. "Foul play here!"

One of the junior masters looked round with a little frown. He walked over slowly, long robes whispering in the hush.

"What seems to be the trouble, Ikuppi?" he said, glancing at Tiamat.

"We need a new die, sir," Ikuppi said. "I'm not happy with this one."

The junior master raised an eyebrow. "All the Egibi dice are carefully crafted to be absolutely fair."

"I know that, sir. But someone's tampered with this one. It gives her all the advantages. Watch, if you don't believe me."

"You refer to your opponent as 'my opposite', Ikuppi," said the junior master with mild reproof. "Whatever her gender."

Ikuppi glowered at Tiamat. "It gives my *opposite* all the advantages, sir," he insisted.

The junior master nodded and surveyed the board. "Your complaint has been noted. White is winning. Play on, and I shall monitor you myself."

Ikuppi clearly didn't like it, but he was forced to play from his disadvantageous position. With the junior master's eyes on her, Tiamat fully expected to lose, as normally happened when she was being watched and got flustered. But every time she picked up the die, her fingers tingled and exactly the right number came up. Even an idiot at strategy could not have lost with her luck tonight, and Tiamat wasn't a complete idiot in spite of what Ikuppi and his friends thought. Growing more confident, she risked landing on one of the Eye Symbols, which were a gamble at the best of times and which even Simeon wouldn't play towards the end of the game. Ikuppi's face, when she guessed exactly how many counters he put under the cup and doubled her score, was classic.

In nine double-minutes, she'd thrashed him.

"See?" Ikuppi shouted, losing all control and throwing the die across the room. "I told you! She and her sneaky little friends have fixed it! This is what happens when you let foreign blood into the Club!"

"IKUPPI! THAT'S ENOUGH."

The boy froze. All heads turned to the door as a tall man wearing a long, fringed robe and sandals with upturned toes swept into the room. His beard was frosted with silver, but his eyes pierced the shadows like stars on a moonless night. Whispers passed round the boards. "Master Andulli's here! Ikuppi's in trouble now."

The junior master stepped back and murmured something to the Egibi Gamesmaster.

"Hmmm," said Master Andulli, stroking his beard and looking thoughtfully at the arrangement of counters on their board. "Tiamat was clever with those last few moves."

"But I'm Egibi champion!" Ikuppi protested. "She's only first rank! It's obvious she was cheating, Master!" He was on his feet, glaring at the Gamesmaster, fists clenched.

Master Andulli stared him out. "Sit down, Ikuppi," he said quietly. "This behaviour does not become a member of the Egibi Twenty Squares Club."

Everyone else in the room had stopped playing. A plump girl called Muna, who was in the Team and obviously well aware of Ikuppi's tricks, smiled hesitantly at Tiamat. Simeon gave her an encouraging wink. The blood rushed to her face. What if they *had* fixed the die? She'd never had such strange luck before, usually quite the opposite.

Ikuppi lowered his gaze and sat down. Master Andulli pressed his lips together and gave them a fresh cube. "Play again," he instructed, folding his arms and positioning himself nearby to watch.

This time Ikuppi couldn't risk cheating, but it would have made no difference. The numbers were on Tiamat's side tonight. Enjoying every moment now, she pulled off a few fancy strategies Simeon had shown her and this time beat Ikuppi in six double-minutes. Only when she looked up from the board to smile at the inner city boy did she realize their game had drawn a silent, awed circle of masters and children.

"So, Tiamat," Master Andulli said softly. "It seems your first win wasn't a fluke, after all. I've not seen anyone with the gods so firmly on their side since young Zazum of Uruk took the Garland back in Nebuchadnezzar's day. Get up,

Ikuppi. You're a bad loser. Go and play two rounds with Simeon. The rest of you, back to your boards. I'm going to test this girl's mettle myself."

More whispers passed round the room as Master Andulli seated himself on the stool opposite Tiamat and arranged his long robes. He frowned up at the lamps. "The light's bad on this table. Someone fetch us another lamp. I like to see my opposite's face when I beat him – or her." His smile, which creased his sunburnt face into hundreds of wrinkles, took the threat out of his words. "Now then, Tiamat. What colour would you like to play?"

Tiamat's mouth dried. *The Team*, was all she could think. If she played well, Master Andulli would make her Team Reserve and she'd be able to help the sirrush.

"Bla— no, White," she said. She managed a little smile. "Seems lucky for me tonight."

"Hmmm," said Master Andulli. "We'll see." He picked up the die and brushed a speck of grit off the board. "Shall we play?"

The next double-hour was the most gruelling Tiamat had spent in her entire life. Master Andulli made her play again and again, frowning when he lost and tapping his finger on the edge of the board when he won. Occasionally, he would tell her off for a careless move, and once he showed her a trick that she hadn't seen before, and she tried it and got hopelessly confused, losing the next game miserably. But in general her luck held – if you could call it luck. By the end of the evening, when Master Andulli rose from his stool and stretched until the bones in his shoulders cracked, Tiamat's head was spinning and the dots on the counters were floating before her eyes.

Master Andulli rested a gnarled hand on the top of her head and smiled down at her. "Tired, Tiamat?"

"Yes, Master." She struggled to her feet, embarrassed to be sitting when the Gamesmaster was standing.

Most of the others had finished their games and were leaning across the boards, chatting while they waited for the junior masters to collect up the counters and dice. A boy called Labinsin had replaced Simeon at Ikuppi's board. The two inner city boys' heads were close together as they discussed something in whispers. They kept casting dark glances across the room at Tiamat. She scowled back.

"Interesting," Master Andulli said, stroking his beard again. "Seems you've somehow acquired a god's favour." He looked thoughtfully at her. "Did anything unusual happen while you were ill? Did you have any strange dreams, for example?"

Tiamat blushed, thinking of the lie Nanname had told for her. "I… er… don't remember, Master."

He stroked his beard a bit longer, then nodded. "This is far too good an opportunity to miss. I'm going to put you in the Egibi Team for this year's Championships, Tiamat. Twenty Squares is a game of both skill and chance. It's entirely possible for someone with your basic level of skill and the gods on their side to win against a much more experienced player – as I believe you proved tonight." Again, that kindly smile. "I'll give you some extra tuition, teach you a few of the simpler tricks so at least you'll know when your opposite is trying to pull them on you. We've almost two weeks yet, so don't panic. And no one's going to blame you if the gods desert you on the night. I'll take full responsibility. You must remember to throw with your left hand, though. Quite apart from the fact that the Championships adhere strictly to the rules and you might get disqualified, your luck's not half as good when you throw with your right."

He swept his robes around him and strode through the departing children to talk to the younger masters. Tiamat stared after him, open-mouthed. Left hand, she thought. Left hand. Something important… Then she realized what Master Andulli had said. On the Team. Not just Reserve. She was going to play in the Championships against all the best players from the cities of Kish, Borsippa, Uruk and Ur, and maybe, if she got through the initial rounds, in the Throne Room of the Royal Palace before Prince Belshazzar himself! It was even rumoured that the King might attend this year, his advisors having tracked him down in his desert retreat to ask what they should do about the Persians.

Her knees wobbled. She sat down again, her excitement fading slightly. How could she possibly help the sirrush if she had to play Twenty Squares? Then she giggled. No, she was being silly. She'd be wiped out in the first round, anyway. Luck like tonight's didn't hold, couldn't hold.

"Tia!" The voice broke into her thoughts. She blinked and focused on a grinning Simeon. "I just heard! Congratulations! That makes you and me, Ikuppi, Enki,

Muna, and Hillalum as Reserve. You're taking Labinsin's place." He glanced at the door and grinned again. "Pity it wasn't Ikuppi who got thrown off the Team. He had some cheek, calling you a cheat and a foreigner in front of everyone like that."

She looked at Ikuppi and Labinsin, who were still muttering by the door. After a final glower in Tiamat's direction, the two inner city boys pulled their cloaks around them and hurried out.

She sighed. "It's bad enough I'm replacing his best friend. He'll hate me more than ever now."

"Don't be silly," Simeon said. "You beat him fair and square. Labinsin was the weakest link in the Team. No one liked him."

"Except Ikuppi."

"They're two of a kind. Inner city snobs!" Simeon pulled a face at the door.

Tiamat gave her friend a sideways look. "You're in a good mood. Did you win against the junior master or something?"

Simeon's grin widened. "He shouldn't have shown me that move. Caught himself in his own trap! I'm going to use it on Ikuppi next time I have to play him, take him down a peg or two."

Tiamat grinned back, feeling a bit better. "I think he was taken down several tonight, being beaten by a girl. I just have to keep throwing with my left hand, apparently."

"And what's so special about that one?" Simeon looked at her hand, which she'd been rubbing without realizing it. A shadow moved behind his eyes. "Sirrush," he whispered.

"What?" Tiamat's heart fluttered.

"That's the hand the dragon licked, isn't it?"

They stared at each other.

"That's got nothing to do with it," Tiamat mumbled, although the same thought had occurred to her. "But at least I'll be able to help them now."

"Not if you're playing, you won't."

"I won't be playing all the time. It's supposed to be a Feast too, isn't it? Lots of fancy food and stuff. I'll smuggle some out to them. There's bound to be something on the royal table they like to eat." Her stomach gurgled loudly at the very thought.

Simeon laughed. "Anyone would think Lady Nanname was starving you! Didn't you have supper before you came out?"

"Yes, but I'm hungry again after all that concentration." She rubbed her hand again. "Master Andulli should give us snacks if he expects us to work this hard. I bet Prince Belshazzar feeds the Crown Team."

Simeon's smile faded. "Grandfather says it's wicked having Feasts. He doesn't want me to play in the Championships."

"But you will?"

"Of course!" The boy paused on the step, his eyes sparkling. "Father's really proud of me. He said I should be allowed to play if I'm good enough. But I'm not just going to play, Tia – I'm going to win! I'm going to be the first Judean ever to take the Twenty Squares Garland. That'll show those inner city snobs we foreigners are just as good as them."

Tiamat laughed. "Maybe you'd better let the sirrush lick *your* hand! Ishtar, but I'm stiff!" She shook her wrists and took a deep gulp of night air. The moon silvered the canal and bathed the outer city houses, making the dirty, smelly alleys shine like the Ajiburshapu Way itself. Needing to stretch her cramped legs, she leapt off the step and broke into a run. "Race you to Marduk Street!"

"Hey! Wait for me!" Simeon plunged after her. "We're supposed to walk home together, remember, in case the Persians get us. Look out, they're coming... GRRRURRR!" His attempt at a barbarian war cry echoed from the walls. A baby started crying and its mother yelled at them to be quiet.

Tiamat laughed and ran faster. "The Persians won't dare come this far downriver. Anyway, they'd never get over our walls."

Neither of them noticed the two cloaked figures lurking in the shadow of Zababa Gate, staring after them. "Don't worry," the taller boy said with a cold little smile. "We'll fix her."

EGIBI TWENTY SQUARES TEAM
4th Tashritu

Gamesmaster

ANDULLI	Egibi Family of Babylon

Team

ENKI	Master Andulli's son, Enlil Street, inner city
SIMEON	Jacob's son, Judean Neighbourhood, outer city
MUNA	astrologer's daughter, outer city
IKUPPI	Zerim's son, inner city
TIAMAT	Nanname's adopted daughter, outer city

Reserve

HILLALUM	farmer's son, country

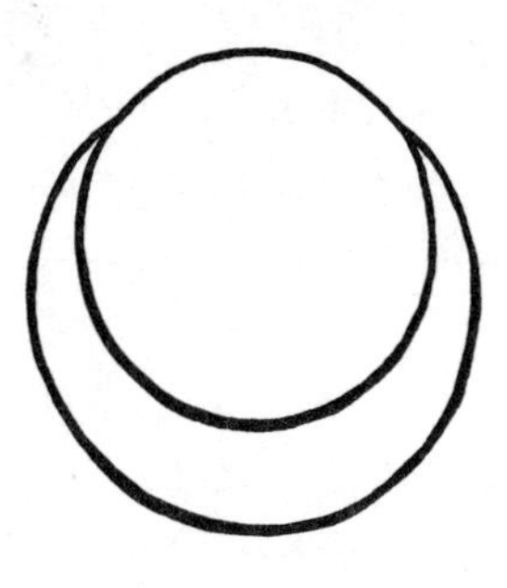

Chapter 5

AMBUSH

May there never approach me the poisons of the evil deeds of men!

BEING IN THE Twenty Squares Team was harder work than Tiamat had anticipated. With less than two weeks until the Championships, Master Andulli arranged extra sessions for the six Egibi competitors and demanded their full attendance on pain of being replaced. The evenings Tiamat wasn't in the princess's garden picking herbs for Nanname, she was at the Tablet House on Zababa Wharf crouched over a Twenty Squares board until her left hand ached from throwing and her head throbbed with trying to keep track of the score.

Although this meant she'd have her chance to explore the Palace, it was also very frustrating. The sentries on Nebuchadnezzar's Wall had been doubled following the Persian victory at Opis, and were patrolling its whole length. She dared not climb across the branch to drop more food for the sirrush. Yet every night she missed taking them food, she was tormented by images of the poor creatures starving to death before she could help them.

She kept expecting her strange luck to desert her. But however badly she might play because she was thinking of the sirrush or her sore hand rather than the game, she didn't seem able to lose. And if Master Andulli caught her trying to throw with her right hand, he quietly transferred the die to her left. "Never give your opposite a deliberate advantage, Tiamat," he said quietly. "Not even in practice."

In fact, Master Andulli treated her and her lucky hand so reverently, Tiamat doubted that he would throw her out even if she didn't turn up for practice. She didn't quite dare try it. Besides, being in the Team wasn't all work. Muna came up on the first night and said how glad she was not to be the only girl any more. Hillalum, the farmer's son who travelled into the city by boat every evening, asked gruffly if her mother would like some onions and didn't seem at all upset he was only Reserve now. Even Enki, who was the Gamesmaster's son and treated everyone with equal contempt, seemed to accept she'd earned her right to play. Nanname sent little phials of perfume in return for the gifts the other parents sent home with Tiamat, which became so numerous that some nights it felt as though they were staggering home from market rather than Twenty Squares Club. Needless to say, Ikuppi took no part in this trade. But the inner city boy was quiet without his friends around and Tiamat learnt to ignore him. She might have started to enjoy herself, had it not been for the constant worry over her hand.

After replacing the seal in the fountain, she'd hidden the tablet with its sirrush picture under the reeds in her bed box. She wondered if the Sumerian writing might contain instructions for a cure, but after what Nanname had said about it being a royal seal, she knew she couldn't risk taking it to a public scribe for translation.

Then she had an idea.

On their next Club night, she slipped the tablet into her pouch before setting out to meet Simeon. "Got to go," she mumbled, snatching up the phials of perfume Nanname had left out for her and quickly dropping them in the pouch on top of the tablet. "I'm late."

Nanname smiled and planted a quick kiss on her cheek. "Remember to stick to the lighted ways. Stay with Simeon, and—"

"—watch out for the Persians!" Tiamat finished for her as she escaped into the alley. "Don't worry – we will!"

She met Simeon on the corner of Marduk Street and whispered her plan to him as they went. He stopped walking, his serious eyes shadowed by the dusk.

"Are you sure that's such a good idea?"

"Why not? I don't expect anyone'll know anything, but there's no harm in asking, is there? Don't worry, no one's going to say anything to the authorities. I'm not stupid. I know the things we trade at

Twenty Squares aren't exactly legal."

"Shh!" Simeon hissed, looking round in alarm. "Talk like that could get the Egibi Family in a lot of trouble."

"Relax. No one's listening."

"Grandfather says there's always someone listening. The Demon's spies are everywhere. That man over there could be one, or... that man." He pointed to a citizen who'd just passed them, his drab-coloured robes swishing around his ankles.

The man in question didn't have a beard. Unease rippled down Tiamat's back. It was rumoured that men without beards had horrible things done to them so they couldn't father a family. It was supposed to make them more loyal to their masters. She giggled nervously. "That's not a real man, silly."

"That's exactly who they use," Simeon said, pulling her through the shadows. "Grandfather says it's wicked, what they do."

"Your grandfather thinks *everything's* wicked!" Tiamat giggled again. "Anyway, you were the one who wanted to know what the writing said. It might explain why I've suddenly got all this luck at Twenty Squares, as well. I'm sure Master Andulli suspects something. He keeps asking about my hand."

"That's because he wants us to win and he wants to be sure you've still got the god's favour."

"No, it's more than that." She frowned, wondering what the Gamesmaster would say if he found out she'd touched the sirrush. But Simeon was checking over his shoulder to see where the beardless man had gone and didn't notice her unease.

"Muna's folks might know something, I suppose," he said slowly. "Astrologers have to study all kinds of ancient lore. Hillalum won't be much use. Most farmers can't read Akkadian, let alone Sumerian. He's probably never even heard of a dragon. Pointless asking Enki, of course, but that's up to you. Only whatever you do, don't let Ikuppi see it! He'll only find some way of getting you into trouble."

"I'm not *that* stupid!"

Simeon eyed her sideways, as if he weren't so sure. Suddenly, he grinned. "Hurry up, then! Or there won't be time to ask anyone anything before slave-driver Andulli gets there."

It was the end of the evening before Tiamat got a chance to show her new friends the tablet. Fortunately, Ikuppi had left early with some excuse that made Master Andulli frown, so she didn't have to worry about him recognizing the seal. But no one knew what the writing said. Muna promised to bring one of her father's Sumerian texts along next time so they could have a go at translating it. Enki ran his finger over the underside of the tablet, gave Tiamat an amused glance and said she'd better not let Master Andulli know what she'd used good Egibi clay for. Hillalum frowned at the picture and said was that some breed of goat under the ziqqurat? Simeon gave her a look that said "I told you so" and heaved his bag of onions on to his shoulder.

"Want me to carry yours?" he offered.

"Don't be silly. That's why I brought my pouch."

Her head still buzzing with what the seal might say about the sirrush, Tiamat carefully packed her share of the onions and cheese into the pouch and wedged the tablet on top to stop them falling out. When Simeon suggested they should take the short cut, she followed him into the alleys without thinking. Then she caught a glimpse from the corner of her eye of something moving in the shadows and hesitated, Nanname's warning echoing in her ears. *Stick to the lighted ways.*

"What's the matter?" Simeon set down his bag and rubbed his shoulder.

Tiamat stared intently at the shadows. "I thought I saw someone."

"Other people are allowed out at this time of night, you know."

"It's just..." She shook her head, unable to explain the uneasy tingle in her left hand. "The moon's going in. Let's go."

As Simeon picked up his bag, a second cloud went across the moon. They both jumped as a dog loped out of the darkness, sniffed the air and vanished down another alley. Tiamat shivered.

"Maybe we shouldn't have come this way tonight," Simeon said. "It's darker than I thought. Hurry, Tia."

She didn't need urging. Her hand was throbbing and cold sweat bathed the back of her neck. She broke into a run, hampered by her full pouch.

They took a turn towards the inner city, where the street beside the moat would be lit by the torches on the battlements. Thinking of the sirrush trapped behind those walls, Tiamat stepped on Simeon's heels. He'd stopped again, staring at a patch of darkness ahead.

"What's wrong?"

"I think someone's lying in wait up there."

"Should we go back?" She twisted her head, suddenly reluctant to re-enter the maze of dark alleys between them and the wharf.

"Maybe we could work our way round another way." Simeon broke off as a slender silhouette in a long cloak detached itself from the shadows and came sauntering towards them.

Tiamat tensed, then let out her breath. "It's only Ikuppi!" She scowled at the boy. "What are you doing here? You scared us half to death! I thought you'd gone home. What do you want..?" Her voice trailed off as more boys stepped out of the shadows to surround them.

"Shut up, Green-Eyes!" Ikuppi snapped. "I'll do the talking now."

Simeon put a hand on Tiamat's arm. "Get ready to run," he whispered. "Let them have the onions if they want."

Angry with Ikuppi for having scared her, Tiamat pushed his hand away. "Don't be silly! They're not having our food." She raised her chin and glared at the inner city boy. "Let us through. The sentries on the wall are watching."

Ikuppi shook his head. "Nice try, Green-Eyes, but

they can't see us here. We picked this spot specially. Drove you to it like cattle."

The other boys closed behind, cutting off their retreat. Five of them, all wearing good cloaks that indicated their parents were rich enough to afford food without going to the trouble of taking it from outer city children. Labinsin was with them, smirking. Tiamat's heart beat faster. Beside her, she could hear Simeon breathing heavily.

"You took my place on the Team," Labinsin said, pushing his face close to hers. "I don't like that."

Tiamat glared back. "Hard luck! Master Andulli must think I'm better than you."

"Tia!" Simeon hissed. "Don't antagonize them."

"They can't do anything," Tiamat said. "They'll be in too much trouble with their mummies and daddies when they get home."

Labinsin flushed. He made a grab for her hair, ripping it from its band. Tiamat swung her pouch and clouted him on the side of his head. He staggered with a grunt of surprise. Two of the other boys flung themselves at her, only to dodge back when she swung the bag again.

"Help!" Simeon yelled. "Guards! Help – *ah*!" His yells ended in a strangled gasp.

Tiamat was too busy fighting off her would-be attackers to see what had happened. Then she saw the glint of the moon in the blade at Simeon's throat. Her pouch suddenly seemed very heavy. She let it drop at her feet, unable to take her eyes from that blade. A proper dagger, she thought in terror. A dagger that a soldier might use to kill someone. The hilt was in Ikuppi's hand. It reminded her what happened to people who challenged the authority of the inner city.

"Everyone shut up and stand still!" Ikuppi snapped.

The boys backed off, eyeing his dagger and one another, as if unsure what to do next. Labinsin's eyes widened. "You didn't say anything about weapons."

"Quiet!" Ikuppi hissed. "Get a hold of her, someone. She's only a grubby outer city orphan who's happened to have a bit of luck. Gamesmaster thinks you've acquired a god's favour, does he? Well, your god's about to desert you, Green-Eyes."

"Run, Tiamat!" Simeon shouted. "Don't worry about me. He won't dare—" He choked as the dagger nicked his neck, drawing blood.

"Don't hurt him!" Tiamat stared in horror at that trickle of blood, which gave two of Ikuppi's friends a chance to dart in and seize her arms.

Ikuppi smiled coldly. "No one's going to shed any tears over a dead Judean. These alleys are dangerous at night. Your fathers should have told you – oh, but I was forgetting! You haven't *got* a father, have you, Green-Eyes? The Persian scum ran off and left your mother up the spout, didn't he?"

"That's not true!"

"No?" Ikuppi raised an eyebrow. "Where else did you get eyes that colour? Who is your father, then? For that matter, who's your real mother?"

Tiamat blinked back a furious tear. "You know I don't know. Let Simeon go! Don't be so stupid, Ikuppi!"

The boys holding her glanced uncertainly at each other. Labinsin was still shaking his head at the dagger. "I think we've gone far enough, Ikuppi—"

"I said shut *up*! You want to play in the Championships, don't you? Or do you want everyone to know a *girl* took your place? Not only that, but an outer city girl, an orphan who was so unwanted when she was born that her real mother left her in the street for the dogs! They'll laugh at you so loudly, you'll be able to hear them even when you're dead."

Labinsin was silent. Tiamat's cheeks burned with helpless shame.

"Right then," Ikuppi said. "This is how you're going to get back in the Team. Get hold of her hand and hang on tight."

Tiamat's skin crawled as Labinsin reached for her nearest wrist.

"Not that one!" Ikuppi snapped. "Her left hand, stupid. The one with all the luck in it. Those that steal people's places on the Team should pay the appropriate penalty."

Only then, seeing Labinsin's slow smile of understanding as he seized her wrist and the way Ikuppi's knuckles tightened on his dagger, did she realize what they meant to do. The penalty for theft, according to the Laws of Khammurabi. Her fingers tingled in terror. She heaved against the two boys who held her, trying to kick them, but the remaining boy put his arms around her waist and dragged her backwards until she lost her balance.

In one silver-quick movement, Ikuppi withdrew the dagger from Simeon's throat, shoved the Judean boy hard against the wall and swooped on Tiamat's exposed wrist.

She screamed, dizzy with the flash of the approaching blade and the boys' tight grip on her arms. Everything slowed down. Simeon's cry of protest... Labinsin's smile... the crazed look in Ikuppi's eye... There was a searing pain in her fingers, as if she'd put her hand in a fire. Then a bright red flare lit the houses and the alley with its piles of dung and rotting vegetables, and suddenly she was free.

Ikuppi gave a wild yell. "I'm cut! I'm cut!" He raced down the alley, still yelling. The red light faded. The remaining boys stared at one another in confusion. Labinsin grunted as something small and round struck him in the stomach. At first, Tiamat couldn't think what was happening. Then her heart lifted. Onions were flying out of the shadows.

Labinsin turned with a shout of fury as a second missile hit him on the ear. "It's only the Judean!" he yelled. "Get him!"

The other boys flung themselves at Simeon, but he darted off into the maze of alleys he knew so well, still flinging onions from his bag and yelling at Tiamat to run. The boys gave chase, leaving Labinsin staring at Tiamat in confusion. There was the tramp of heavy feet and two soldiers rounded the corner at a trot, carrying torches that trailed smoke in the night. Labinsin fled after his friends. Hardly able to believe she could still use her hand, Tiamat snatched up her pouch and ducked round the corner, leaving the soldiers to investigate the spilt onions and drops of blood in the dust.

She waited a bit longer for Simeon, but he must have gone straight back to the Judean Neighbourhood. Still in a daze, she washed her hand in the moat and stumbled the rest of the way home. She thrust the onions and cheese at Nanname and hurried up to bed, her injury hidden in a fold of her skirt. Only then, getting undressed one-handed in the smoky glow of her lamp, did she realize the worst.

Sometime during the struggle in the alley, the tablet with its sirrush impression had fallen out of her pouch.

Chapter 6

THE DEMON

I am afraid, I tremble and I am cast down in fear!

TIAMAT SLEPT LATE the next morning. When she woke, scented steam was already curling up the stair. She leapt out of bed in a rush of guilt, grabbed her work dress, and yelped as the scab that had formed overnight on her hand broke open and started to bleed again.

The pain brought back every detail of the ambush in the alley. She muttered a few curses for Ikuppi, bit her lip, and wound one of her hairbands around her injured hand, tying it with her teeth. She couldn't manage the pins to put up her hair and settled for braiding it loosely. Then she hurried downstairs to the laboratory, where Nanname's quiet singing drifted through the steam.

The song broke off as Tiamat ducked through the doorway. "So, you're awake at last. What happened last night?"

Tiamat hid her injured hand behind her back. "Nothing."

"I'm not blind, you know." Nanname wiped her fingers on her skirt and limped across. "How did you hurt your hand?" She pulled it gently from behind Tiamat's back and frowned at the blood soaking through the linen.

"It's nothing, really. I... uh... fell and cut it on a piece of broken pot. That's all."

Nanname had already unwound the makeshift bandage and was examining the wound. "Broken pot? Looks more like a knife wound to me." She shook her head. "Oh, Tia, what am I going to do with you? I thought that Club would give you a nice interest with people of your own age, keep you out of trouble. What really happened?"

Tiamat recalled the wild look in Ikuppi's eyes as he'd wielded his dagger above her wrist. That red light... What exactly *had* happened? She needed to talk to Simeon as soon as possible. "It was an accident," she mumbled.

Nanname released her. Still shaking her head, she reached a bowl from under the bench and filled it with liquid from one of the vats. "I bet it has something to do with those inner city boys. Doesn't look too deep, fortunately, but those extra sessions go on far too long. If the Egibi Family can't make better arrangements for the safety of their young players, they'll just have to find someone else to play in their Team. It might be all right for the boys to roam the streets at night, but I'm not having my daughter— " A pause as she waited to see that

Tiamat understood. "—put in danger over some silly game. Hold still. This'll sting a bit."

"It's not a silly game." Tiamat sucked in her breath as Nanname poured the hot herbal water over her wound. She blinked away tears. "I'm good now, really I am. I even beat Master Andulli once! And I'm not the only girl, anyway. There's Muna—"

"What Muna's parents let their daughter do is no concern of mine."

Nanname patted her hand dry and examined it again. As she retied the bandage, Tiamat drew a deep breath.

"Nanname?"

"Mmm?"

"Was my mother... I mean, did you ever meet my real mother? Or my father?"

Nanname looked up sharply. "So that's what this is all about, is it? Who's been saying what?"

Tiamat bit her lip. "Ikuppi said my father was a Persian. He said he ran off and left my mother pregnant, and that's why she abandoned me to the dogs."

"Ikuppi's a fool!"

"But he's right, isn't he? Black Heads don't usually have eyes my colour."

The perfume-maker's lips tightened. "If I knew who your real parents were, Tia, I'd have told you before now, you know that. As to you having foreign blood, of course it's possible – Ishtar knows there are enough foreigners living inside our walls these days. But that boy's got no right to go around spreading rumours like that, particularly at a time like this." She gazed at the door and sighed. "I can't read the stars like Muna's father to see if you'll be safe. But I can take other precautions. You're not going to that Club any more."

Tiamat stared at her in despair. "But— "

"No buts." Nanname's voice softened. "I only want what's best for you, Tia. When you've children of your own, you'll understand."

Tiamat bit her lip. She resisted a cruel urge to remind Nanname that she wasn't *her* child. "But all my friends are in the Club!" she protested. "Master Andulli won't be very happy if you don't let me play." Ikuppi and Labinsin would be, though. Gloatingly, ecstatically happy.

"I'll speak to Master Andulli."

Nanname's tone warned that the conversation was over. She rummaged under the bench again and produced Tiamat's empty pouch. "There's not much point you helping in the lab today, not with that hand. I've had an order for some more Ishtar's Tears. You can go to the garden and collect the rose petals we need. White ones. No bruises. But be back here by sunset. The streets are obviously not as well patrolled as they used to be. No doubt the city guard are all up on the wall instead of doing their job down here. The sooner this stupid war's over, the better for all of us."

The first thing Tiamat did was go looking for Simeon. She kept seeing him throwing onions, yelling to call the boys off her, fleeing into the dark alleys with Ikuppi's gang hard on his heels... trapped in some corner...

Ikuppi's dagger slicing down like a crescent of the moon... It was a relief to discover Simeon was at the Tablet House learning his numbers, although it meant her questions would have to wait. Not feeling up to another argument with the Egibi wardum, she worked her way slowly through the crowds, searching for the alley where they'd been ambushed last night. Everything looked different by daylight. When she thought she'd found the right place, there was a new pile of refuse steaming in the sun but no sign of blood or Simeon's onions. She searched through the rubbish, holding her breath against the smell and pushing away eager dogs who thought she was helping them dig for scraps, but it was obvious the tablet wasn't there. Eventually, with the sun nearing its zenith, she had to give up.

She called at Zababa Wharf to see if Simeon's lesson had finished, only to discover that his family had collected him in an ox-cart. When she asked where they'd gone, the wardum told her with a snooty smile that Judean business was none of his concern. Tiamat sighed and made her way to the garden. At least she knew Simeon was all right. She'd call at his house again on her way home.

By mid afternoon, she had filled her pouch with waxy white petals and was feeling a bit calmer. She finished up at the secret fountain. There was a bench in the grotto that provided a good place to think. Sun filtered through the leaves, water dripped, swallows swooped on the other side of the vines that shaded the entrance.

She fought her conscience a moment, then pushed her hand into the hiding place under the fountain and pulled out the cylinder-seal. She lay back on the bench and rested it on her knees, watching the shadows play over the dark blue stone and thinking of her unknown parents.

What would she do if she found out who they were? How could she love a mother who had left her for the dogs? She shook her head. No matter what Nanname said, she had to go back to the Twenty Squares Club. It was the only way to help the sirrush.

She never meant to fall asleep, but it was so peaceful in the grotto, the air warm and heavy with scent, and she was so tired after last night. Before she knew it, her eyelids closed.

She woke with a start from a muddled dream of the sirrush mouldings on the Ishtar Gate coming alive and fighting the tiny blue sirrush on her seal. She was trying to stop them, and their tongues were licking her left hand. Only this time, it wasn't a cool kiss they gave her but burning red flame, and when she looked down her hand had gone. Blood pumped from her wrist as Ikuppi brandished his dripping dagger above it, laughing evilly…

She jerked upright on the bench, her heart thudding. The grotto was dim and chill. Her hand had flopped into the fountain. The seal lay in the cracked basin beside her pouch.

Someone was still laughing.

Her breath caught in alarm. Holding the jasmine aside and peering into the grotto was a man with no beard. He wore baggy riding breeches under a short, fringed tunic with two belts that crossed over his chest. A short sword swung at his hip. Although she couldn't see his eyes in the shadows, she could feel them looking at her. Her skin prickled.

"Who are you?" she demanded. There was no time to put the seal back in its hiding place. She knocked it quickly into her pouch and swung herself off the bench. "What do you want?"

The laughter stopped. "Up here!" the man called to someone below, before returning his attention to Tiamat. "You took some finding, Tiamat Nanname-daughter, I must say."

"Who are you?" she repeated, her heart still thudding. "How do you know my name?"

The man came into the grotto with a curious, snake-like movement, took her elbow and steered her out on to the terrace. The sky was deep mauve, the sun low and red above Nebuchadnezzar's Wall. Tiamat transferred her despairing gaze from the sun to her captor. He wasn't nearly as young as she'd thought, but the fierce glint in his eyes made up for the silver in his curls. "I know everything about you, Tiamat," he said softly, releasing her elbow. "It's my job."

A sandal scraped behind her. She twisted her head. Two soldiers blocked the steps, their swords glittering in the low sun.

The sight of those exposed blades brought back all the terror of the attack in the alley. She made a dash for the edge of the terrace, only to be brought up short when one of the soldiers leapt across to cut her off.

"Don't be stupid, Tiamat," said the beardless man. "How far do you think you would get? I have men all over these gardens and a hundred more on the Wall, should you fancy another expedition up there."

Ice trickled down her spine. "I – I have to be home by sunset," she stammered, hating herself for sounding afraid and cursing herself for falling asleep. "I haven't done anything wrong! I've permission to be here and collect flowers! Lady Nanname's got a sealed tablet from the King."

"I know," said the beardless man, descending another step. "I authorized it myself. But right now I'm far more interested in another seal." He pulled two halves of a small, round tablet from a pouch at his waist. "Recognize this?"

Tiamat stared at it in despair. "No."

His eyes narrowed. He crept towards her with that snake-like gait. "Oh, I think you do."

Tiamat thought fast. "That's not mine. It's Egibi clay. There's a stamp on the back– " Too late, she realized her mistake.

A raised eyebrow. "Really? And how would you know that, I wonder?" He nodded to the men behind her. "Search her."

"But I've only got rose petals!" She whirled, only to

find her way blocked again by those two swords. She stared wildly down the terraces. Other soldiers could be seen picking their way through the shadowed greenery below.

The beardless man sighed. "Your name is on the List of First Offenders, Tiamat Nanname-daughter. If necessary, I have the right to arrest you. I'm sure you would prefer to cooperate with me voluntarily?"

Tiamat bit her lip. "Who are you?" she whispered again.

He smiled coldly, his face wrinkling, but not in the kindly way of Master Andulli's. It looked more like the entrails of a sheep when the diviners were doing a reading. "Don't you know? I'm King Nabonaid's Ensi. I believe some people call me the Demon."

Tiamat swallowed.

Another cold smile. "I see you've heard of me. Good. Perhaps now you'll be sensible?"

Left with little choice, she watched as one of the soldiers took her pouch and rummaged through the rose petals, bruising them with his callused fingers. When he found the seal, he presented it to the Demon with a triumphant smile.

"I didn't steal it, sir!" she said quickly. "I found it in the fountain."

The Demon examined the lapis lazuli cylinder closely, looking from the broken tablet to the seal and back again. "Yes," he whispered. "This looks like it."

"I was putting it back, really I was! I only made the

impression because I wanted to know more about the sirrush."

The Demon's gaze darted from the seal to her face. "What have you heard about the King's sirrush?" he hissed, the gleam back in his eyes.

"N – nothing. I mean, I know they run between the walls at night. I take them food… that is, I used to before I got caught."

"I see." The Demon looked at her bandaged hand. Still considering her, he put the broken tablet back into his pouch and dropped the seal on top. He glanced thoughtfully at the setting sun, then nodded. "Bring her. I have some more questions for the girl and this is not the place to ask them."

Tiamat's heart thumped faster. "But Lady Nanname's expecting me back! I can't go with you."

The Ensi was already slipping down the steps with his creepy, snake-like gait. One of the soldiers caught Tiamat's arm and dragged her after him. The other followed, his hand resting on his sword. Back on the terrace, a third soldier she hadn't noticed stepped out of the bushes and picked up her fallen pouch. Tiamat dug in her heels, all the stories she'd heard about the Demon spinning inside her head.

"Please," she begged. "I have to go home. Lady Nanname will be worried about me– Ow! Stop it! You're hurting my hand."

The soldier dragging her down the steps, tiring of her struggles, had produced a leather cord which he began to wind around her wrists.

"No!" she shouted, really frightened now. "Sir Ensi, please! I haven't done anything! Please tell him to stop."

The Demon turned and frowned at the soldier. "Put that away," he said.

"But she's resisting arrest, sir."

"She's not under arrest." He looked hard at Tiamat. "Yet."

This gave her the strength to go with the soldiers out on to the Ajiburshapu Way, where the Demon turned right and led the way at a smart pace between the rows of moulded lions to the Ishtar Gate. The high, blue arch, shadowed now the sun was going down, was like the mouth of a monster waiting to swallow them alive. The bulls and sirrush that decorated it seemed ready to leap off the bricks and trample her. This was the first time Tiamat had entered the inner city through the Ishtar Gate and it made her feel very small, but she straightened her shoulders and tried to look as if she came this way every day. She felt the eyes of the guards watching her curiously as the Demon led the way under the first arch, along a narrow passage, through an open central court, and along a second passage under the inner wall. The soldiers' sandals echoed. No one challenged them. The great, bronze-barred gates swung shut behind them with a thud that made Tiamat jump. She gazed up at the battlements that surrounded the inner city, suddenly aware of how difficult it would be to get out again until morning.

When the Demon turned off the Ajiburshapu Way and led them down some shadowy steps to a door in the wall of the Old Palace, she hung back again. "Sir Ensi?" she whispered. "Can you please send someone to tell Lady Nanname I'll be late home? She'll be worried about me."

She thought he hadn't heard. The soldiers jerked her on, across a courtyard surrounded by high walls to another door. Tiamat caught a glimpse of stone pillars and arches rising into the sky with iron bars across the openings, but she wasn't given time for a proper look. The Demon hurried them down a smoky, torchlit passage and through another door, where he finally turned with a cold smile.

"We have already visited the Lady Nanname," he said as Tiamat stared nervously around the vault. "She led us to believe the seal was hidden in her house. My men wasted a lot of time searching, but I think I understand now why she was so reluctant to tell us its whereabouts. It always amazes me what lengths a mother is willing to go to in order to protect her child – and you're not even her own flesh and blood." He shook his head.

It was difficult to take in this and her surroundings at the same time. The room was some kind of storage vault, cold and gloomy with an arched roof. A single, smoky oil lamp swung from a bronze chain, doing little to light the shadows. There were old stains on the floor. The whole place smelled – of oil, bitumen, and something else that was vaguely familiar. Three of the walls were of solid stone. The fourth was barred. Beyond the bars lay a thick, heavy darkness.

Tiamat wrapped her arms around herself and shivered.

The Demon motioned the soldiers to take up positions at the door. Thankfully, they didn't close it.

"Do you know where you are, Tiamat?"

She blinked at the Ensi. "In… in the Old Palace?"

"You haven't heard of this place? It's the only stone building in Babylon. One of the ancient kings had it built for his pets."

"I don't know much about the inner city."

"It's in disrepair now, of course. It's been a long time since a king brought anything back from his travels worth storing down here. But this place has other uses. Some people call it the House of Silent Screams. Do you know why?"

She shook her head. Her mouth was too dry to speak.

"Perhaps you can guess?"

Tiamat didn't want to think about it. "Why have you brought me here?" she managed in the end.

The Demon smiled. "I'd like to tell you a story, Tiamat. It's about King Nebuchadnezzar's favourite wife, the Persian Princess Amytis. I assume you've heard of her? It was her garden you were sleeping in when I found you, after all."

If he was watching for a reaction, he wasn't disappointed. "Persian? But I thought— " She bit her lip.

The Demon chuckled. "You didn't know she was a

Persian, did you? Nebuchadnezzar married her in an attempt to form a peaceful alliance between our peoples – not that it lasted long. Things were already deteriorating when the people saw sense and put Nabonaid on the throne. But old Nebuchadnezzar was soft enough on her at the time. He had the garden built and planted it with exotic flowers and trees to remind the Princess of the mountains of her homeland. What not so many people know is that King Nebuchadnezzar also gave his beloved Princess a cylinder-seal made from lapis lazuli as a wedding present. A very ancient and special seal which contains the secret of opening the gates that lead beyond the Earthly Ocean."

A seal, a lapis lazuli seal.

The Demon paced the vault as he spoke, the gleam back in his eyes.

"According to the legends, the King of Babylon journeyed beyond the Earthly Ocean to bring back leaves from the Tree of Life for the Twenty Squares Garland. He also brought back a sirrush egg at the same time. Of course, no king of Babylon has journeyed beyond the Earthly Ocean in thousands of years. The secret of opening the gate is supposed to have been forgotten, yet the answer's right there on the seal for those who have eyes to see."

He paused to stare through the bars.

"The priests guard their secrets closer than silver, but I believe a special sirrush was hatched at the New Year Festival and kept in here until the Championships, when the priests used the creature in their Gate-Opening Ritual so the King could collect leaves for that year's Garland and another egg, thus ensuring immortality for the Champion, the City, and himself. King Nabonaid and I have been sacrificing sirrush on the night of the Twenty Squares Championships for years. Unfortunately, however, it appears the creatures' blood is not enough. I've been wondering for a while if the seal itself might be important to the Ritual, but although the Princess left plenty of documents in the Palace archives with its impression rolled across them, the actual seal was lost during the riots when Nabonaid took the throne."

He turned to Tiamat with a cold smile. "So you can imagine my interest when a student tablet turns up in the outer city bearing an impression from the past. At the same time, I hear reports of a girl who has been caught climbing between the walls when the sirrush were out and survived to tell the tale. Not only that, but she seems to have acquired an abnormal amount of luck and can use the Eye Symbol in Twenty Squares with the uncanny accuracy of the legendary players."

Sacrificing sirrush for years.

"How – how do you know that?" she whispered.

The Demon smiled again and slithered towards her. "I have my sources. The Egibi Gamesmaster is up to something, so naturally I'm keeping an eye on him. But something puzzles me. Was it Lady Nanname or Master Andulli who sent you up on the wall to try to touch the sirrush?"

Her stomach churned. "No one sent me. I just wanted to feed them. And I didn't know it was Princess Amytis' seal, I swear!"

"Shh." He put a finger over her trembling lips. "I forgive you. You led me to the seal, after all. But you know something about the King's pets, don't you? I'd like to know why they didn't attack you when you went over that wall. We need to have a little chat about that."

"I don't know anything," she whispered, glancing at the open door and the two impassive soldiers guarding it. How far would she get before they caught her? It occurred to her that this was an opportunity to find out more about the sirrush, but all she wanted right now was to be safe back in her bed in the outer city with perfume wafting up the stairs and Nanname singing below. That smell...

"Maybe you do. Maybe you don't. It's my job to find out." The Demon lifted her injured hand, unwound the bandage and examined the cut with interest. "You were lucky," he said. "A little deeper, and you'd have lost the use of your thumb. Does it hurt?" He squeezed until she winced, then smiled and let go. Tiamat snatched her hand to her breast, prickles going down the backs of her legs.

"It was Ikuppi, wasn't it?" she whispered. "He told you about my luck." She had an even colder thought. "You were the one who told him to cut off my hand!"

The Demon's lips tightened. "Your juvenile quarrels are nothing to do with me. This attitude is not helping your case, Tiamat."

"You can't keep me here," she said, fighting tears. "You said I wasn't under arrest."

"No, but you might be able to help your King open the gates that lead beyond the Earthly Ocean. All loyal subjects should help their King if they can. You are a loyal subject, aren't you, Tiamat? I'd hate to think those green eyes of yours indicate rebellious blood."

Her breath came faster. "I don't know anything about your stupid gates!"

"I'll be the judge of that."

The Demon crossed to the bars and gazed through them. "Now then, let's have the truth, shall we? Why exactly did you climb between the walls of the inner city on the 26th night of Ululu?"

Tiamat blinked back a tear. "I only wanted to show the sirrush to Simeon. He didn't believe they were real."

"Ah, yes. Your little Judean friend. Weren't you afraid?"

"I knew they wouldn't hurt me."

"Why?" The Demon turned and looked at her with interest.

She shook her head helplessly. "I just… knew."

"You know they're poisonous?"

"Yes… maybe…"

"And you still weren't afraid? Come over here, Tiamat, and put your hand through the bars."

She stared at him in renewed terror.

"Come on. I want to test something."

She shook her head.

"If you won't do it voluntarily, I'll have to ask my men to help. They might hurt your hand again."

Tiamat eyed the soldiers and shuddered. "What's in there?" she whispered.

"Can't you guess?"

That smell...

"Oh!"

She was across the vault in a flash, peering into the darkness beyond the bars. Yes, there! A gleam of red. A lidded eye. Her heart twisted. Lying on a pile of reeds at the very back of the barred vault was a sirrush. Its scales were dull. Its tongue flickered listlessly. Its tail lay in its own dung, crusted with scabs.

"What's wrong with it?" Tiamat demanded, turning on the Demon, her fear forgotten at the sight of the poor creature. *Trapped. Starving.*

"It's dying."

"What have you done to it?"

He smiled. "Nothing. I merely locked it in here in the dark with no food and no water according to the instructions in the Ritual. By the time we come to spill its blood, it won't put up much of a fight."

"You – you— " The tears she'd fought so long blurred Tiamat's eyes. "Let it go!"

"Don't be silly. It won't be much use between the walls in that state. This way, it can serve its King as it was hatched to do. Put your hand through, Tiamat, there's a good girl."

She clenched her jaw and stretched her good hand as

far through the bars as she could. The soldiers at the door stiffened. She still couldn't reach the poor sirrush, which did not move from its bed. Its eye opened a little wider and its tongue flickered in the gloom, but that was all.

The Demon sighed. "All right, you can take your hand out again now. It was an interesting experiment, but I always suspected that part of the Ritual was obsolete. Not that you're likely to have royal blood, anyway. When I put Nabonaid on the throne, I dealt with most of Nebuchadnezzar's family before they could breed."

Tiamat turned on him, furious and trembling at the same time. "At least let it have something to drink! It'll die before the Championships if you leave it to suffer like that."

The Demon shook his head. "And have it get wild again? My King would never forgive me. Besides, if it dies, we've six more to play with. This war has its uses, if only to persuade the priests to hatch more eggs for us."

"The King's crazy! The whole city knows it! And you're as mad as he is! When I get out of here, I'm going to tell everyone what you're going to do to that poor creature, and they'll – they'll—"

Another shake of the head. "They'll what, Tiamat? Do you really think anyone's going to care about the fate of a single sirrush with the Persians knocking at our gates?" He was watching her again with that slightly amused, cold look. She clung to the bars, trembling again.

"That's better. For a moment I thought you'd forgotten who I was. All right, let's go back to what happened on the wall. How close to the creatures did you get, exactly, before the sentries came?"

As Tiamat was wondering whether to admit the sirrush had licked her, feet echoed outside and a third soldier came into the vault. He glanced at Tiamat and cleared his throat. "Ah, Ensi..."

The Demon frowned. "What is it?"

"There's a man at the gate from the House of Egibi. He's asking for the girl. He knows she's here."

Another frown. "Tell him to wait. I haven't finished."

The soldier looked at Tiamat again. She held on tightly to the bars as he crossed the vault and whispered something in the Demon's ear.

The Ensi cursed softly. "Tell him— oh, never mind. I don't think the girl knows anything useful, anyway." He gave Tiamat an exasperated look. "Come along, Tiamat Nanname-daughter. Time to go home."

"You're letting me go?"

It was too much, too many shocks on top of one another. She gripped the bars tighter and stared one last time at the dying sirrush.

The Demon chuckled softly and motioned for the soldiers at the door to help her. "Doesn't want to leave her pet," he said. "No doubt she'd prefer it if their positions were reversed."

The soldiers laughed as they hoisted Tiamat between them. They had to carry her because her legs refused to work. The night air and the stars that had come out while she'd been inside made her dizzy. Her teeth began to chatter.

Master Andulli was waiting alone in the courtyard, his face stern. He took one look at Tiamat and put his arm around her shoulders, drawing her under his cloak. Without a word, and without acknowledging the Demon's sketchy hand-to-nose greeting, he turned his back on the King's Ensi and guided Tiamat through a door the soldiers held open for them, out on to the Ajibursharpu Way.

In silence, he supported her past the golden and white lions and into the shadow of the ziqqurat. The whole way, Tiamat's legs felt as if they belonged to someone else. Only when they'd turned their backs on the ziqqurat and descended into Marduk Street did Master Andulli draw her under an archway and let her stop.

Embarrassingly, the Gamesmaster's arms slipped around her, pressing her cheek against his fine robes. She resisted briefly. Then all the terror and desperation of the past double-hour came out in a huge gulp, and she was telling him everything between uncontrollable sobs, shivering and shaking and apologizing for wetting his clothes, while Master Andulli held her close and murmured soothing words into her hair.

He let her cry herself out, before pushing her back to examine her hand, which had begun to bleed again without its bandage. "Did the Demon do this?" he asked, his voice hard.

Tiamat sniffed. "No, no... that was an accident, yesterday..."

"He didn't hurt you at all?"

"No, not really."

Master Andulli's lips remained tight and stern. "What did he want?"

Tiamat shook her head. She felt like crying all over again when she thought of the sirrush. "The seal. The princess's seal. But he had a sirrush in there, Master Andulli! He was starving it, and he's going to sacrifice it on the night of the Championships, and he... he kept asking me..." She sniffed, unable to make sense of it all. "I'm sorry, I was so frightened. I just want to go home."

Master Andulli held her close again and smoothed her hair. "Shh now, shh. I think it'll be better if you stay with me tonight. The city gates are shut and my house is closest, but I'll send someone to let Lady Nanname know you're safe. She was the one who alerted us as to where you might have been taken." He paused, staring along the torchlit street. "She's fine. Don't worry."

There was a catch in his voice. Tiamat was too weary to work it out. She relaxed a little. "Thank you, Master Andulli," she whispered, remembering something. "I – I'm sorry I can't come to Twenty Squares Club any more."

He frowned at her. "Shh, Tiamat," he said. "Shh.

Don't think about that now. We'll work it out. We'll work everything out, and I'll make sure this sort of thing doesn't happen again. The Demon's got more sense than to antagonize the Egibi Family. Even Kings and Ensis have to eat."

Chapter 7

SUMERIAN RIDDLE

Let me have knowledge!

SUNSHINE, STREAMING THROUGH the grille of a window that overlooked a private courtyard, woke Tiamat. There was laughter below the window and the sound of splashing. She lay with her eyes closed, reluctant to move. Last night had been a blur of red-framed doorways that she didn't have to duck to walk through, lamplit rooms and strange faces. Someone had bandaged her hand properly while she slept and for the first time since Ikuppi's attack it didn't hurt. The bed was a proper wool-stuffed mattress on a wooden frame. Beside it was a chair and a small carpet. Under the window was a table bearing a bowl of figs.

Tiamat stared at the carpet, trying to imagine how rich Master Andulli must be to afford one. Its yellow and red design showed the flowers of Ishtar. She leant over to stroke the soft pile then slipped out of bed and, careful not to tread on the expensive floor covering, attacked the figs. She was part way through her second, the dark juice dribbling down her chin, when the door opened and a girl of about her own age came in. She wore her hair braided on one side of her head and a plain yellow tunic. A crescent had been burned into the back of her right hand, pale against her dark skin.

While Tiamat stared in horrified fascination at the brand, the girl stared back. "Don't they feed you in the outer city or somethin'?" she said, looking at the fig juice on Tiamat's chin. "Hurry up and finish it, then. I'm supposed to show you the you-know-what in case you don't know how to use things, which I expect you don't." She giggled.

With an effort, Tiamat tore her gaze from the girl's hand. "Things?"

Another giggle. "The Egibi Family don't crouch in the street with the commoners, you know. C'mon, it's this way."

Tiamat stepped carefully around the edge of the carpet and followed the girl, finishing the fig on the way. "Are you one of Master Andulli's daughters?" she asked.

The girl gave her a strange look. "Don't be silly! I'm one of his wardum. He bought me from the temple at Ur. It's in here, look. You sit on that plank, and when you've finished you got to pour this water down to clean the pipe. Don't forget! 'Cause if it blocks up, I'm the one who has to clear it, an' it stinks worse than the Palace sewers when the wind's in the wrong direction, I can tell you!"

She pulled such a face, Tiamat couldn't help but smile, though she felt stupid and embarrassed. Of course a daughter of the Egibi Family wouldn't be branded like a temple slave! And it felt wrong to be sitting in such a beautiful room for what, in the outer city, people used the public area beside the nearest open sewer.

"Wait!" she called, when the girl made to close the door. "Where's Master Andulli? I've got to get home. Something bad happened last night."

The girl glanced down the passage and returned to crouch behind the door, her eyes gleaming with curiosity. "What did the Demon do to you? We heard the Egibi men talking after you'd gone to bed. They said the Demon's harassing all the foreigners in the city because the Persians are gettin' so close. The Master was real angry. Said it was time for the citizens of Babylon to stand up for their rights. Course, Humusi – she's head of the house wardum here – thinks it's a bad idea, 'cause the Demon'd only drag the lot of us into his lair like he did during the riots after King Nabonaid took over and stopped the New Year Festivals, and then things'd be even worse than before. Humusi says it's always the poor folk who suffer, not the fine Masters with their grand ideas, and you only have to look at what he did to the perfume-maker. But I think—" Misinterpreting Tiamat's expression, she broke off. Her tone turned sympathetic. "Does your hand hurt? Mine hurt somethin' awful when they branded me. I screamed so loud they had to stuff linen into my mouth, and the priestesses said the moon god would hear me and be angry I'd woken him from his daytime sleep! But it'll get better. I hardly ever think about mine now. It must have been horrible in the House of Silent Screams, though. Were you terribly scared?"

Tiamat scrambled off the toilet and seized the girl's shoulders. "Never mind my hand! What happened to Lady Nanname?"

The girl pressed back against the door, her eyes wide. "I thought you knew— "

"WHAT DID THEY DO TO HER?" Tiamat pushed past her and looked wildly for a way out of the house.

"You forgot to flush." The wardum's reproachful voice followed her down the stairs. "Come back! I'm supposed to take you to the study next. Master Andulli said you're not to go home without him seeing you."

The outer door was barred. Tiamat struggled to lift the heavy cedar plank one-handed, but it was too much for her to manage alone. The wardum girl, seeing she wasn't going anywhere, went back to flush the toilet. Tiamat sank on the bottom stair, cradling her injured hand.

That was where Master Andulli found her when he came in from the courtyard. "Ah, there you are!" His concerned expression dissolved in a mass of kindly wrinkles as he joined her on the stair. "How are you feeling this morning? How's your hand? I had an asipu work a spell over it while you were asleep. Don't worry, we'll have you back playing Twenty Squares in no time."

"What happened to Lady Nanname?" Tiamat said in a tight voice.

Master Andulli sighed. "So tongues have been wagging, have they? She's fine, Tiamat – don't worry. I wouldn't lie to you."

"But the girl who showed me the toilet said—"

"Khatar?" Master Andulli called up the stairs. "What have you been saying?"

The wardum girl appeared, looking defensive. "I didn't know you hadn't told her, Master!"

Master Andulli sighed and put an arm around Tiamat's shoulders, drawing her to her feet. "It's my fault. I should have explained. I'll send you home very soon, Tiamat, but there's something I'd like you to help me with first." He looked back up the stair, where the wardum girl was still listening, her eyes bright in the gloom. "Go and clean the guest room, Khatar."

As the wardum went, Tiamat squared her shoulders. "I want to see Nanname!"

Another sigh. "The Demon's men made a bit of a mess. Nothing that can't be mended, but I think Lady Nanname would appreciate a little time on her own this morning to clean up. Don't worry. She knows where you are."

"Poor Nanname! It's all my fault."

"No, Tiamat, it's not your fault. Don't ever think that. But we need to find out why the Demon seems so interested in you all of a sudden. Now, come on through and let's see if we can make any sense of that seal you found."

The last thing on Tiamat's mind was the princess's seal. As far as she was concerned, it had brought nothing but trouble and the Demon was welcome to it. She was still worried about Nanname, but Master Andulli promised that they'd be finished within the double-hour and firmly steered her into a long room with doors that opened on to the sunlit central courtyard.

The room smelt of clay. Benches lined the walls, groaning under the weight of tablets still sealed in their thick, clay envelopes. More tablets showing grids of wedge-shaped writing were scattered over a large, cedarwood table. Their empty envelopes were stacked on the floor nearby. In the centre of the table lay an old, dusty transaction tablet verified with a cylinder-seal impression. Tiamat's heart beat faster as she recognized the sirrush under the ziqqurat. At the end of the table sat a man she didn't know. He wore the fringed sash of a scribe and was pressing neat wedges into fresh clay with a wooden-handled reed, breaking off now and again to frown at the tablet bearing Amytis' seal and to check through his piles of texts. Muna perched nervously on one side of the table, staring at her clasped hands and biting her lip. Enki lounged on the other side with his feet on one of the chairs. When Master Andulli entered, he swiftly put them on the floor.

Muna half rose. "Tia! Are you all right…?"

"She'll be fine," Master Andulli said. He raised an eyebrow at the scribe. "How are you doing?"

Tiamat slid into the chair next to Muna, glad to see a

friendly face. As the scribe shuffled through his tablets to show Master Andulli something he'd found, Muna reached for Tiamat's uninjured hand and squeezed. Though she knew it must have been Muna who had helped identify the seal, Tiamat flashed her a smile of gratitude.

Enki regarded them coolly across the table. "Finally!" he muttered. "I thought you were going to sleep all day! I've no idea why Father's wasting valuable Egibi time on this seal nonsense. I should have been at school half a double-hour ago. If I get whipped for being late, it'll be your fault, Green-Eyes."

"Shut up, Enki!" Muna hissed. "Tia's been through quite enough lately without putting up with your whingeing!"

Enki blinked at Muna, clearly taken aback that an outer city girl would dare talk to him like that in his own house. He glanced at Master Andulli and the scribe, scowled at Tiamat, and went back to picking splinters off the edge of the table.

Muna whispered, "Simeon told us what Ikuppi tried to do to you, the snake! Just wait till next Club night!"

Tiamat frowned. After the terror of the Demon's vault, she'd almost forgotten the attack in the alley. She glanced at the end of the table. "Does Master Andulli know?"

"He does now." Muna's face was set. "I hope he throws Ikuppi out of the Club completely! He might be our best player, but he never helps anyone else. He cheats, too, if he thinks he isn't going to win. That'll get us all disqualified if he does it in the Championships. The whole point of having a team is so we can help each other. Inner city people never seem to grasp that, somehow." She looked meaningfully at Enki.

Tiamat rubbed her injured hand. She had enough problems without Ikuppi.

Enki pulled a face and hissed across the table, "Ikuppi and his so-called friends are nothing to do with me! Just because we both live in the inner city doesn't mean we have anything in common. Ikuppi failed the entrance exam for the Temple School. Don't ask me which school he and his gang go to. I don't care. And for your information, I want Egibi to win just as much as you do. More, actually."

"Could have fooled me," Muna muttered.

But Tiamat leant forward, interested. "You go to the Temple School? Really?"

"Where did you think I went?" The Egibi boy's eyes were wary.

"Do you learn about the sirrush there? Do you know anything about their blood being used to open gates?"

Enki sat back with a laugh. "The King's Ritual, you mean? Not content with getting herself arrested and her mother's laboratory smashed up, now she wants to know Temple secrets as well! Do you think the priests tell *us*?"

"I did not get arrested—" Tiamat began, then realized what else he'd said. Her stomach gave an uncomfortable turn. "What do you mean, 'smashed up'?"

Master Andulli looked round with a frown. "Quiet, you three. Now, listen. These Sumerian texts can be tricky, but Shamshi thinks he has the translation right now. This is what the text on Princess Amytis' seal, which the Demon seems so interested in, says in Akkadian... Shamshi, if you will?"

The scribe pulled the tablet he'd been writing on and the one bearing Amytis' seal towards him. He cleared his throat.

"I might have some of the minor wording wrong. This tablet's been gathering dust in the Egibi archives a long time and the impression is worn in places. Also, it's written in the ancient Sumerian riddle style, which means it's about as clear as the Palace sewers after a royal feast." Muna giggled, which seemed to throw him off his stride. He glanced at Master Andulli and cleared his throat again. "Well, er, here it is...

A garden with a foundation like heaven,
A stairway where Shamash and Sin stroll hand in hand,
A gate which like a copper drum has been covered with skin,
Blessed of Marduk has opened it,
Ishtar's Gift comes out of it."

As he quoted the words of the riddle, the scribe's voice took on a sonorous tone that sent shivers down Tiamat's spine. The fingers that the sirrush had licked began to tingle again. She gripped the bandage tightly. Muna, assuming her hand was hurting because of the injury, flashed her a sympathetic look.

There was a short silence. Then Enki, looking interested for the first time, said, "The third line's obvious. It's from the school riddle. The drum covered in skin is what the diviners use to talk to the gods. It means something is hidden and the right rituals have to be used to find it, otherwise it'll remain hidden. At school, it means we all have to behave otherwise we won't learn anything." He pulled a face. "Our teachers love that line."

Tiamat glanced at him in surprise. For a moment, she thought Enki was actually about to grin. But he quickly reassumed his haughty expression.

"Hmmm." Master Andulli curled his beard around his little finger and frowned at the scribe's tablet. "The first line's almost the same as the school riddle, too. That seems to suggest the garden in question is within the Temple precinct, maybe one of the priests' herb gardens? The stairway's obviously supposed to be the ziqqurat. Where Shamash and Sin walk hand in hand might mean a day when the sun and moon are both in the sky together. We'll have to ask Muna's father to look at his astrology tablets. Blessed of Marduk has opened it..." He stared thoughtfully at Tiamat, then shook his head. "Sumerian riddles, eh? Enki, have you any more ideas?"

Enki shrugged.

"Muna? Tiamat?"

Muna shook her head. Tiamat sat very still. "Blessed of Marduk means the sirrush, doesn't it? The Demon said he was going to sacrifice one of them to open the gate."

Master Andulli's lips tightened. "That's obviously his interpretation. But as I understand the legend, and Shamshi agrees, it was always a princess who opened the gate for the king. Maybe it means she was blessed by Marduk during the Ritual. I must ask the High Priest about it." Again, he gave Tiamat a thoughtful look.

Her heart lifted, briefly overcoming her worry for Nanname. "Then the Demon doesn't need to kill the sirrush, after all! We have to tell him!"

Enki gave her a withering look.

Master Andulli sighed. "I doubt the Demon would listen, Tiamat. It's no secret that he and Nabonaid are searching for the Tree of Life that the ancient kings used to defy age and death, and if that means killing every last creature, man, woman, and child in Babylon, then I'm afraid they'll do it. If I didn't know better, I'd suspect they'd even started this war to aid their quest – they're certainly using it for their own purposes. Strangely enough, though, if you look at the riddle, the Demon could be on the right track. Ishtar's Gift is Life, after all."

The scribe, who had been chewing the end of his reed, cleared his throat. "There are some who would say Ishtar's Gift is Death – she's the goddess of war as well as love, remember. But I might have muddled some of the words. 'Drum' could also mean 'kettle'. And 'gate' might mean 'neighbourhood'."

"Which makes even less sense!" Enki said, scraping

his chair as he got to his feet. "I'm very late for school, Father."

Master Andulli gave his son an exasperated look. "Sit down, Enki!"

Enki sat, scowling.

Master Andulli paced the room, winding a finger in his beard. "Tiamat acquired her luck after finding Amytis' seal... Let's assume for a moment that the legends are true. Suppose the seal really does have power? Suppose the Demon somehow manages to use it to open the gate beyond the Earthly Ocean, and Nabonaid brings back leaves from the Tree of Life for the Twenty Squares Garland like the ancient kings used to? Can you imagine the city's reaction? No one would care how mad Nabonaid was if they saw him complete the King's Ritual and gain the favour of the gods. Part of the reason the Persians have got so far without much of a fight is because our army's divided down the middle. Many people in this city would like to see Nabonaid dethroned. A united Babylon is the last thing we need at this stage – it could throw all our plans out. Except... maybe there's a way we can turn this to our advantage. Mmm, I wonder..."

Tiamat and Muna stared at the Egibi Gamesmaster. The only other time they'd seen him look so disconcerted was when an Egibi player lost a Twenty Squares Game they should have won. On the other side of the table, Enki shifted in his chair and frowned at his father.

The scribe looked uncomfortable. "Er, sir?" he said, glancing at Tiamat and Muna. "Do you think it's a good idea to talk about...? With the children...?"

Master Andulli stopped pacing. He gave the scribe a distracted look, sighed and returned to the table. He rested one hand on Tiamat's shoulder and the other on Muna's. "I'm sorry. I get carried away sometimes. I should let you girls go home and Enki get along to school. It's later than I thought. Tiamat must be exhausted."

Tiamat mumbled something, embarrassed. Enki gave her another scowl. Muna frowned.

"I'm afraid I have to get to the temple urgently," Master Andulli went on. "But I'll send Khatar with a pass to see you through the Marduk Gate so there's no trouble – if you'll just write a quick one for me, Shamshi?"

The scribe extracted a small tablet from his bucket. He frowned at Tiamat as he pressed her name and Muna's neatly into the clay. Master Andulli unclipped his own seal from his wrist and rolled it across the bottom.

"There!" He smiled at them both, a mass of wrinkles. "An Egibi pass will get you anywhere in the city! Give my apologies to the Lady Nanname, Tiamat, and tell her I hope to see you at Twenty Squares Club tomorrow night. You'll have to throw with your other hand for a while, but it'll be good practice for your strategy." He added quietly, "And don't worry about Ikuppi. He's in a worse state than you, by all reports. As from today, he's off the Team. Labinsin's back in as Reserve, on the condition he remains strictly on his best behaviour – so any more funny business, you let me know immediately. Understand?"

Tiamat nodded, her head spinning. She remembered Ikuppi running into the alleys, screaming "I'm cut! I'm cut!"

Muna's expression said she hadn't known about Ikuppi, though Enki's smirk suggested he had. Master Andulli called Khatar, who appeared suspiciously quickly, and handed her the pass. He turned back for a word with the scribe and the four children escaped into the street.

Even the dazzling glare and heat of midday seemed welcome after that strange meeting. They stood in the shade of the palm trees that lined Enlil Street, staring awkwardly at one another.

Enki shook his head. "Father must have flipped! No one really believes in that Tree of Life stuff. We learn about it in the Temple School, of course, but it's just some old legend like the one about the ancient kings using the ziqqurats to travel between cities without having to step outside the walls. Bedtime tales for babies, huh!"

Muna glared at him. "You were interested enough in the riddle, I seem to remember. Anyway, I thought you said the priests didn't tell you their secret rituals, so how do you know?"

Enki put his nose in the air. "You don't have to know

the details to know what's possible and what isn't. If you ask me, old Nabonaid's not as mad as everyone thinks, refusing to take part in the New Year Festival – at least he's never had his beard tugged and been slapped around by the priests and had his favourite wife come back smelling of sirrush!" Seeing the expression on Tiamat's face, he grunted. "I haven't time to stand out here in the sun explaining things to uneducated girls. Some of us have important lessons to get to. I only hope you didn't let that creature in the Demon's vault lick you, Green-Eyes. Everyone knows what happens to the princess in the legend if the sirrush dies before the gate opens." He drew a finger across his throat.

Feeling a little sick, Tiamat watched Enki disappear into the shadow of the ziqqurat. Heat shimmered from its brightly-painted tiers, forming a rainbow haze over the temple precinct. At its summit, the House of Heaven on Earth gleamed gold like a second sun.

"Egibi snob!" Muna scowled after the boy.

Tiamat bit her lip and thought of that almost-grin. "He knows his riddles."

"Not half as well as he thinks he does!" said a voice behind them. They'd forgotten Khatar, who had been lurking on the step with Master Andulli's pass.

"I know what that Ishtar line means," she said. "The women in the temple at Ur were always goin' on about it. Ishtar's the goddess of love, so Ishtar's Gift is someone who... you know." She giggled at their blank expressions. "The princess used to sleep in the shrine at

the top of the ziqqurat and in the night a ma
come. Then he'd go away again, and when the p
got pregnant everyone would say it was the god." She giggled again. "They must think we're all stupid."

Muna blushed furiously.

Tiamat stared at the wardum girl. "You were listening!"

Khatar smiled. "Course I was listening! How else am I expected to find anything out? You wouldn't believe some of the things that go on in the Egibi house, I could tell you—"

"Ishtar's the goddess of war as well as love," Muna said, cutting her off. "And you shouldn't spread stories about your masters."

Khatar scowled at her. "Goin' to tell on me, are you, *mushkenum*?" She used the rude word for people who lived in the outer city.

"I just might, *wardum*."

"Stop it!" Tiamat said. "I don't feel very well."

The midday sun reflecting off all the bricks made her dizzy. Her head spun with strange legends and riddles. Her hands trembled. *I only hope you didn't let that creature lick you. Everyone knows what happens to the princess if the sirrush dies.* Had Enki been making it up to scare her or was it really part of the legend? And how true were the legends, anyway?

Muna turned to her in concern. She told Khatar to take Tiamat's other arm, which the wardum did with a stiff glare that made it obvious she wasn't helping because Muna had told her to, and the three girls made their way along the palm-lined streets to Marduk Gate.

At the sight of the sentries' uniforms, Tiamat broke into a cold sweat. But the gates stood open, traffic was passing freely in both directions and there was no trouble. They didn't even have to show their Egibi pass – maybe just as well, since the clay was still wet. In the courtyard between the walls, they stopped to let a cart laden with vegetables creak past and Khatar seized the opportunity to whisper in Tiamat's ear.

"If you'll give me your ankle beads, I'll let you keep this." She brandished the Egibi pass.

Tiamat blinked at the tablet. It was a struggle to think.

Muna pushed the girl away. "Leave her alone, wardum! Can't you see she's had enough? C'mon, Tia, let's go."

"No, wait."

Tiamat untied the string of luck-beads she wore around her left ankle. Khatar snatched them with a grin and dropped the pass into her lap. "Thanks, Persian-Eyes! Hope you have as much luck as I do!" She winked at Tiamat and darted back into the passage under the wall.

Muna watched her go, lips set. "Why did she call you that? It's not funny. And why did you give her your beads? They're worth a lot more than that silly tablet!"

Tiamat shook her head as she pulled her friend through the second gate to join the outer city crowds. "You heard Master Andulli. An Egibi pass will get us anywhere in the city."

"But we're already out. We don't need it now. That wardum's sneaky. I don't trust her." Muna was frowning at the alleys. "Which way's your house, Tia? I'm taking you all the way home. You look like you're about to faint. Are you sure your hand's not infected? I'll bet you anything Ikuppi's dagger was dirty."

Tiamat slipped the pass into her pocket. "It's fine," she said, making an effort to stand on her own two feet. "I'll be all right, Muna. I'm just hungry." *And frightened I'm going to die*. "You don't have to take me home. You must have plenty of other things to do."

Muna shook her head. "Nothing important. I'm coming, all right? I've always wanted to see how perfumes are made."

Neither of them mentioned how unlikely it was that Lady Nanname would be making perfume today.

EGIBI TWENTY SQUARES TEAM
12th Tashritu

Gamesmaster

ANDULLI	Egibi Family of Babylon

Team

ENKI	Master Andulli's son, Enlil Street, inner city
SIMEON	Jacob's son, Judean Neighbourhood, outer city
MUNA	astrologer's daughter, outer city
TIAMAT	Nanname's adopted daughter, outer city
HILLALUM	farmer's son, country

Reserve

LABINSIN	Ikuppi's best friend, inner city

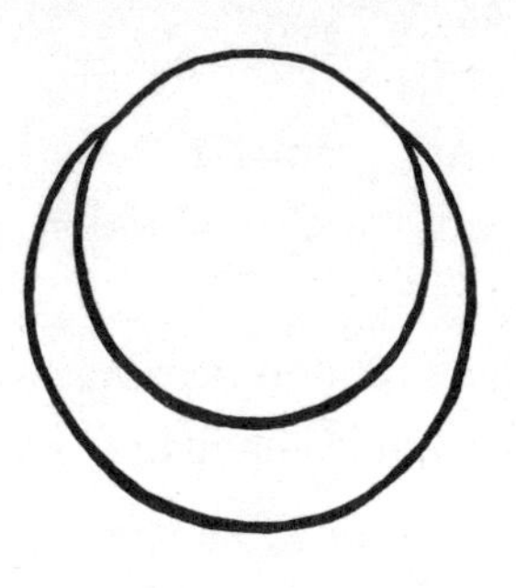

Chapter 8

MARDUK'S BLESSING

Free me from my bewitchment!

TIAMAT'S STOMACH TIGHTENED as she led Muna to the only home she'd ever known. She didn't need the warnings to tell her something was wrong. For the first time since she could remember, the alley did not smell of boiling greenery.

A large pile of broken glass and pottery partly blocked the door. A mastiff that she used to feed was scratching through it, snuffling at the strange smells. The dog came towards her expectantly, wagging its tail. She chased it off with a furious yell, picked a phial out of the rubble and stared at it. The stopper was missing, the precious glass cracked, the perfume she and Nanname had worked so hard to make gone for good. She clenched her fist, filled with anger. The Demon had done this.

Muna, who had been staring at the rubble in shocked silence, whirled in alarm as a figure leapt the pile and flung itself at them. Tiamat raised the phial, ready to fight, then dropped it with a shudder.

It was Simeon.

"We were expecting you back ages ago," he said. His eyes flickered to Tiamat's bandaged hand. He bit his lip. "I was so worried about you, Tia! By the time I got rid of Ikuppi's gang and worked my way back through the alleys, you were gone. Then yesterday I had lessons, and then I had to go to the synagogue. When I finally got away and came round to see if you were all right, there were soldiers in your house! I tried to help Lady Nanname, but there were too many of them, and—"

"Is Lady Nanname all right?" Muna said quickly.

"Yes, she's inside. I'm helping her clear up." He glanced uncertainly at Tiamat. "It's – er – quite a mess in there."

"I know. I heard."

Simeon and Muna exchanged an awkward glance. Tiamat pushed past them and rushed inside.

Nanname leant against the wall of the laboratory, her hair stuck to her cheeks in sweaty tendrils. She wore her oldest work robe with the sleeves rolled up. There were dark circles around her eyes and her fingers were bleeding from handling the broken glass. The vats were empty. Splintered holes in their sides showed why. The chest where they kept their stock of perfumes and oils was smashed too, though the floor had been swept clean. A few stray rose petals, curling at the edges, had been collected in a cracked bowl and placed on the bench. What for, Tiamat didn't know.

"Nanname..." She gulped. "I'm sorry."

The perfume-maker's warm arms folded her into a hug. Nanname stroked her hair and murmured, "It's not your fault, Tia. We should have handed that seal over to the authorities straight away, admitted you'd found it." She paused before saying quietly, "I couldn't think what they were looking for at first. They just barged in and started smashing things. Then they showed me the tablet, and I knew." The hug tightened. "Oh, Tia! I was so frightened for you! I tried to get to the garden to warn you, but the soldiers wouldn't let me leave the house, and I can't run with this stupid leg of mine."

"I'm all right. They didn't hurt me."

"Thank Ishtar for that!"

"It was Master Andulli who got me out."

Nanname examined her carefully from all sides as if she were a rare flower, and managed a smile. "It seems we have a lot to thank the Egibi Family for."

"The Demon said—" Tiamat broke off, noticing that Nanname was not putting any weight on her bad leg. She saw the blood crusted on the hem of her robe and clenched her fists, the anger returning. "They hurt you!"

"It was my own fault. I tried to delay them."

"But—"

"I'm all right, Tia. It could have been a lot worse."

There was an uneasy silence. The shadows in Nanname's words scared Tiamat. Part of her wanted to race back to the House of Silent Screams and kick the Demon until he couldn't walk properly, either. Shout at him. Make *him* bleed. The other part never wanted to go near the inner city again.

"The Egibi Family are going to lend Lady Nanname the silver to buy new phials and things," Simeon said behind her. "So you can still live here and make perfumes, and we can still go to Twenty Squares Club, and you can still play in the Championships. It'll be all right, Tia, you'll see."

Tiamat looked questioningly at Nanname, but the perfume-maker's proud face gave little away. "It's true," she said. "I can hardly refuse to let you play when Master Andulli's been so good to us, can I? He's agreed to arrange an escort to see you safe home afterwards, so there won't be any trouble with those inner city boys or – other people."

Tiamat didn't know if she was glad or not. Playing in the Championships would mean going into the Palace, which was what she'd wanted, but that was before she'd met the Demon. Not noticing her unease, Muna and Simeon exchanged smiles.

"There's a carpenter coming this afternoon to mend the vats and make us a new chest," Nanname went on. "He's one of Simeon's father's friends, so I know he'll do a good job. We'll see about ordering some more tubes and oil tomorrow." She managed another smile. "I've just about finished clearing up in here, but we should get that broken glass to the rubbish tip before someone walks on it and cuts their feet. That'd be a useful job you could do for me this afternoon – only watch out for the Persians if you're going near the wall."

They hardly heard the old warning. After what had happened, the possibility of an attack from outside seemed as remote a threat as the sun falling from the sky.

By the time they'd carried three loads of broken glass through the Judean Neighbourhood to the rubbish tip in the shadow of Nebuchadnezzar's Wall, Tiamat had told Simeon and Muna everything that had happened to her since the attack in the alley, and heard all the gossip from their side. A chill crept over her as she began to realize the full implications of what she'd done that night on the wall. Meanwhile, Simeon wanted to know all about the meeting in Master Andulli's house and why Muna had been included.

"I think he just wanted Tia to have a friend there," she said, giving Tiamat a quick look.

They all knew why he hadn't asked Simeon. Judeans in the inner city without a good reason caused awkward questions, and questions were the last thing Master Andulli wanted right now.

"He's planning something," Muna added, glancing up at a sentry patrolling the battlements overhead. "Something to do with the Championships."

Simeon smiled. "He wants Egibi to win, you mean."

"No, it's more than that. If you'd been there, you'd know. Tia, what do you think?"

Tiamat gazed at the dusty path that led along the

inside of the wall to the tip. Further down, two shaven-headed wardum were shovelling the rubble into a cart ready to transport it outside the city. The ox between the shafts looked as bored as they did, swishing flies with its tail. It was quiet out here at this time of day, the smells trapped in the shimmering heat under the wall. "I'm not sure. I didn't understand all that stuff about the gates. But I think I know what Marduk's Blessing is now." She paused, shivered, and said firmly, "Feeding the sirrush isn't enough, not any more. I've got to get them out of the Palace before the Demon kills them."

Muna and Simeon glanced at each other.

"I don't think that's a very good idea, Tia."

"Nor do I!" Muna shook her head forcefully. "Not after what the Demon did to you."

Tiamat set her jaw. "I have to get them out. You don't understand. I can't leave them in there, not now."

Simeon sighed. "I know you care for them, Tia. But throwing scraps over the wall is one thing. Stealing the King's dragons is quite another. It's sad that one of them is going to be sacrificed, but all sorts of animals are sacrificed in the temples every day. You can't save them all."

"It's more than that." She curled her left hand, took a deep breath. "Enki said that if the sirrush died before the gate opened, then so did the princess it had licked – and one of them licked me! Simeon saw."

Muna frowned. "That was just Enki being stupid. He said it himself – no one believes the old legends. It's only a story, Tia."

"No, listen. What if it's true? Why am I so hungry lately? I normally don't eat anything when I'm frightened and worried. I think it's the sirrush, *making* me hungry. I feel what they feel. Trapped. Half starved. They're Marduk's creatures, aren't they? And they gave me all that luck at Twenty Squares, which is sort of a Blessing. It makes sense, Muna! And if the Demon kills the sirrush that licked me, I might die too."

Voicing her fears helped.

Muna was still shaking her head, but Simeon chewed a nail and stared at her thoughtfully. "When Ikuppi tried to cut Tia's hand in the alley, *he* was the one who got injured. Maybe the dragon's poison does contain some ancient power. Grandfather says all legends are based on truth."

"But that's silly!" Muna protested. "Master Andulli said it was the seal that gave you your luck. Anyway, I thought you told us the Demon's only going to sacrifice the sirrush in his vault? That one couldn't have licked you if it was locked in."

"He said he'd use one of the others if it died before the Championships. We can't risk leaving any of them, Muna! Besides, he'd kill the one that licked me eventually. Next year, the year after that... or the Persians will, if they try to get in and meet them between the walls." She bit her lip. She might have known they wouldn't understand.

But Simeon said slowly, "Tia had the seal with her when she climbed between the walls. What if that's part of the magic? The princess holds the seal so the dragon knows it's supposed to bless her? That would make more sense than expecting it to know if someone has royal blood or not by smell or something."

Tiamat gave him a grateful look. "So you'll help me get them out? We'll have to do it before the Championships." She pulled out the Egibi pass. "We can use this to get into the Palace. Maybe we should do it tonight."

Muna's eyes widened. "So that's why you wanted the pass! Suppose I'd better help, since my name's on there as well." She grinned, though she looked scared.

Simeon shook his head. "Hold on! You can't just go rushing in there. Even if you do manage to get into the Palace without anyone arresting you, which is unlikely, how are you going to get out again with a herd of wild dragons?"

"They're not wild," Tiamat said. "They'll follow me. I know they will."

"Follow you where, exactly? Those creatures are bigger than full-grown camels! You're not going to be able to hide them in your secret fountain, you know."

Tiamat sank on to a pile of broken bricks. Simeon was right. Her vague idea of hiding the sirrush in the princess's garden wouldn't work. The Demon would simply send his soldiers to fetch them back. And next time he might do something worse than smash up Nanname's laboratory.

"There must be a way," she whispered. "I don't want to die."

The other two looked at each other.

Muna's arm went around her shoulders. Simeon sat on her other side and held her good hand. The sentries patrolling the wall took no notice of the three children sitting beside the rubbish tip. To pass the time in the midday heat, the men had scratched a Twenty Squares board in the shade of one of the lookout towers and were playing the simple, non-scoring version with stones as counters. They obviously weren't expecting an attack today. Their confidence made the children feel a bit better.

Muna said gently, "You're not going to die, silly! Maybe that's what Master Andulli's planning – to get the sirrush out? Did you tell him one of them had licked you?"

"I..." Hope stirred. "Yes, I told him last night, after he rescued me from the Demon."

"There you are, then! He doesn't want you to get hurt, so obviously he's going to make sure the Demon doesn't kill them."

Tiamat shook her head. "If Master Andulli was going to rescue them, I'm sure he would have said something."

Simeon's forehead creased in the way it did when he was considering which stratagem to play in Twenty Squares. "I've been thinking... The dragons have the run of the inner walls between sunset and sunrise, right? They must be able to get through the gateways or they'd be trapped in just one section of the wall, and that would defeat the object if they're supposed to be guarding the inner city."

"The sentries probably leave the side gates to the courtyards between the walls open at night," Tiamat said, not sure what he was getting at.

"Yes, that's what I think, too. So to let the creatures out, we only have to open one gate. There won't be much point letting them out on this side of the river, since they'd be trapped in the outer city. They'd cause a real panic, and we'd still have to get them past Nebuchadnezzar's Wall somehow. But what if we managed to open one of the outer gates on the other side of the river? They'd be free then, out on the plains. No one would ever catch them out there."

"But how are we supposed to open the gate?" Muna said. "They're designed to keep an army out!"

Simeon smiled. "That's where your Egibi pass comes in. Hillalum says there's always a queue to get in at Lugalgirra Gate at sunrise. There's a sort of unofficial camp outside, where people who have travelled a long way can stable their animals until the city opens. I bet you anything the sentries open that gate just as soon as they can to start letting people through. If we're lucky, there'll be a few double-minutes when the dragons are still between the walls, being driven back to their pen or whatever. We'll have to time it exactly right. You girls can flash your pass, pretend you're on important Egibi business and need to get through ahead of everyone else. The rest of us will keep the outer gates open while Tia calls the dragons. If she's right, and they do have a magical connection with her, then they'll break free when they hear her call and make for the gate. When we see them coming, we duck back outside and run like mad. It'll be chaos. No one will realize what's happening until it's too late."

Tiamat shivered in excitement. "What if they don't come when I call?"

Simeon regarded her levelly. "Then you'll know you've nothing to worry about, won't you?"

She curled her bandaged hand and nodded. Typical Simeon-style stratagem. The rescue plan was also a test to see if she was right about being magically connected to the sirrush.

"The rest of you?" Muna asked, frowning.

"You'll need someone to jam the gates open so the sentries can't close them quickly. Hillalum and I could probably manage it between us."

"We'd have to be outside the city at night."

"Yes."

Tiamat glanced up at the battlements. She'd never spent a night outside the city walls before. The thought frightened her more than she liked to admit. "Nanname would never let me," she said. "She thinks there are Persians behind every brick, waiting to gobble me up."

"My parents are the same," Muna said. "Father reads the stars every night to see if there's going to be an attack on the city."

Simeon nodded. "That's why it'll have to be tomorrow. It's our last Club meeting before the Championships. We'll tell our parents we have to stay on for a final practice after everyone else has gone home, and that the session might go on all night, so they won't worry. Then we'll get out of the city on Hillalum's boat. He says the sentries are never as interested in boats going out as they are the boats coming in. I'll have to hide, of course, but you girls can use your Egibi pass."

It sounded as if a lot of things could go wrong, and Tiamat couldn't imagine Master Andulli's reaction once he found out what they'd used his pass for. But she seized on Simeon's plan because she couldn't think of anything else. "What about the sirrush in the Demon's vault?" she said.

"We can't help that one," Simeon gave her his level stare. "But it's not the one that licked you, is it?"

"And what about our escort home?" Muna asked.

The boy frowned. "I'd forgotten about that... We'll have to let them walk us home then sneak back to the Wharf, tell Hillalum to delay the boat until we've given them the slip. Shouldn't be too difficult."

Tiamat shivered again. Lie to Nanname. Creep through the dark alleys where Ikuppi had ambushed them. Spend a whole night outside the city walls. Hope the sirrush came when she called. And after that, they still had to get back into the city and face everyone's wrath. Then she realized something else.

"The day after tomorrow's an evil-day, she whispered. "The fourteenth... that's when we'll be letting the sirrush out."

Muna went pale. "She's right! We can't do the rescue

on an evil-day! Something's bound to go wrong."

Simeon sighed. "Grandfather says only wicked people believe in evil-days. It's our best chance. Do you want to rescue your dragons or not?"

Muna looked from one to the other of them, biting her lip.

Tiamat made the decision. "Let's do it," she said.

Chapter 9

OUTSIDE

Thou art the judge of my actions.

TIAMAT AND SIMEON arrived early at the Egibi Tablet House the following evening, hoping to outline their plan to Hillalum before the session started, only to find he hadn't turned up yet. The other Club members crowded round to ask if Tiamat's lucky hand was still working. She growled at them to leave her alone, which merely made everyone more curious about the bandage. In the end, to get rid of them, Simeon had to invent a story that the bandage was to stop her luck running out before the Championships. Tiamat wasn't sure they believed this, but at least they stopped asking questions. Enki turned up on his own and gave her a strangely wary look, before removing his cloak and seating himself at the board nearest the door. He fiddled with the counters as he waited.

Muna arrived out of breath and rushed across.

"Well?"

Tiamat shook her head in frustration. "He's not here yet. I hope he's coming."

"He will," Simeon said. "You know Hillalum's always late for everything."

But when one of the junior masters clapped his hands and told them all to settle down and play, there was still no sign of the farm boy. Since tonight was a full Club session, it took Tiamat another moment to realize that Labinsin hadn't turned up, either.

Unable to concentrate, she took the stool opposite Muna. Simeon gave them a warning glance and settled down to play Enki. By the time the Gamesmaster's robes whispered through the door, all three of them were tense enough to jump. Tiamat dropped the die. It rattled noisily across the floor, coming to rest beneath the upturned toe of one of Master Andulli's sandals.

Muna stiffened. Tiamat's cheeks burned as Master Andulli's gaze rested on her. She felt as if their plans must be pressed into her forehead with a reed. But the Gamesmaster simply nodded to her and moved his toe. A girl in a yellow tunic darted past him and retrieved the die. As she placed it back on their board, the crescent on the back of her hand shone in the lamplight. "That's a good trick to fiddle the score, Persian-Eyes," she said, winking at Tiamat. "Have to remember that."

Muna scowled. "Khatar! What are you doing here?"

"Come to practise, haven't I?"

"Where's Hillalum?"

"He's just outside, helpin' unload the boat. Brought a lot of stuff in for Master Andulli tonight."

Even as she spoke, the broad-shouldered farm boy came in, wiping seeds off his tunic. But before they had a chance to talk to him, Master Andulli cleared his throat.

"Everyone, this is Khatar. She'll be replacing Labinsin as Reserve on the Egibi Team this year, since I've been informed that Labinsin and Ikuppi have both defected to the Crown Team." He turned to Simeon and Enki with a smile. "That means they'll be your opponents in the Championships, boys. Try not to forget that, will you?"

There was a ripple of uncertain laughter, followed by whispers of amazement that an untried wardum should be picked for the Team. There were quite a few grumbles, too, but no one dared question the Gamesmaster. Khatar stood with folded arms, smiling at the room.

Master Andulli indicated Enki should rise and nodded to his vacant stool. "Take over White opposite Simeon, Khatar. We'll see how your game holds up against our star player."

It was true, Tiamat supposed. Now that Ikuppi had gone, Simeon was the best player in the Egibi Team. As if it mattered, now. None of them was likely to be playing in the Championships after tonight.

As Khatar took his place, Enki shook his head and muttered loudly, "Great! We lose our best player over some stupid outer-city quarrel, and now we get a wardum as Reserve. This whole Team's gone crazy. Now we haven't a hope of winning."

Khatar didn't seem to hear, or maybe she was used to ignoring such comments from the likes of Enki. *Stupid outer-city quarrel.* Tiamat clenched her good fist. Was that all he thought it was? Even now?

Across the board, Muna gave a little cough. "Ignore him, Tia."

Tiamat still wanted to thump Enki, but her anger evaporated when Master Andulli, after inquiring about her hand, said she should play Hillalum next. She seized the opportunity to outline their plan in whispers, losing shamefully to the boy in the mean time because her attention wasn't on the game.

Hillalum listened in silence, and for a horrible moment she thought he was going to refuse to help. But as they rose from their stools to make the formal hand-to-nose gesture across the board, he whispered, "I'll delay the boat as long as I can. But if you're not there when the water gate opens, we'll have to go. Otherwise we'll get locked in for the night, and Father won't let me come again."

Tiamat could hardly sit still long enough to complete the rest of her allocated games. As soon as the junior masters had collected up the counters and dice, she rushed to be first out of the door, closely followed by Simeon and Muna.

But the Gamesmaster was waiting on the step. "Not so fast, Team!" he said, catching Tiamat's elbow. "I need a word with you, Tiamat." He looked at the other Club members dispersing in small groups along the dark street. "I think we'd better go back inside. This might take a while to explain."

Tiamat cast a desperate look at the canal. A wind had sprung up, ruffling the dark surface of the water and making the bitumen-coated barges moored for the night knock against one another. Hillalum's boat was at the end of the row, piled with reeds, but there was no sign of a crew. She spied Hillalum on his way to the wine-shop where the boatman waited for his charge to finish practice, and willed the boy to walk slower. The wind lifted Master Andulli's oiled ringlets and blew Tiamat's hair across her eyes, bringing a whiff of sirrush from between the walls. Her fingers started to itch. *Trapped.*

"I really ought to go straight home, Master Andulli," she said innocently. "Lady Nanname's worried about me after what the Demon did, and with the Persians so close and everything. I'll be all right walking back with Simeon and Muna now Ikuppi and Labinsin have left. There's no need for your men to waste their time taking us home."

The Gamesmaster gave her shoulder a little squeeze. "Don't be silly, Tiamat. That's all the more reason for you to have an escort. I promised your parents I'd see you all got home safely, and an Egibi never goes back on his word." He looked at the other two, who were darting worried glances at the canal, and sighed. "But maybe you're right. It is getting rather late and you youngsters need your sleep. Tell you what, I'll come and see Lady

Nanname tomorrow and we can talk about it then, how about that?" He smiled at her as she scratched beneath the bandage. "Your lucky hand's getting better, is it? Good! You're our secret weapon, Tiamat. We have to look after you."

It took forever to get rid of the Egibi bodyguards. But the two men finally left to go about their own business, after being persuaded that Tiamat and Simeon were safe enough when they reached the Judean Neighbourhood and there really was no reason to walk them all the way to their respective doors.

"What did Master Andulli want?" Simeon hissed as they worked their way back through the alleys. "I thought he was going to ruin everything."

"How do I know? He probably wanted to examine my hand again." Tiamat broke into a run. "We've got to find Muna and get back to the canal before Hillalum gives up on us. If they'd made us walk any slower, we'd have turned into statues!"

"What I don't understand is why they went that way." Simeon kept turning his head to frown back the way they'd come. "It makes no sense. They left us right outside Marduk Gate. That's the quickest way to Enlil Street, isn't it?"

"Who cares?" she snapped, tension making her short-tempered. "I expect they've got other things to do— Look, there's Muna!"

The girl was hugging herself on the corner where they'd agreed to meet, looking nervous and cold. Her round face melted into an expression of relief when she saw them. "I thought you were never coming," she said.

"Simeon wanted to stay and watch the Egibi men. Says they're acting illogically."

Simeon scowled. "I only said it was a strange way for them to get back into the inner city, that's all."

Muna gave them a distracted look. "Have you brought the Egibi pass?"

Tiamat patted her pouch. "Of course."

"I expect Hillalum's gone by now."

The same thought was in all their minds as they hurried back through the dark streets to Zababa Wharf. Muna had almost sounded hopeful when she said it. Tiamat couldn't really blame her.

Before she had time to feel guilty about getting her friends into trouble, they spotted the barge making its slow way along the canal towards the water gate. Hillalum must have already told some tale to the boatman, because as soon as he saw them racing along the towpath, he steered his vessel to the bank and grinned at them without surprise. Three of his front teeth were missing. "Hop aboard, then," he said. "Make yourself comfy under them reeds, plenty of room for everyone."

"It's all right," Tiamat said stiffly. "I've got a pass. We don't have to hide."

She wondered if it was such a good idea for Simeon to come. Those reed bundles wouldn't stop a spear, and she thought she could see the ones at the far end moving. Rats, probably. Or snakes. She shuddered. But Simeon was more concerned about the tunnel under the wall ahead of them.

"Do you think anyone can see us here?" he whispered to the boatman.

"Won't matter if you've got a pass."

"My name's not on the pass."

With a Judean's talent for slipping out of sight, he wriggled under the reeds and pulled them over his head. Hillalum arranged a few bundles on top of the boy and sprawled across them, feigning sleep. "Just in case," he explained as the boatman cast off again.

Tiamat's heart thudded as the barge glided along the canal towards the shadowy arch beneath the wall. The water flowed freely to join the moat outside, but their passage was barred by a bronze grille that could be raised and lowered by the sentries at the New Zababa Gate. Hillalum and the boatman seemed quite casual about it all, as if they transported illegal people out of the city every night. Perhaps they did. She supposed it wasn't so different from transporting illegal goods in.

She sat very still while the boatman steered from the back with his paddle. Because the reeds took up most of the length of the vessel, she and Muna were squashed near his feet, with Hillalum lying on the bundles in front of them. Their combined weight made the stern end of the barge ride low in the water, and the boatman grunted as he paddled.

"Heavy lot, aren't you?" he remarked as they glided into the shadow of the wall. "Get that pass ready, girlie. They mightn't check, but you never can tell what mood they're in."

Tiamat pulled out the pass and hid her bandaged hand under a fold of her skirt. She felt Muna stiffen as their graceful prow nudged the grille. Water plopped and echoed in the darkness. The bricks seemed to press down on them like wet clay. Tiamat shivered.

Trapped...

"Having a party tonight, huh?"

The sentry's voice, startlingly loud in the enclosed space, made her jump. A cloaked man stood on a ledge under the wall, holding a torch. Its flame rippled red and gold across the water and cast eerie shadows on to the bricks. Behind the sentry, a flight of shadowy steps led up to the guard room.

"It's his birthday, ain't it?" The boatman prodded Hillalum and treated the sentry to his gap-toothed grin. "Showin' his fine city friends the delights of the countryside, ain't he?"

The sentry laughed. "Hope you all like insects, then – you'll get bitten to death out there at this time of night!" He strolled to the front of the barge and poked his spear into the reeds. There was a rustle and Tiamat was certain she heard a faint yelp. Her heart stood still. Surely he couldn't have speared Simeon from there? Hillalum looked startled, but had the presence of mind to break into a bout of coughing, and fortunately the sentry didn't seem to hear anything unusual. He wound a handle in the shadows and the grille raised, letting them through. "Watch out for the Persians!" was his parting comment as they slipped beneath Nebuchadnezzar's Wall and emerged under a sky ablaze with stars.

Tiamat's breath came faster. So much space. No houses, no walls, only reeds and open plain and the occasional wind-ruffled palm as far as she could see. She gazed up at that sky and gripped Muna's hand, suddenly dizzy. Muna squeezed back, staring around with equal dismay.

They paddled without speaking for ten double-minutes, their prow crackling through reeds that grew as tall as a man, using the network of irrigation channels to work their way towards the river. Only when the walls were safely out of earshot did the boatman allow his barge to bump to a halt on a mud bank. "All right," he said, jumping ashore and running to the bows, where he dragged bundles off his load with startling speed. "Out you come!"

Simeon had already emerged from his hiding place with reeds sticking out of his hair. He blinked at the boatman's back in confusion. Hillalum frowned, then a look of slow understanding crossed his face. Tiamat was too busy shivering at all the open space and trying to see if Simeon was hurt to wonder at the boatman's strange behaviour. But Muna's eyes widened. "I don't believe it," she whispered.

Tiamat looked round in time to see the boatman drag

a girl in a yellow tunic from under his load, holding her easily by one arm. "I *thought* my boat was heavy tonight," he said in satisfaction. "I suppose your name wasn't on the pass, either?"

As everyone stared, Khatar snatched her arm free of the boatman's grip and tugged her tunic straight. "So what you all lookin' at?" she said. "Supposed to keep an eye on you, aren't I? How I'm supposed to do that when you take it into your heads to sneak out of the city in the middle of the night like a gang of thieves, I don't know!" She slapped at a midge and scowled at the moonlit plain. "Sin's rude bits, but I hate the country! What you all doin' out here, anyway?"

Simeon and Muna exchanged glances. Hillalum looked as if he were trying not to laugh. The boatman frowned at Khatar's hair, which was mussed from being under the reeds but still recognizably braided in the wardum style.

Tiamat sighed. "Suppose we'd better tell her."

"And have her go running straight back to Master Andulli with our plans?" Muna scowled at the wardum girl. "Go home, Khatar. You're not wanted."

"Can't get back in till morning, can I?" The wardum smiled sweetly at Muna. "Sorry."

"You should have thought of that before you smuggled yourself out."

"I'm only doing what I'm told."

"Ha! And if Master Andulli told you to jump off the highest tier of the ziqqurat, I suppose you'd do it?"

"A wardum has to do everything she's told, but I don't expect a *mushkenum* to understand that."

"I understand you do plenty of things you're not told! I wonder what Master Andulli would say if he knew you were listening in on our meeting the other day?"

There was more of the same, but Tiamat was too tense to follow it all. Simeon was trying to pacify Muna. Hillalum had hold of Khatar's arm, holding the two girls apart. They might have argued all night, had not the boatman grunted and seized Khatar's wrist.

"That's a temple mark!" he exclaimed, turning the crescent brand to the moonlight. "And you're a wardum! Have you any idea what sort of trouble you'll be in if someone catches you out here? They'll think you've run away, and then I'll be in trouble for helping you."

"Have to make sure they don't catch me then, won't you?" Khatar gave him a cheeky grin.

Muna fought free of Simeon and lunged at the girl. "Why, you little—"

"STOP IT!" Tiamat shouted. She sprang to her feet, fists clenched. The barge rocked wildly. Everyone turned to look at her in surprise.

"Just stop arguing," she said, still dizzy with the thought that there was nothing to protect any of them from attack by lions, Persians, or any other dangers that might be hiding out here on the vast, shadowy plain. "Please. We're outside and Khatar's here. We can't change that now. I think we should let her come. She can help hold the gates open."

The boatman gave her a suspicious look. "I didn't hear nothin' about opening any gates. What are you youngsters up to?"

Tiamat looked at Simeon. He bit his lip and nodded. Muna folded her arms and stared across the plain. Hillalum sighed. "Tell them, Tia."

She explained as quickly as she could. The boatman frowned, but Khatar looked at her with new respect. "Really? A sirrush really licked you?"

"We wouldn't be out here otherwise," Tiamat said, curling her hand. "So will you help us?"

Khatar grinned. "Don't think I'm goin' to miss this, do you?"

The boatman shook his head, though Tiamat thought she saw a flicker of admiration in his eyes. "You're all quite crazy! If you've got any sense, Hillalum, you'll come straight back to the farm with me and let your city friends get on with it."

Hillalum folded his big arms.

The boatman sighed. "Might as well argue with a half-trained onager, as usual!" He looked at their determined faces, then suddenly grinned. "Let the King's dragons out, eh? That'll be something to see! If I can't talk you out of it, I can at least take you safely across the river. You haven't any floats and I don't suppose any of you can swim. Also, you'll blend in better at the gate if you're carryin' something. You can take some of my reeds –

they've served their purpose tonight. But if anyone asks, I'm warning you now, I'll deny all knowledge of what you're up to. Smugglin' goods is one thing, but I'm getting far too old for this sort of caper."

Tiamat threw her arms around the boatman's neck and kissed his leathery cheek. He stiffened, but picked up his paddle with a small smile. "Hop aboard, then, girlie. Them dragons are waiting."

EGIBI TWENTY SQUARES TEAM
14th Tashritu

Gamesmaster

ANDULLI	Egibi Family of Babylon

Team

ENKI	Master Andulli's son, Enlil Street, inner city
SIMEON	Jacob's son, Judean Neighbourhood, outer city
MUNA	astrologer's daughter, outer city
TIAMAT	Nanname's adopted daughter, outer city
HILLALUM	farmer's son, country

Reserve

KHATAR	Master Andulli's wardum, Enlil Street, inner city

Chapter 10

RESCUE

Hearken to my cries!

THE CAMP OUTSIDE Lugalgirra Gate was as Hillalum had described – a rough reed fence surrounding huts constructed in the plains style to shelter both animals and people. But it was overrun with refugees from the north. Some were already rolled in their travel-stained blankets, twitching uneasily in their sleep. Others huddled around fires, talking in quiet voices or weeping softly. The few merchants among them sat apart, spitting out the shells of pistachio nuts and scowling. Three heavily-laden carts were parked nearby, guarded by their drivers. With so many people of all ages from all sections of society, no one looked twice at the five children when they staggered in from the direction of the marshes, bent under their reed bundles.

"There aren't usually this many people here," Hillalum said, looking round in confusion.

Simeon frowned at the refugees. "It's because of the war. We should have thought. But we needn't change our plans – there'll be even more confusion when the gate opens. We'll just have to make sure we get inside first."

Tiamat clenched her left hand and shivered. This was starting to look more and more like a bad idea. She eyed the crowds nervously and looked for a quiet corner where they could wait for sunrise. But Khatar grabbed the arm of a boy in a ragged tunic and demanded, "What's goin' on? Where are you all from?"

The boy stared at her in amazement. "Haven't you heard? The Persians took Sippar. The stupid sentries just opened the gates and let 'em in! Father says we'll be safe in Babylon." He gave them a suspicious look. "Where are you from? I thought the whole country knew."

"Just one of the farms," Simeon said quickly, pulling Khatar away before the boy could ask any more awkward questions. "We never hear any news out there."

They found a place near the bridge and settled down. Simeon suggested they should try to sleep in turns, with two of them staying awake to keep watch. But after what they'd heard, sleep was impossible. In the end, they huddled round their bundles and discussed the bad news in whispers, hiding their faces whenever the sentries patrolling Nebuchadnezzar's Wall paused to tease the refugees.

"Nice and comfortable down there, are you all?" they called. "Persians'll be here soon, I expect. Sleep well!"

Then they'd laugh before continuing with their patrol. Sometimes people shouted back, but the merchants, who had traded with Babylon before and knew the sentries' sense of humour, ignored the taunts.

Simeon tried to get Khatar to tell them why Master Andulli had sent her to spy on them. But the wardum girl said how in Sin's rude bits would she know? She just did the dirty work while the masters got rich. Then she somehow got hold of Muna's hairband, which started another fight until they realized she wanted it to cover the temple brand on the back of her hand. "Now I look just like Tiamat!" Khatar said, holding up her bandaged hand and pointing to her grubby foot. Tiamat realized the wardum was still wearing the luck-beads she'd traded for the Egibi pass on their way through Marduk Gate. She looked away before she could start thinking about omens and evil-days.

Muna shifted closer. "I still don't trust her," she whispered. "When the sun rises, we should turn her in as a runaway. It'd be a good way to get the sentries to open the gate."

Tiamat blinked at her friend in disbelief. "We can't do that!"

"It's not a bad idea, actually," Simeon said, glancing at Khatar, who was showing Hillalum her ankle beads. "With all these people, we're going to need something to get us noticed. Don't worry, she won't be in trouble if Master Andulli really did send her to spy on us."

"No!" Tiamat frowned. "The soldiers might hurt her!

They do all sorts of horrible things to runaway wardum."

Muna muttered something about it serving Khatar right for spying on them if they did. But Simeon sighed. "No, Tia's right. It would be a mean thing to do. We'll just have to watch her when that gate opens."

"I'll be watching her, don't you worry," Muna said, her eyes resting on the wardum girl. "Every double-moment."

After that, Tiamat must have dozed off in spite of her nerves. One moment, she was watching Hillalum and Muna giggling together and wondering what they could possibly find to laugh about at a time like this. The next thing she knew, Simeon was shaking her awake.

She leapt to her feet and stared at the ziqqurat silhouetted against the paling sky above the walls. The House of Heaven on Earth at its summit, the first place in the city to see the sun, already showed a blush of colour.

"We're too late!" she cried. Her head felt muzzy, her mouth like fur, and her fingers were itching like crazy beneath their bandage. "Why didn't you *wake* me?" She stumbled to her feet.

Simeon pulled her back. "Calm down, Tia! I am waking you, aren't I? There's plenty of time yet and you needed the sleep. You looked terrible last night." The concerned look in his eyes told her she didn't look much better this morning, but he gave her an encouraging smile. "Now then, Muna's got the pass and Hillalum's in position. Don't worry about Khatar. We'll look out for her. You just concentrate on calling your dragons. Here, drink this."

He tipped a cracked bowl to her lips. Whatever it contained tasted awful, but she gulped it down because she was so thirsty. Her empty stomach complained, and she eyed the fruit and vegetables one enterprising merchant was selling to the refugees at extortionate prices from the back of his cart, but there was no time to think about breakfast. Already, the refugees were pressing across the bridge towards the gate, anxious to be safe inside Babylon's walls before the Persians came.

Tiamat pushed the bowl away and fought her way through the crowd. She caught up with Muna at the bronze-bound gates, where the girl was holding the Egibi pass to the spy slot and demanding to be let in. Over one shoulder, Muna carried her reed bundle. Tiamat realized she'd forgotten hers. No time to go back for it now. She closed her eyes and thought hard of the sirrush.

Come, she willed. *You have to come.*

The bridge softened under her feet and her ears buzzed.

"What's wrong with your friend?" asked the sentry, peering through the slot. "Is she sick? We can't risk letting the plague into Babylon, Egibi pass or not."

Tiamat made an effort to stand straight. She wiped her hair out of her eyes and gave the sentry what she hoped was an innocent smile. "I'm just hungry, sir! We've been travelling for days without food." At least, she felt as if she had.

The sentry snorted. "Hungry, eh? I suppose you can't have the plague if you've an appetite. What you got in the bundle, girl?"

"Just reeds, sir," Muna said with downcast eyes, winking at Tiamat.

There was a scrape as the bars behind the gates were lifted. Agonizingly slowly, they began to open. Tiamat tensed, her eyes on the growing gap between them. The great city wall loomed overhead, making her dizzy again. She sidled towards the opening.

One of the waiting refugees, a well-dressed man covered in dust like the rest, grabbed her hair from behind. "Wait your turn!" he growled, elbowing her and Muna apart. Tiamat, still dizzy, staggered and nearly fell into the moat.

Muna whirled, hampered by her bundle. Then a yellow streak dodged across the bridge. "Leave my friend alone!" Khatar leapt on the man's back, fastened her arms around his neck and clung on, kicking her bare feet in the air. He growled in fury, but the gates were open far enough now to admit a person on foot. Before anyone could stop her, Tiamat was through.

"Hey!" the sentry called, making a grab for her as she ducked under his arm. "Where do you think you're going? All incomers must be searched, Ensi's orders!" A second sentry blocked her way with his spear. Muna threw her reed bundle at him, knocking the spear flying.

Tiamat dodged past and raced along the shadowy passage to the central Lugalgirra courtyard.

"Sirrush!" she shouted at the top of her lungs as she ran, her cry echoing between the walls. "Come, sirrush!" At the same time, she felt a bit silly. Call them, Simeon had said. He hadn't said how.

Behind her, the sentries on the outer gate had their hands full with the refugees, who had seen the children get through and thought they would try the same tactics. One of the sentries had grabbed Muna when she threw the reeds but had to let her go again so he could deal with the sudden surge of people and animals.

For perhaps half a double-minute, the central Lugalgirra courtyard was deserted, the sentries on duty at the inner gate yet to realize the trouble at the outer. Still calling for the sirrush to come, Tiamat darted left under the arch that would take her between the walls – and slithered to a halt in dismay. A bronze grille blocked her path, closing off the courtyard from the strip of ground where the sirrush ran. Her heart sank. Of course they would have made sure the creatures couldn't get out before they opened the outer gates with so many people around. She'd been stupid to believe otherwise.

"Up here, Tia!" A breathless shout broke through her despair. Simeon raced across the court and sprang up a flight of steps in the shadows at the side of the arch. "I think it's the same mechanism as the canal gate. We should be able to lift it from above."

Tiamat looked at the top of the grille, where it

vanished into the brick arch. She hadn't even thought to observe how the grille beneath the New Zababa Gate had been raised to let their boat through last night.

"Don't just stand there!" Simeon hissed. "They're coming!"

At first she thought he meant the sentries on the inner gates, who had finally noticed the disruption and were running down the passage towards them. Then a familiar smell wafted into the courtyard and she realized. Her heart leapt. She scrambled up the steps after Simeon and grabbed the other side of the winding handle.

She'd thought it might be difficult, but the mechanism was well oiled and the grille raised with hardly a squeak. From the top of the arch, they couldn't see what was happening between the walls, but she saw the sentries' heads turn as they entered the courtyard and their mouths fall open. Yelling in alarm, they spun round and raced back the way they'd come. They skidded into their guard house and slammed the door.

At the outer gate, the first few refugees had got past the sentries. One of them was dragging a laden onager up the passage at a reluctant trot. The beast smelled the sirrush and reared, ripping its halter rope out of its owner's hand and whipping round so fast that the men behind didn't have a chance to get out of the way. The onager knocked them aside and galloped back the way it had come, hooves echoing under the wall and pieces of its load falling behind it in the dust. Screams sounded outside as the panicked animal burst through the camp and out across the plain. Simeon fixed the winding handle in its "up" position with a tight smile.

In a rush of shadowed scales, six sirrush streamed under the raised grille. As one, they turned their horned heads to the outer gate, tongues flickering to taste the air. Tiamat's heart sang. The battlements spun dizzily against a glowing pink sky. The sirrush that had licked her was right below them at the front of the herd. She could feel its heart beating, its wild excitement at being free. Its scales rippled like fire as a shaft of early sunlight cleared the wall. It tossed one of the onager's dropped bundles high into the air with its horn. Seeds showered out. It shook its head and hissed. Then its head raised and it stared directly at Tiamat.

Simeon sucked in his breath. "Stay very still," he whispered. "I don't think they can climb up here."

"Run, stupid sirrush!" Tiamat yelled, shrugging off Simeon and waving her arms at the creatures. "Why don't you run?"

By this time, the sentries at the outer gate had recovered from the onager's flight. They'd recruited some of the merchants and were advancing warily in a line up the outer passage with spears and staffs held across their bodies. When they saw the sirrush had stopped, the men shouted and beat their sticks against the walls.

"Drive them back in!" called one of the sentries. "You two up there! Get ready to lower that grille soon as they're back inside! You're bloody maniacs, lettin' them out! Just wait till I get my hands on you!"

Tiamat had heard enough. Unable to think of anything except that the men mustn't be allowed to drive the poor creatures back into their cruel prison, she flung herself off the arch and on to the leading sirrush's back.

"NO, TIA!"

Simeon's anguished cry came from a long way off. The sirrush's scales were surprisingly supple and warm beneath her legs. Its neck snaked in front of her, a mane of red-gold spikes ending in two curly horns and locks of fiery hair that hung around its ears. Its central horn spiked the sky. For an instant, it was rigid with surprise. The other five swung their heads and flickered their tongues at her. Tiamat cringed, terror replacing the wild excitement that had urged her to jump. But she swallowed the fear and dug her heels into the scaled sides. "Go!" she sobbed. "Don't let them drive you back."

Her mount reared and leapt at the line of men who blocked its path. Tiamat clung on desperately as one clawed forepaw caught a merchant on the shoulder and he went down screaming. Another man was tossed high into the air by the creature's horn. His body crashed against a wall and fell, broken and still. The other men threw down their sticks and spears and fled for the outer gate, yelling for someone to close it. Those refugees who had got through into the passage turned and fled, too. The sirrush raced after them towards the rapidly diminishing gap, heads and tails stretched low.

Tiamat crouched over the leading sirrush's back, her eyes squeezed shut in excitement and terror. The lowest spike of its mane cut into her unbandaged hand and its muscles rippled beneath her, not at all like the sedate donkeys, camels and onagers she'd begged rides on as a little girl. The speed and power of the creature took her breath away.

Shouts tore past her ears.

"Merciful Ishtar, there's a child on its back!" ... "What does she think she's doing?" ... "Jump, girl! Jump!" The shouts grew more frantic as they came closer. "Look out!" ... "Turn them, can't you?" ... "Get that gate shut!" ... "Marduk's Teeth, they're OUT!"

She knew they were through the gates without needing to see. The sudden warm wind, the thud of claws and talons on the bridge, people screaming as they leapt out of her way, brightness on the other side of her eyelids, dust in her throat... Unable to believe she was still mounted, she risked a look back. They had lost one of the herd over the side of the bridge. She could see it thrashing in the moat surrounded by men who, frightened for their families, clubbed it over and over again until the water boiled red. She looked away, her throat tight.

A dark line of shadufs blurred past as the sirrush turned north along the bank of the river. A huge, red sun reflected in the canals and burnt the dust of the distant plain. More refugees, fleeing to Babylon by boat, pointed at the creatures in amazement and shouted things Tiamat couldn't hear. Goats whirled from their path and bolted, bleating. *Jump off*, she thought. *Must jump off*. But every time she thought this, her legs trembled and she clung on tighter.

She tried to talk to her mount, at first in a soft voice as she would a wary street-dog, then shouting at it to stop or at least slow down. It took no notice of her. It was running at full stretch and seemed to have forgotten she was there, while the others had obviously accepted her as some kind of insignificant growth on their leader's back.

At some point, they left the river and swerved along a track through marshy fields, heading for the open plain. A new fear came over her. How far was it to Sippar? What if the Persians were already on the march downriver? Her mount was limping. Its speed slackened slightly. She shifted her weight and looked for a soft place to land. Then she heard a noise that chilled her blood, a low growl in the reeds.

Lions.

The sirrush she was riding shuddered. The others hissed at the sound and fought to be closer to their leader. Tiamat abandoned the idea of jumping off and urged her mount faster. She hardly heard the lions' attacking rush, but the sirrush at the back of the herd went down. The others echoed its screech of anguish and her mount sprang forward, even faster than before. She stared back in horror at three lionesses fighting over the creature's carcass, ripping chunks off its haunches while the dying sirrush gurgled in pain and tried to reach them with its horn. Tears blurred her eyes and she pressed her face into her mount's scaled neck.

"You're supposed to be fierce," she sobbed. "Why don't you fight?"

More lions, alerted by the smell of the blood, loped towards them. A second sirrush went down without even being attacked, losing its hind legs in a ditch and somersaulting, its neck twisted beneath its body. It did not get up again. The lions stopped to investigate, allowing the three surviving sirrush to race on. But the creatures were tiring fast, their tails dragging on the ground and their muzzles low. The one Tiamat was riding was making a terrible rasping noise and its limp had grown worse.

"Stop," she sobbed, terrified that her mount would stumble into a ditch as well. "Please stop. You're killing yourselves, you stupid things!"

It was all going wrong. They should never have attempted the rescue on an evil-day. When she felt her mount swerve, and saw one of the others plunge into the reservoir behind a nearby dam, where it floundered for a moment before disappearing beneath the surface in a cloud of steam, she simply leant her head against her mount's neck, too overwhelmed to deal with this new death. "You can't even swim, can you?" she whispered. "What sort of creatures are you?"

Then she saw the reason for the swerve. They'd come through the reeds to the edge of the plain. In the distance a vast wall shimmered across the marsh. A line of chariots was racing towards them out of the sun, each drawn by a pair of horses with brightly-tasselled harnesses, kicking up clouds of dust that turned to spray as they hit the marshy area. The chariots slowed, then came on again urged by whip cracks and excited shouts. Each carried a driver and a passenger armed with a bow. They split up as they entered the reeds and seemed not to have noticed the sirrush, but the shouts and whip cracks grew louder again as they swung round in a wide circle and came towards them from behind.

Tiamat realized what they intended. "Stop!" she shouted. "Stay in the marsh!" She flung her arms around her sirrush's neck and tried to drag it to a stop. But her mount and the other survivor were already crashing out of the reeds in panic and running across the open plain, fleeing the strange, wheeled monsters. Several lions loped out after them and bounded alongside, the concerns of hunter and prey momentarily put aside in their need to escape the common enemy.

Behind them, triumphant shouts, whip cracks, drumming hooves, and the rumble of wheels warned that the chariots were giving chase. There was a sigh in the air and one of the lions went down, an arrow sticking out of its neck. Another arrow struck the riderless sirrush on the haunch. It gave an angry hiss and turned on the nearest chariot with lowered horn. The driver shouted and the bowman released another arrow that pierced the sirrush between the eyes. It collapsed, scrabbling at the dust with its clawed forepaws, eyes closed, tongue flickering in and out. Other chariots caught up and circled at a safe distance, while the men pointed and exclaimed. They released more arrows into the crippled sirrush and jumped down to investigate the strange creature. The rest of the chariots abandoned the lions to chase after Tiamat's mount.

"No!" she yelled, her voice hoarse with dust and fear. "Don't kill it! Please don't! You don't understand! It licked me I'll die— "

The leading chariot was so close now, she could see the red lining of the horses' nostrils and the rolling whites of their eyes. The driver crouched over his reins, while the other man fitted an arrow to his bow and shouted something Tiamat couldn't understand. He wore strange, tight pants and a bronze helmet that glittered in the sun. His eyes, as he took aim at the sirrush, were fierce and determined. Again, he shouted. A chill dried the sweat on Tiamat's back and her arms lost all their strength. Even as her grip on the sirrush's mane loosened, she heard the arrow release. There was a whirl of sky... scales... flying hooves... wheels...

She hit the dust in a whoosh of breath and her head cracked on a rock. She had a blurred image of a helmeted, bearded face peering down at her. Then everything slid away into the dark.

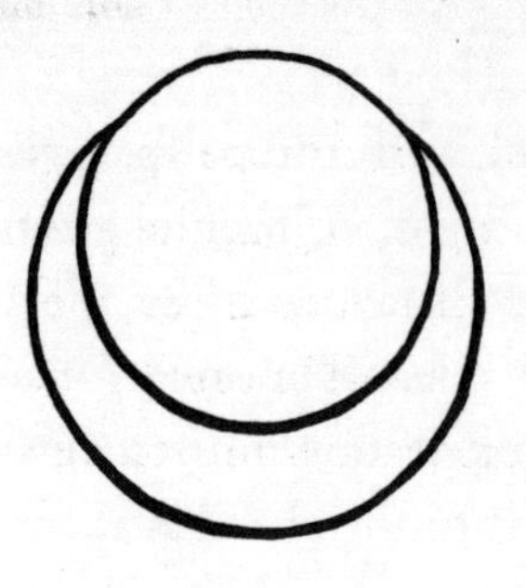

Chapter 11

PERSIANS

A lord art thou, and mighty is thy word!

THE LOW MURMUR of men's voices woke Tiamat. She had little interest in what they were saying. A sore throat and a thumping headache demanded her whole attention. She was lying on a rug beneath some bright orange material that rippled in the wind. The heat brought smells of smoke, horse sweat and roasting meat.

The last thing she remembered clearly was racing across the plain, chased by strangely-dressed men in chariots. Something horrible had happened.

She lifted her head. A triangle of blue sky was blocked by a bearded silhouette wearing a helmet and leg-hugging pants. A sword swung at his hip and he carried a spear.

I'm in a tent, she thought. Then: sirrush! They killed my sirrush!

Had she been stronger, she would have thrown

herself at the man, spear or no spear. But as she pushed herself into a sitting position, the ground began to spin and she flopped back with a moan. The guard turned his head and looked at her. He caught the arm of a passing soldier and muttered something to him, before resuming his watch.

Tiamat closed her eyes, counted to sixty and opened them again. A jug with a golden handle had been left beside the rug. Cautiously, she rolled over and reached for it. Water sloshed inside. It was warm and tasted strange, but she finished the whole jug and lay back to wait for her strength to return. This time, the guard took no notice of her.

Think. Must think.

She wasn't dead, that much was obvious. Did that mean her sirrush was still alive, too? The voices she could hear were speaking a mixture of Akkadian and the barbarian tongue the men in the chariots had shouted at her. Fighting her fear, Tiamat made herself lie quietly and listen.

"Our master is worried about how long it'll take you to divert the river," a man was saying in Akkadian. "There'll be lots of people travelling to the city by water for the Twenty Squares Championships, to say nothing of all the refugees. They're bound to notice something and it could reach the Demon's ears."

"The river is Babylon's only weakness," a gruff voice with a thick accent replied. "We've been over this a hundred times already. My men will be in disguise. The number of people travelling and the excitement will work to our advantage. No one's going to look twice at a gang of peasants clearing the canals. They won't realize who we are or what we're doing until it's too late. The men are ready, Sire. I wouldn't recommend changing our plans at this late stage."

A deeper, richer voice said something that sounded like a question, and the gruff voice answered in the barbarian tongue. Respectful, but also forceful.

"We realize it's rather sudden, my lord," the Akkadian speaker broke in. "But we've only just discovered this way might be possible ourselves. Our master sent this map. It's a copy of the one at the top of Babylon's ziqqurat. As you can see, all the gateways are clearly marked..."

"Let me see that!" A pause, followed by rough laughter. "Sire, this map is a joke! These gates are about as real as the Babylonian Tree of Life!" His tone turned threatening. "Does your master think we're stupid?"

"It's no jest, my lord, we can assure you. Our master has discussed the matter at length with the High Priest, and he believes the Earthly Gateways represent the safest way into the city for you and your men. It's a very old map, and granted some of the ziqqurats no longer exist – it's unfortunate the priests at Sippar destroyed the shrine before they let you in, but there are others we can use. See this circle here? That's Borsippa, a short distance downstream from Babylon and easily taken by a small force. We'll send messengers to the priests of the

Borsippan god Nabu and they'll aid you. All you need to do is wait in the temple at the top of the Borsippan ziqqurat until we open the gate, then step through into the heart of Babylon. The Earthly Gateways haven't been used in thousands of years. You'll achieve complete surprise."

The gruff voice started to protest, but the one they called "Sire" silenced it and spoke in careful, perfect Akkadian.

"General Gobryas has a point. It's true we could take Borsippa tomorrow. But I'm not sure I like the idea of relying on ancient magic to open a gate that you yourselves admit hasn't been opened in thousands of years. Seems to me your ziqqurat could become a trap as easily as a gateway."

"No, my lord! We swear by Marduk's Name it's no trap!"

"And how do you propose to open this gate? Have you tested it to make sure it works?"

A small cough. "Our master is dealing with that side of things even as we speak. Be assured that it will be fully tested before you make the passage. If you don't trust the magic, maybe you'd prefer to send your General through with some of your best men, and then you yourself can enter the city through one of the more traditional gates when they've gained control of the walls."

Tiamat lay motionless, hardly able to breathe. *Step through into the heart of Babylon.*

The General's gruff protest, that all magic was trickery and everything had a perfectly normal explanation if men only knew the facts, sparked off another discussion in the barbarian tongue. Then she heard something that sent prickles of fear through her.

"My General is naturally cautious." The leader sounded amused. "But I think even he would agree there are some things in this world we can't explain. Wasn't your training exercise interrupted by strange beasts only this morning, Gobryas? And one of the creatures being ridden by a barefoot girl with no harness to control it?"

"Bloody crazy," the General muttered. "Certainly wasn't magic, though. The girl had no control over the beast that I could see."

A soft chuckle. "I'll keep your map. But I want you to take the girl back with you. She must have come from one of your farms – you can drop her off on your way. A war camp is no place for a child. Now, I think it's time you gentlemen left..."

Tiamat sat up, rigid with terror. There was no longer any doubt who the men in the strange clothes must be. And someone from her own side was helping them! The knowledge made her tremble with rage. The tent no longer spun, but she still felt terribly weak. Must get out, was all she could think. Must get back to Babylon and warn Master Andulli.

Only there was nowhere to go. The guard snapped to attention as a tall, surprisingly young man ducked into the tent. He wore a flowing robe of pink and gold stars thrown negligently over his leg-hugging pants. His beard was black and curly, and he had bright green eyes. Behind him hurried an older man, dark and muscular, still dressed in the dusty uniform he'd worn for the hunt, though he'd removed his helmet. They were followed by two men dressed in the Babylonian style, their cloaks stained from travel. Tiamat was so busy staring at the leader's eyes, she didn't recognize the Babylonians until one of them sucked in his breath and said, "Isn't that the girl we—?"

He bit the words off, but the green-eyed Persian missed nothing. His head turned sharply and he raised an eyebrow.

"I see you three know each other already," he said in a dangerously soft tone. "Would one of you care to explain?"

Tiamat stared at the Babylonians in shock and confusion. They were the Egibi bodyguards from last night – the men Simeon had seen heading along Marduk Street in the wrong direction.

"Traitors!" she hissed.

"What's going on?" The dark man growled.

The Egibi men glanced at each other. "Sh – she looks a bit like a girl we know from the city," one stammered. "But it's impossible— "

"Riding a strange creature?" whispered the other. They looked more carefully at Tiamat, then glanced at each other again. Something passed between them. "You're right, my lord," said the first man. "We should take her back with us at once."

Tiamat struggled to her knees and from there to her feet. She swayed slightly, but managed to stay upright. Heart thudding, but concentrating on those green eyes, she gave the Persian leader a formal hand-to-nose greeting. "Sir, please don't send me away with these men! They'll kill me!"

"Don't be so stupid, girl!" hissed the nearest Egibi man, grasping her elbow.

"No!" Tiamat dug in her heels. She appealed again to the green-eyed leader. "They won't take me back with them, I know they won't! They'll be too afraid I'll tell on them. I know their master, you see. He's our Club Gamesmaster and he'd be furious if he knew they were here. Please, Sir, let me stay as your prisoner! I won't be any trouble, I promise, and– " She swallowed the lie. "I won't try to run away."

The dark man shook his head. The leader frowned. "Do you know who I am?"

Tiamat bit her lip. The Egibi man had let her go, but his gaze still rested on her in a furious manner. "You're the Persians, aren't you?" she whispered.

The leader smiled. "A clever girl, I see. I'm King Kyros, ruler of the New Persian Empire. This is General Gobryas who commands my army. And those two men you seem to think will hurt you are helping us get into Babylon because they believe I'll make a better job of ruling the city than your old King who, I've heard, likes to spend his time in the desert eating grass while his son sits on the throne and eats you all out of house and home. They're going back to the city now. Why don't you want to go with them?"

Tiamat shivered. "Because they're traitors," she whispered.

"And I'm your enemy. Why do you think I won't kill you?"

Tiamat shivered again. "You haven't, not yet. And... you've got my eyes."

Kyros stared at her, startled. Then he laughed. "Got your eyes! So I have. Will you look at that, Gobryas! The girl's got the eyes of a royal princess!"

The General scowled.

The Persian King looked thoughtfully at Tiamat. "What's your name, girl?"

"Tiamat," she told him warily, caught off guard by the change of subject.

"Tell you what, young Tiamat. If you go back to the city quietly with these men and don't tell anyone what you've heard here, I'll make sure no one hurts you or your family. If they try, they'll answer to me. Is it a deal?"

She turned to the Egibi men, a terrible suspicion dawning. "Does Master Andulli know you're here?"

They glanced at each other.

"*Does he*?"

One of them shrugged. "She'll have to be told soon enough."

"Of course he knows!" said the one who had grabbed

her arm earlier. "What did you think? That the Egibi Family is split down the middle like a pistachio shell? I've no idea what you're doing out here, but one thing I do know. If we don't get you back to Babylon before tomorrow night, Master Andulli is going to be madder than old Nabonaid on an evil-day!"

He turned to Kyros. "I can assure you that map's genuine, my lord. As to whether the gate will work after so long, no one can tell, not even Marduk's priests. We need to experiment and for that we need this girl. We'll send word as soon as we know more."

Gobryas scowled again. "Only two days until we move on Babylon and you're going to start experimenting?"

Kyros held up a hand. Though he addressed the Egibi men, his green eyes rested on Tiamat. "You claim this Earthly Gateway of yours would be a safer way into the city than diverting the waters and fighting our way under the wall?"

"Quicker, too. The river plan will get you into the outer city all right, but you'd still have to fight your way into the inner. This gate will get your men into the heart of Babylon with not a single sentry to pass and not a single man dead, if it works."

"If it works." Kyros sighed. "There we have the truth of it. Very well, take this girl back with you and carry out your experiments. Meanwhile, General Gobryas and his men will continue with our original plan. Call me a traditionalist if you must, but I tend to have more faith in the strength of my army and my men's skill with bow and sword than any priestly magic. After all, traditional methods have worked well enough for me so far." He chuckled.

Gobryas folded his arms and looked pleased. But the Egibi men shook their heads. "Babylon's different, my lord," one said.

"Every people thinks their city is different before it falls."

They seemed to have forgotten Tiamat. While the men were talking, she edged towards the open flap. She still didn't trust the two Egibi, despite what they said about Master Andulli knowing where they were. And Nanname had warned her too many times about the Persians for her to feel anything except fear when she looked at their swords. King Kyros didn't seem to be the monster everyone in Babylon said he was, yet his men had killed the sirrush and now he was talking about capturing her home. When King Nebuchadnezzar had captured Simeon's grandfather's home, he'd broken every last brick and carried off all the people.

She made it through the flap and out under the burning plains sun before anyone noticed her. The soldier posted outside, taken by surprise, gave a shout and the men inside the tent spun round. Tiamat ducked under a rope and ran.

The camp was a haze of smoke and rippling orange tents. Horses were tethered in long pickets, swishing their tails and shaking their heads to get rid of flies. They shied and snorted as Tiamat ran past. Soldiers hurried towards her in answer to Gobryas's furious order. A chariot that had been circling the camp at a slow trot speeded up to cut off her escape. Tiamat changed direction, her legs trembling. The soldiers followed. She had nowhere to go and no way to fight them, and they knew it. They smiled as they surrounded her. The man closest to her put his sword away and reached out a hand.

Tears in her eyes, Tiamat kicked him on the shin and dodged under his arm. "Sirrush!" she shouted as she fled. "Sirrush! Where are you?"

–scorchingskinhungrythirstyitchy–

She stopped, overcome by a sudden wave of dizziness. An arm went around her throat from behind and lifted her off her feet. She kicked, but it was hopeless. Another wave of weakness made her head spin. By the time the Persian King arrived with his dark General and the two Egibi in tow, she was leaning against her captor, needing his support to stay on her feet. Her hair hung in tangles across her eyes. She didn't have the strength to wipe it away.

Kyros wasn't smiling any more. He shook his head at her. "I'm afraid you have to go with these men, Tiamat, willingly or otherwise. It seems you're crucial to the magic – though I must say I don't understand why you're making such a fuss. I'd have thought you'd be glad to go home."

She blinked back tears. "What have you done with my sirrush?"

Kyros frowned. One of the Egibi men muttered something in his ear. The green eyes flickered. "Ah! The creature you were riding, of course. General?"

Gobryas scowled. "It collapsed when you fell off. I got rid of it. The smell of the creature was driving the horses crazy."

Tiamat managed to stand straighter. "Where is it? You... you didn't kill it, did you?"

"Of course he didn't kill it," Kyros said impatiently.

"He killed the other one!"

"Steady, girl," growled Gobryas. "That's the Emperor of all Persia you're talking to."

"I don't care! The sirrush are dying. The lions got one, and one fell and broke its neck, and the first one didn't even get over the moat! And then your men chased one into the water so it drowned, and they put arrows in the last one until it couldn't get up, and then they... they chased me, and..." She buried her face in the soldier's chest. "Oh, it's all going *wrong*! It wasn't meant to be like this!"

The soldier awkwardly handed her over to the Egibi men, who seemed to have as little idea of how to comfort her as he did. "There, there," one said. "Don't upset yourself. We don't need the sirrush now, anyway. Master Andulli will explain everything when we get back. All we want you to do is help us open the gate, and then you can go home."

"I haven't a clue what you're talking about!" Tiamat pushed him away. "I'm not going anywhere until I've seen my sirrush!"

Gobryas's eyes darkened. "You'll do what you're jolly well told, girl!" He turned to the Egibi men. "I'll lend you some rope. It's not very comfortable to travel tied on a horse, but the girl needs to be taught proper respect for her elders. It's most careless of you to let her run about out here, considering she's so important to your plans. I hope the rest of your master's so-called 'aid' is better thought out."

The Egibi's grip tightened and Tiamat tensed. But Kyros held up a hand and said, "An unwilling travelling companion will slow you down. Why don't you take her to see the creature? It won't take long and it's not far out of your way. Gobryas will give you directions." He looked hard at Tiamat. "Despite what you seem to think, I wouldn't deliberately kill anybody's pet. My men were on a training exercise, hunting lions to keep their aim sharp. They had to kill the creature they'd wounded because it was a danger to the horses. As to the one you were riding, don't expect too much. I doubt you'll be able to take it back to Babylon with you, at least not yet."

Tiamat met the Persian King's direct green gaze. "I don't want to take it back," she said. "Not ever."

Chapter 12

SKIN

Uprooting and destruction are in my house!

THE EGIBI MEN, Harrim and Igmil, were in a hurry to leave the Persian camp and strode off towards the picket line before the General had finished giving them directions to the sirrush's hut. Tiamat, who had been listening carefully, lagged behind hoping to hear more details. But the General ducked back into his tent, shaking his head and muttering something about teaching these arrogant Babylonians a lesson in manners once he got inside their walls. Tiamat bit her lip.

The soldiers in charge of the picket had obviously been instructed to water the Egibi horses while the visitors were with the King, but to save time they hadn't removed the animals' bridles or their dusty riding-blankets. Tiamat found the Egibi men fretting at the delay while a soldier bridled a small black gelding clearly intended for her.

"She probably can't even ride," muttered Harrim, the one who had seized her arm back in the tent.

"She'll just have to manage, won't she?" Igmil replied. "She's too big to ride up front with one of us."

"She's bound to slow us down. What in Marduk's Name was she doing out here with a sirrush, anyway, that's what I'd like to know? Why can't these youngsters ever do what they're told?"

"I thought they were quiet last night. I told you we should have seen them all the way home."

"Guard them, Andulli said, not nursemaid them! They're plenty old enough to look after themselves. How were we to know the girl would decide to leave the city at a time like this?" He raised his voice. "How much longer is this going to take? Get a move on there, man!"

The soldier muttered something in his barbarian tongue that didn't sound very polite and picked up a tasselled riding-blanket. Tiamat watched with a mixture of excitement and apprehension as it was secured on the gelding's back.

"If I can ride a sirrush, I can ride a horse," she said stiffly. "I won't slow you down."

"You'd better not," growled Harrim. "Or I'll take the General's advice and strap you on that horse's back like a bundle of reeds, make you ride back to Babylon upside-down. Serve you right for all the trouble you've caused us."

Tiamat raised her chin and glared at him. "Just you try!"

"Stop it," Igmil said quietly, putting a hand on his friend's arm. "We should get going. It'll be late enough when we get back as it is. We'll be lucky to make the gate before sunset."

"We'll make it," Harrim muttered, casting a dark glance at Tiamat as he vaulted on to his horse. "Or she'll be sorry."

Tiamat let the soldier leg her up on the gelding and gathered up the reins. In spite of what she'd told the men, this was the first time she'd sat on a real horse. After the sirrush, it seemed small and jittery. Harrim and Igmil immediately kicked their mounts into a canter. Tiamat's gelding tossed its head, snorted and sprang after them. She dropped the reins and grabbed the mane in alarm, but the horse turned out to be a much more comfortable ride than the sirrush. Its mane was longer and easier to hold on to, its canter was smooth once she became used to the rhythm, and the blanket stopped her slipping. She relaxed a little and started to look for the hut where the sirrush was supposed to be stabled. According to the General's directions, it couldn't be far now.

The Egibi men, after satisfying themselves she wasn't going to fall off, rode without speaking. This suited Tiamat fine. Her left hand was tingling under its bandage. When she half closed her eyes, she could almost smell the sirrush's snake-like odour on the hot plains wind.

"I'm coming," she whispered. "Wait for me."

They reached the irrigated area at the edge of the marsh and passed several round-roofed farm huts. But most of these were deserted, their owners having joined the refugees heading south to Babylon. Those still in use were occupied by frightened families who clutched their children close as the horses galloped past.

"How much further?" she called, twisting her head to look back the way they'd come.

The men glanced at each other but didn't answer. They kicked their horses closer, forcing hers to canter between them. Tiamat's hand tingled again. Suddenly suspicious, she let go of the mane and dragged on the reins. The gelding threw up its head in surprise, banging her on the nose, which started to bleed.

"You're supposed to take me to see my sirrush!" she said, trying to hold her nose and control the gelding at the same time. "King Kyros said."

"I don't care what King Kyros said!" Harrim wheeled his horse and seized her reins. "We haven't time to go chasing after some sick dragon. We've got to get you back to the city. There are more important things for you to do."

Tiamat tried to turn the gelding, but Harrim had got its reins over its head and was dragging it after his own horse. Igmil rode behind to keep it going. "You can come back and see your sirrush after the Championships, Tiamat," he called over the thundering hooves. "It'll be safe out here, don't worry."

The lie was obvious. No creature was safe out here with the Persians and the lions.

"Let go of my horse!" She leant along the gelding's neck and tried to snatch her reins back, but she couldn't reach. "I don't care about your silly Championships!" she yelled. "I wish I'd never joined your stupid Twenty Squares Club! I hope Egibi loses!" She eyed the ground flashing under the gelding's hooves. But it was like when she'd been carried by the sirrush. The more she thought about it, the harder it was to jump.

"The game has nothing to do with it, you idiot girl!" Harrim shouted back through the dust, his words coming in gasps. "It never did have. The only reason Master Andulli's entered a Team this year is so he can help the Persian King get into the palace. Think he cares who wins the Twenty Squares Garland?"

"That's not true!" Tears pricked Tiamat's eyes, because after what she'd heard in the camp, Harrim's words made chilling sense. "Master Andulli cares about the Team more than anything else in the world! You can't make me go back with you. I'll jump off!"

The men still had control of her mount. But making a led horse gallop is hard work, and their speed had slackened, allowing an unmistakable odour to come to them on the wind. It was coming from a lone hut off to their right at the edge of the irrigated area. Tiamat swung a leg over the gelding's withers and shut her eyes.

"This is ridiculous!" Harrim wrenched his horse to a stop and dragged her gelding to a halt beside him before she could fall. Igmil reined up on her other side. Shaking his head, he pushed her safely back on the gelding's blanket. All three horses danced and snorted, their sweat surrounding Tiamat in clouds of steam. She felt sticky and dirty, her hand itched, and she thought she might be sick. She looked at the hut again. It was a long way to run.

Harrim glared at her, panting. "You are going to behave yourself, girl. You're going to ride back with us to see Master Andulli, and we're not going to hear another word about that dragon. I can't believe a girl of your age is acting like such a baby. I know one thing. Master Andulli would be thoroughly ashamed of you if he could see you now."

Tiamat hung her head, one hand over her nose to catch the blood. It was true, what he said. But it was also true she couldn't abandon the sirrush. "Give me my reins," she said in a small voice.

Harrim continued to glare suspiciously at her. Tiamat gave him what she hoped was an innocent look. He sighed and tossed the reins back over the gelding's ears. "About time you came to your senses. Maybe now we can—"

Tiamat wrenched the gelding's head round and kicked it hard in the ribs. It barged past Igmil's horse and fled diagonally across the plain. Tiamat crouched low over its neck, praying it wouldn't stumble, urging it towards the hut. She didn't look back, but she heard the thud of hooves coming after her.

She reached the hut ahead of the men and flung herself off the gelding while it was still moving. She landed in a cloud of dust, rolled once, and threw herself at the door without stopping to think. It gave way beneath her weight and she half stumbled, half fell into the shadows beyond.

The smell inside was so strong, it made her head spin. She staggered to her knees in a pile of something dry and crackly. The sun shining through tiny holes in the reed roof made a pattern of dots inside the hut. Dust drifted in the sunbeams.

No sirrush.

Stamping hooves and snorts outside warned her that the Egibi men had arrived. At the same time, she realized what she was kneeling in.

"No..." She gathered the crackly, dull red folds to her breast in despair. "Oh, no."

The men burst through the door, swords in hand, but stopped when they saw her kneeling there. They stared at what she held.

"What the...?" exclaimed Harrim.

"Looks like a snake skin," Igmil said. "Except I've never seen one so big." He frowned. "You don't think...?"

"He killed it." Tiamat hugged the red scales closer. "He lied to me! He told his General to kill it and skin it, and he gave it to his soldiers to eat. I thought they were roasting lion meat— " She swallowed, too choked to cry. "I hate him. I hate him so much."

The men put their swords away. They glanced at each other. Igmil came into the hut and helped her to her feet.

"Leave it," he said gently. "You can't help it now. Come on, let's go catch your horse before it runs back to the camp."

Tiamat stared at the skin. It looked exactly how she felt. Empty, hollow, dried-out. Finished. Useless.

"I'm thirsty," she whispered.

Harrim shook his head at her. "I'm not surprised!" Seeing her expression, he sighed and passed her his water pouch. "Here," he said gruffly. "Use some to wash that blood off your face. But don't drink it all. We've a good way to go yet."

Tiamat cried for the sirrush during the ride back to Babylon. The Egibi men must have seen, but they pretended not to, and for that she almost forgave them the way they'd tried to trick her earlier. When her tears dried, she questioned them about Master Andulli's plans and why he was supporting the Persians. But they would say little more than she already knew, telling her Master Andulli would explain the rest when they got home. They then kicked their horses into a gallop, making further questions impossible. They reached the city just as the sun was slipping beneath the plain, entered the inner city through the Adad Gate, and crossed the river using the central Purattu Bridge. Their sweaty, dusty condition went unnoticed amidst the crowds of refugees who thronged the streets.

Overhead, the House of Heaven on Earth shone

above the city in the last rays of the sun as if it were floating in the air, but Tiamat was far too miserable to notice her surroundings. All dead, she thought. Every sirrush I tried to rescue is dead. And the Demon's going to sacrifice the last one in his vault. She didn't even notice her hand had finally stopped hurting. The only thing she cared about now was making sure the treacherous Persians stayed out of her home.

They rode straight to the house in Enlil Street, where their horses had barely clattered into the courtyard before Master Andulli rushed out to meet them.

"Thank Ishtar!" he said, hurrying across to catch Tiamat as she slid off the gelding's back. "Where did you find her?"

Harrim and Igmil muttered something about the sirrush and the Persian camp.

"Not here – inside!" As he supported Tiamat towards the door, Master Andulli unwound the grubby, blood-stained bandage and looked carefully at her hand. "Could be worse," he grunted. "At least you had the sense to keep the bandage on. I know you're tired, Tiamat, but we want you to try something for us tonight. I imagine you know something of our plans by now, but when we get to the ziqqurat the High Priest will explain better than I can. Meanwhile, you can have something to eat and get cleaned up. I've got to hear my men report." He patted her hand in a distracted fashion. "Don't worry, we won't let the Demon find you. That episode at the Lugalgirra Gate was unfortunate. I wish you'd come to me first – I'd no idea you were so determined to free the sirrush. But you're here now. Even if the Demon does get anything out of Khatar, it won't change our plans at this late stage. She doesn't know any details. Now then, you run along with Humusi and I'll come and collect you as soon as I'm done here..."

Before she'd caught up with half of what he was saying, Master Andulli had handed Tiamat into the care of a large wardum woman, who bustled her upstairs, clucking her tongue.

"You poor mite," she said, picking Tiamat's hair off her face. "Look at the state of you! It's not right involving youngsters in business like this. And now our poor Khatar's locked up and her a branded wardum with no rights at all – it's just too bad!"

Humusi already had Tiamat's blood-crusted tunic off and was sponging her body from a bowl of warm water. Dazedly, Tiamat recognized the room where Khatar had brought her to use the toilet. There had been bad news then, too.

"What happened to Khatar?" she asked, shivering as she made sense of the wardum's words. "Why's she locked up?"

Humusi sniffed. "That poor girl! She was always a bit on the wild side, but I never thought she'd get mixed up in anything so stupid. What she thought she was doing, sneaking out of the city in the middle of the night and lettin' them dragons out at a time like this, I'll never know."

"It wasn't her fault," Tiamat said quickly, beginning

to suspect what had happened. "I made her help. And it was all useless, anyway, because they're all dead."

"Oh, no, dearie." Misunderstanding what she meant, Humusi put her big arms around her and gave her a comforting squeeze. "No, dearie, I'm sure they're not dead. They got arrested, that's all. Muna's parents are respectable citizens. Her father's an astrologer, isn't he? The young farmer's son will be all right, too – the Prince likes his food too much to risk trouble in the countryside. The little Judean might have it a bit harder, but not even Judeans can be locked up indefinitely these days. We're civilized people. We have Laws. Master Andulli will get them out just as soon as he can. It's Khatar I'm most worried about."

"*Arrested*? Who's been arrested?"

Tiamat wrenched herself free and stared at the wardum, the shock pushing the Persians and what had happened to the sirrush to the back of her mind.

Humusi sighed. "Didn't you know, dearie? It's all over the city – how a gang of outer city children let out the King's sacred dragons! Half the inner city thinks it's dreadful and they jolly well ought to be punished. The rest are petitionin' the Palace to let the children go."

Tiamat swayed on her feet. She thought of Simeon, Muna and Hillalum locked in the dark in the House of Silent Screams, all because of her. Khatar, too. *Even if the Demon does get anything out of her*. Master Andulli's words suddenly took on a chilling aspect.

"We've got to get them out of there!"

"Calm yourself, dearie. The Master will get them out very soon – don't worry. He's got plans."

Humusi tugged a clean dress over her head. It was the prettiest dress Tiamat had ever worn, with red flowers embroidered around the neckline and sleeves, but she wouldn't have noticed if Humusi had dressed her in a sack. "I've got to go home!" she said, guiltily remembering the lie she'd told Nanname to explain her absence last night. "My mother probably thinks I've been arrested, too!"

"Shh, silly… Here, eat this before you faint." Humusi steered her from the bathroom to the bedroom where Tiamat had woken after her own visit to the House of Silent Screams. She thrust a pomegranate into Tiamat's hand and gazed at her with pity. "I'm sure the Master will get your mother out as well."

Tiamat's legs wobbled. "Lady Nanname's been arrested?" she whispered. "But she hasn't done anything!"

"I expect they were looking for you, dearie."

"Then I've got to tell them it's a mistake!"

The wardum pushed her down on the bed and placed the fruit bowl beside her. "Eat!" she said, hands on hips. "You're not leaving this house until you do. Where do you think you're going to go, anyway? It's after sunset. The gates are all shut. When the Master's ready, he'll take you to the ziqqurat so you can practise your magic, and when the Persian King gets here he'll deal with the Demon for good. Do try to eat something, dearie. You're paler than the face of Sin. The Master'll never forgive me if I let you pass out on him now."

Finally, it hit her. Tiamat sat very still, staring at the torches hurrying about in the courtyard beyond the window grille. Her hunger had gone. The pomegranate rolled unnoticed from her hand. *When the Persian King gets here, he'll deal with the Demon for good.* "Can't Master Andulli deal with the Demon on his own?" she whispered.

Humusi sighed. "No, not this time. I thought you understood. It's gone too far for that."

Tiamat closed her eyes.

"The Persians killed my sirrush," she whispered. "They lied to me."

But the wardum simply replaced the pomegranate in her lap and patted her clenched fist. "I know you're frightened, dearie. So am I. It's always us women and the young ones who suffer when men make their grand plans. But maybe it'll be better when the new King comes. I'm sure the Master wouldn't be letting him into Babylon unless he believed so."

Chapter 13

ZIQQURAT

That the law of all the gods thy hand should hold!

MASTER ANDULLI WAITED until it was fully dark before throwing a cloak over Tiamat's head and hurrying her across the Ajiburshapu Way to the temple complex. The Gamesmaster had confirmed what Humusi had told her earlier, and went on to explain that letting the Persian King into the city was the best way to help her friends and Lady Nanname. Tiamat listened in silence, which Master Andulli took to be nerves. But tonight was only an experiment. She mightn't be able to open the gate. And even if she could do it, she didn't have to let the King in when the time came. There had to be another way to free her friends.

As Master Andulli knocked on the temple gates, Tiamat peered nervously at the battlements that surrounded the ziqqurat and its outlying buildings. Marduk's temple was like a third city inside the inner one, a place where the common people never went. Those who wished to worship Marduk had to go to the public House of Headraising on Nabu Street. The Temple School, which Enki attended during the day, had its own street entrance so that the children need not enter the complex and disturb whatever rituals the priests carried out behind their high walls. The knowledge that she was probably the first outer city dweller to set foot inside the forbidden temple did not make her feel any better.

Master Andulli exchanged a few whispered words with the young priest on duty and hurried Tiamat through. Only when the gate had thudded shut behind them did he remove the cloak from her head.

Tiamat caught her breath. She'd never been this close to the ziqqurat before. So far overhead that she got a crick in her neck from staring up at it, the House of Heaven on Earth was a mere glimmer against the stars. Seven tiers of painted brick marched upwards to the shrine, their colours muted in the moonlight. Three wide staircases ascended the first tier, meeting on the first level before continuing up the remaining six, growing smaller and smaller in the distance. Shaven-headed priests in long robes whispered silently up and down these stairs, bearing torches that floated through the night like fireflies.

"Come on, Tiamat," Master Andulli said gently, pulling at her hand. "Don't keep the High Priest waiting."

With a start, she realized a tall, bearded priest had crossed the courtyard to meet them and was looking down his long nose at her. "This the girl?" he asked in a tone that made it obvious what he thought of her. Master Andulli had barely started to say, "Yes, this is Tiamat—" before the High Priest was marching towards the ziqqurat, calling over his shoulder as he went. "Bring her on up then, Andulli! Let's get this over with. I haven't got all night."

The Gamesmaster pressed his lips together. But he gripped Tiamat's hand tighter and pulled her after him. The High Priest led the way up the ziqqurat at a fierce pace. Tiamat's legs, already suffering after the ride back to Babylon, soon began to ache. Her heart pounded with effort and breathing so deeply and quickly made her throat sore. Beside her, Master Andulli was puffing, too. He squeezed her hand. "Count them as you climb," he advised. "Pretend they're a Twenty Squares score. It helps."

Not really believing anything could help her get to the top, Tiamat began to count the steps in her head. There were six hundred in the first tier. As they started up the second, she stole a look at the Gamesmaster's flushed face. *It helps.* How many times had he been up here before?

They climbed so high, they could see clear across the outer city and the wide battlements of Nebuchadnezzar's Wall to the moonlit plain beyond, glittering with canals. The river wound northwards like a silver ribbon into the darkness where the Persian King had his camp. The topmost tier of the ziqqurat had been coated in gold, the thin leaf peeling off the bricks where it had been scorched by the sun. At its centre, the domed roof of the House of Heaven on Earth gleamed under the moon. The actual shrine was smaller than it looked from below, perfectly round, with one plain doorway and no windows. Inside, torchlight flickered and strange shadows moved.

Tiamat stopped to catch her breath, holding a stitch in her side. Her legs were trembling after the climb. She fixed her eyes on the shrine, afraid that if she looked at the view she would fall over the edge. "What's in there?" she whispered.

"Come and see." Master Andulli pulled her forwards.

There was nowhere else to go except down again, and she couldn't face those steps again so soon. She allowed Master Andulli to lead her into the shrine. At once, the door thudded shut, making Tiamat jump and her heart start up afresh until she realized it was only the High Priest closing it, not some strange enchantment.

After the moonlight reflecting from all the gold outside, it took a moment for her eyes to adjust. When they did, she frowned. The mysterious House of Heaven on Earth, the heart of Babylon's power, was empty.

The High Priest took a torch from a bracket on the wall and stepped past them. "I took the liberty of removing the bed," he said. "It's hardly appropriate for our purposes." Again, he gave Tiamat that down-the-nose look. "The only girls we normally allow up here are princesses who come to spend their obligatory night with the god. Not that there's been anyone up here since Amytis, of course – and she failed like all the others," he added, giving the Gamesmaster a pointed look.

The priest's attitude made Tiamat's blood rise. She lifted her chin and pulled her hand free of Master Andulli's. "What am I supposed to do?"

The priest sighed and looked down at his sandals. "This is a map of the Seven Islands between the Earthly Ocean and the Heavenly Ocean. No one's used it in my lifetime, and if you want my opinion, I think this is a waste of time. But the Egibi Family seem to think you can open the gate that no girl of royal blood has been able to open since the reign of Gilgamesh, whatever any of them might claim." He gave Master Andulli another look, as if challenging him to contest this.

When the Gamesmaster said nothing, the priest sighed again. "I suppose we'd better get this over with. Come over here, girl, and I'll explain the symbols." He lowered his torch until the flame nearly touched the floor.

Tiamat frowned at the priest. Symbols? Then she saw something glint beside his foot and looked down in sudden understanding.

His sandals were touching a triangle carved deeply into the limestone that covered the bricks of the topmost tier of the ziqqurat. The groove was lined with gold. It was part of a circle of seven triangles arranged like the points of a star around an inner double-ring that enclosed several smaller circles and lines. "This is Babylon," said the priest, using his toe to trace the golden lines beneath his feet.

In spite of her reluctance to help, Tiamat peered curiously at the map. This must be the map the Egibi men had given a copy of to the Persian King, the one that had made General Gobryas laugh out loud. "Babylon" was a rough rectangle crossed by two parallel lines like a small child's attempt to scratch out a board of Twenty Squares.

"This is our River Purattu, of course," said the priest, tracing the cross lines. He pointed along these to where another rough rectangle was crossed by a curve. "And that's Ur next to the Lower Sea. Master Andulli's standing on the Upper Sea. The circles you can see are other ziqqurats – in other cities," he added, as if Tiamat were stupid. He frowned and carried the torch across to one of the small circles. "From what I remember, this is Borsippa, not that it really matters at this stage." He straightened to look at Tiamat. "Now you know all you need to. Have a go at opening the gate, then maybe we can put this nonsense out of our heads and return to our original plan. I can hardly believe the Persians are considering this."

Tiamat stared at the small circle the priest had indicated. It didn't look much like a gateway to her.

Master Andulli smiled and gave her a little push. "Go on, Tiamat. You can do it. Remember the riddle on the princess's seal? *A stairway where Shamash and Sin stroll hand in hand*. That's the ziqqurat. *A gate which like a copper drum has been covered with skin*. The hidden gateway between cities. *Blessed of Marduk has opened it*. That's you, Tiamat. Marduk's creature blessed you. According to the legends, it's the princess who offers her hand to the sirrush so she can open the Earthly Gateway for her king. The High Priest doesn't agree with me, but I don't see why the sirrush shouldn't bless a girl of non-royal blood if she happens to be in the right place at the right time, like you were. Just use your lucky hand."

Tiamat stared at her hand, then at the map. "If I open this gate, the whole Persian army could come through it, couldn't they? The sentries on the walls won't even know until it's too late."

Master Andulli was nodding, still smiling. "That's the idea. Kyros's men will hide right here in the temple until we're ready. There's a tunnel from the ziqqurat leading into the Palace. Originally, we thought they would have to fight their way in here, which would have alerted the Prince. This way is much better. Once Kyros is in charge of the city, he'll free your friends, don't worry."

Tiamat had a vision of the dark General leading his men through the streets with their swords dripping blood, hunting the people of Babylon as he'd hunted the sirrush. "How do you know he'll help us?" she said. "He might just be saying that, to get us to let him in."

The Gamesmaster's smile faded. "Come on, Tiamat, try, please. We haven't much time."

"But he— "

"Just do as you're told, young lady!" The High Priest's eyes glittered dangerously. He seemed to have forgotten he didn't think she'd be any use.

He turned his glare on Master Andulli. "I'm not surprised the perfume-maker's been arrested – she's obviously no idea how to bring up a daughter. Maybe after things have settled down, I'll offer to take the girl to serve Marduk. A brand on that 'lucky hand' of hers might help tame her."

All kinds of things flashed through Tiamat's head. Foremost was Nanname with her hurt leg, helpless in the Demon's vaults. Would she know the other members of the Egibi Team were prisoners, too? One thing she was sure of. Khatar knew a lot more about what went on in his house than Master Andulli suspected. If Khatar was persuaded to tell all, the Demon would find out about his plans and stop the Persian King from entering the city. But he'd have to hurt Khatar to make her tell. The Demon was worse than King Kyros, wasn't he? Except Kyros had lied to her and his men had eaten the sirrush... Maybe.

She didn't realize the priest had moved until he gripped her elbow and dragged her across the floor. "Get on with it, girl!" he snapped, flinging her to her knees on the Babylon rectangle.

"Don't hurt her!" Master Andulli was beside her at once, pushing the priest away. He put an arm around Tiamat's shoulders. "She'll do it – won't you, Tiamat? I haven't had time to explain things properly. It's no wonder she's a bit confused. Give her a chance to catch her breath."

She shrugged the Gamesmaster off, struggling with tears.

"I'm not confused! Harrim was right. You don't care about any of us, do you? You don't care about the Team. You're only using us to get your Persian friends into the city!"

For a moment, Master Andulli looked taken aback. He glanced at the High Priest, then took her shoulders and gently but firmly turned her to face him. "Listen, Tiamat. I'm doing this *because* I care. The Persian King has promised that if we submit the city to him without a fight, there will be no unnecessary bloodshed and he'll free all captives. He'll even let us worship our own gods as before. We haven't had a proper king in Babylon in years. The only difference is that we'll have a Persian Governor in charge instead of Prince Belshazzar. King Nabonaid and his Demon will be imprisoned where they can do no harm. The Egibi Family's not the only family in Babylon to support King Kyros. He's promised us all a fresh start. It's exactly what we need to revive trade and make our city glorious again."

"But you don't understand. He'll break his promise! He lied to me. He killed my sirrush. I saw its skin."

The High Priest, who had been watching in aloof amusement as they argued, sucked in his breath. "You saw its *what*?"

Ignoring the priest, Master Andulli looked into

Tiamat's eyes. "My men told me what happened. It's a pity about the sirrush, but I'm sure it was a misunderstanding. I know you cared for the creatures, and I know you'll hate me for saying this, but they're not as important as people. I think you realize that. As soon as King Kyros is in charge of the city, he'll release your friends and Lady Nanname. This is the best way, maybe the only way, you can help them now. What else do you expect me to do? Storm the House of Silent Screams with my wardum and a handful of junior masters?" He smiled.

The very thought made her shudder. "The Demon let me go when you came for me before," she said in a small voice.

Master Andulli sighed. "Ah, Tiamat, I thought we'd been over this already... The Demon released you to me that night because he didn't think you were of any use to him once he'd got his hands on the seal. Also, he knew where to find you if he wanted you again. Obviously, the seal didn't give him the power he was hoping for. I'm very much afraid that he's discovered the sirrush licked you and is starting to think along the same lines we are. It looks as though he's using your friends and Lady Nanname to lure you to him. The last thing he's going to do is release them to me."

Tiamat's heart pounded. Deep down, she knew he was right. It was true she couldn't help the dead sirrush now. But Master Andulli's words had given her an idea. Maybe there *was* a way she could help her friends without letting the Persian King into the city.

"What does the Demon want me for?"

Master Andulli glanced at the High Priest. "Probably the same thing we do, only with a different gate. The Tree of Life is supposed to grow beyond the Earthly Ocean... but it won't work. Opening the Earthly Gateways is one thing, opening the Gate of Heaven quite another."

She licked her dry lips. She could barely get the words out. "Then if I give myself up, he'll let the others go."

"Absolutely not!" Master Andulli hugged her tightly. "That's a very brave thought, Tiamat, but I forbid it. The Demon plays to his own rules. Anyway, we need you here."

"Only if I can open your magic gate."

"Which you can." He guided her left hand down to the Babylon rectangle and gently spread her fingers. He clambered to his feet and backed away. "Feel anything?"

Tiamat shook her head with a mixture of relief and disappointment. She was about to remove her hand and tell the priest it was all a waste of time, after all, when a glimmer in the outer circle caught her eye. Amidst the shifting shadows, something familiar seemed to move. "Sirrush," she whispered. "That's a carving of a sirrush, isn't it?" Even as she spoke, the stone beneath her hand warmed and her fingers tingled. Golden light glowed beneath them.

The High Priest took a hasty step backwards. Master Andulli's eyes opened wide. "Yes!" he hissed, like a boy winning his first game of Twenty Squares.

The golden light spread across the map like forks of summer lightning, heading towards the little sirrush-carving in the outer circle.

"No!" cried the High Priest, leaping between Tiamat and the carving. He swung his torch across the golden lines to erase them. "Never look outside the Earthly Ocean – I mean, outside this ring!" he shouted, stamping on the double ring that separated the triangles from the rest of the map. "It's very, very dangerous. Understand?"

Tiamat lifted her hand. The golden light died. She stared at her fingers, wriggled them in wonder, and raised her eyes to the priest. "You didn't tell me that before."

Master Andulli spluttered behind his hand – a laugh that turned into a cough when the priest scowled at him.

"I'm telling you now. All sorts of things live outside the Earthly Ocean, besides sirrush. Now then, try again. And this time, concentrate on Borsippa... here." He tapped the little circle he'd indicated before and stepped back. But this time he watched with real interest, not down his nose as he had done before.

Tiamat pressed her hand to "Babylon" again. This time, she was expecting the golden lightning and found she could control it better. By staring at the small circle of "Borsippa", she made it glow gold, too.

"Marduk's Holy Teeth!" breathed the priest. "I think she's really doing it."

Master Andulli nodded, as if he'd never doubted this. "Open the gate, Tiamat," he said softly. "We should be able to see into the shrine at Borsippa. Once we've seen it open, you can close it again until King Kyros's men are in position. Wouldn't want to alert anyone unnecessarily."

Tiamat stared at the golden circle. Her whole being was tingling with power, yet she felt as helpless as when she'd been carried on the sirrush's back. "But I don't know how."

The High Priest knelt stiffly beside her. "You should be able to see the gate if you look straight along the path of light you've created between the two cities. Just reach out and push it open." He gave her a strange look. "Are you sure you haven't any royal blood?"

Tiamat was in no mood to think about it. She squinted into the golden light. He was right. There was a tiny ghostly gate, an exact replica of the city gates. She tentatively pushed it open with a fingertip. Beyond was a miniature courtyard like the one between the walls around the inner city. And beyond that, another gate. Closed.

She stretched, but she couldn't reach it without taking her hand off "Babylon". When she did, the golden light died and the entire gateway vanished.

The priest sighed, climbed to his feet and quietly replaced the torch in its bracket on the wall. "This explains something that's been puzzling me about the ancient tablets," he said to Master Andulli. "It must be a security measure to prevent kings using the Earthly Gateways to travel between ziqqurats without permission from the other city. For the gateway to exist, she has to open both sets of gates. I think this one will stay open until she closes it. But you'll need to take her to Borsippa to open the other."

Master Andulli curled his beard around his little finger. "I'd hoped to avoid that. The Demon's men are searching for the girl. At the moment, they still think she's outside the city so that's where they've concentrated their search. Harrim and Igmil said they were lucky not to be stopped on their way back from the camp. We can thank our Persian friends for that, creating so many refugees. But further travelling will be dangerous. I'd hoped to leave her here with you until tomorrow night."

"Staying here will be dangerous, too. The Demon's not stupid. It won't take him long to realize who's hiding her."

Tiamat stood shakily and faced the two men. "The only way to open the gate for the Persian King is if I go to Borsippa?" she asked.

The High Priest and Master Andulli exchanged a glance. "Yes."

"Otherwise he'll have to fight his way into Babylon?"

"Well, the sentries won't be expecting an army to come along the river bed, so he should get into the city all right – but yes, he'll have to fight if we fall back on our original plan."

"They'll be expecting him," she said flatly.

Both men frowned. "How do you know?"

"Khatar. She spied on our meeting about the riddle. If you've been discussing your plans in the house, she'll know all the details, I'm sure of it. She'll tell the Demon."

Master Andulli's fingers moved faster through his beard. "It's possible," he admitted at last. "That girl's ears have always been bigger than her brain." He closed his eyes. Suddenly, he looked very old. "Maybe I should have told you all what I was planning. I thought it was safer not to. How was I to know you'd decide to sneak out of the city and let out the sirrush?"

Tiamat made her decision. It was her fault her friends had been arrested. She owed them this. She took a deep breath. "I'll go to Borsippa and open your gate for you. Then King Kyros can come and rescue Nanname and the others, and everything will be back to normal again."

She let Master Andulli hug her and call her brave, but inside she knew it was a lie. Once she opened that gateway, nothing would ever be the same again.

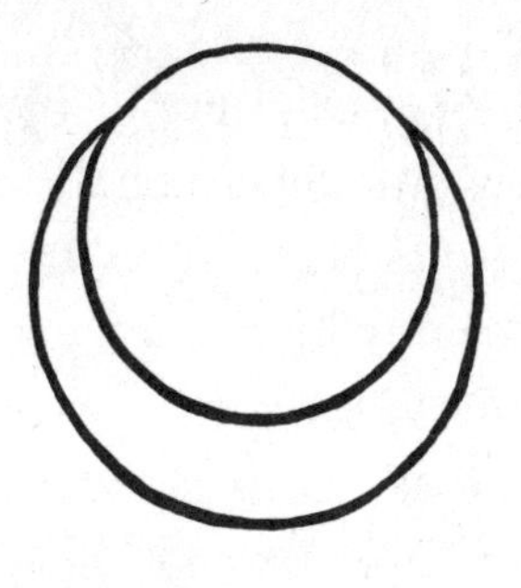

Chapter 14

BORSIPPA

A cry and a shout of joy.

IT WAS AGREED that Tiamat should remain in the temple the following day in case the Demon should come looking for her at Master Andulli's house. She would then make the journey to Borsippa on the morning of the sixteenth, when the High Priest undertook his ceremonial journey along the canal to bring back the statue of Nabu so the Borsippan god could witness the garlanding of the Twenty Squares Champion. This meant they wouldn't have a chance to test the entire gateway beforehand. But after witnessing Tiamat's success with the Babylonian side of the gate, both the High Priest and the Gamesmaster were confident it would work. "There's less danger of alerting the Demon to our plans if we stay away from Borsippa until the last moment," Master Andulli explained when Tiamat protested. "Besides, the sixteenth's a luck-day. What could possibly go wrong?"

Tiamat could think of plenty of things, but held her tongue. She knew Master Andulli's words concealed worries just as deep as her own, so she didn't even argue when he sent Harrim and Igmil to the temple to stay with her until it was time to leave.

The waiting was worse than the vigil outside Lugalgirra Gate. At least then she'd had her friends with her. Igmil tried to interest her in a game of Twenty Squares, saying she should practise for tomorrow night. But both of them knew she wouldn't be playing, and although Igmil proved to be terrible at the game, Tiamat lost to him every time. They were confined to an inner room of the complex with Harrim guarding the door. The room had no windows and was dimly lit. She had no idea if the Demon's men tried to search the temple for her, though at one stage they heard shouting and running feet in the courtyard outside, making Harrim and Igmil draw their swords. A shiver went down Tiamat's back. But the commotion faded and the Egibi men put their weapons away.

None of them slept much. Before sunrise, silent priests escorted Tiamat down the steps to the canal, where they helped her on board an enormous gilded barge, told her to lie down, and pulled a heavy sheet over her head. Her heart pounded and her palms grew sweaty as she remembered the way the sentry had spiked the reeds in Hillalum's boat. But once everyone had boarded and the barge had started to move, it didn't stop. The sun came up and it became stifling under the sheet, but still Tiamat dared not move. She could hear the priests talking, people on other boats shouting, the slap of water against the paddles, and someone playing a harp. Then, after what seemed an age, the barge slowed and bumped the bank. Someone jumped aboard. As they cast off again, the sheet was suddenly dragged from her head.

She sat up in a panic, blinded by the sunlight reflecting off the water and the golden trappings of Marduk's barge. But the Gamesmaster's familiar voice said, "Steady, Tiamat, it's only me. You can sit up now, but be ready to hide again if we spot a patrol."

Her heart slowed as Master Andulli sat beside her and put an arm around her shoulders. She squinted at the sunlit canal. They were weaving their way through a mass of river craft, refugees scraping bows with travellers heading for the Twenty Squares Feast. In any other boat it would have been impossible to make such swift progress against the traffic. But one look at the High Priest standing in the bows, dressed in his full ceremonial regalia, was enough to send the smaller boats scurrying out of their way. As they recognized him, people raised their hands to their noses in respect.

"Priests do have their uses," Master Andulli whispered with a little smile, nodding at the High Priest's back. "While he's with us, only the King himself would dare stop us. Even then, I have a feeling I know who would come off worst."

Tiamat glanced at the Gamesmaster in surprise. "You don't like him either, do you?"

Master Andulli sighed. "Like I said, he's useful. Those who seek to rule Babylon need to keep on the good side of her priests. It's always been the way."

Tiamat bit her lip as she watched the palm trees that lined the Borsippan canal slide past. "I bet the Demon would dare stop us."

"Maybe. But the Demon doesn't know where we are."

After that, they lapsed into silence, listening to the young priest playing the harp. He was really good, but Tiamat was too nervous to enjoy the music. The day grew hotter as the sun climbed in the sky and the flow of refugees increased. The Gamesmaster frowned at them, but didn't say anything until their barge slid unopposed under the Borsippan wall and drew up in the shadow of the ziqqurat. He pointed across the complex, where a coil of smoke showed above the temple wall. "I was afraid of this. Come on, Tiamat, quickly."

She peered up at the ziqqurat. It was very similar to the one in Babylon. But instead of priests, Persian soldiers ran in disciplined ranks up the staircases towards the shrine, bows slung across their backs, carrying spears that glinted in the sun. The priests of Nabu clustered nervously in the courtyard below, watching the soldiers, while above the temple walls more smoke curled ominously into the blue sky. Tiamat heard screams in the streets and her stomach clenched.

"They're burning the city!" she said in horror. "I thought you said they wouldn't hurt anyone!"

"No." Master Andulli looked grim. "The ones starting

the fires aren't Persians. They're the Demon's men in disguise. He's trying to turn the people against Kyros."

Even as he spoke, a torch sailed over the wall and fell into the roof of one of the temple buildings, which crackled into flame. The priests gave a cry of alarm and raced to the canal for water.

"Climb!" said the High Priest, pushing Tiamat ahead of him up the first staircase. "Run!"

Run up more than three thousand steps in the burning heat of midday? He had to be joking. But as she raced up the first tier, the temple gates burst open to admit the men from the streets, who she saw now were wearing Persian tunics over the top of their Babylonian uniforms. A beardless figure sidled through after them, giving Tiamat a strength she hadn't known she possessed. "The Demon's here!" she gasped.

Master Andulli grasped her hand. "We won't let him touch you, don't worry." He seized the arm of a genuine Persian soldier. "Who's in charge here? We need some men to guard the way up. The girl needs time to work on the gate."

"King Kyros is in charge," the man answered. "He's in the shrine with the Borsippan priest."

"The King himself is here?" Master Andulli's eyes widened.

The solider grinned. "The General's taking the rest of the men along the river bed, but we volunteered to try the magic gate. What's good enough for King Kyros is good enough for me!"

"Good man!" Master Andulli slapped the soldier on the back. "It'll work – trust me."

As they hurried on past, Tiamat heard the soldier organizing some of the men into a blockade across the staircase behind them. With Persian bows and spears between her and the Demon, she felt a bit safer.

The top tier of the ziqqurat was crowded with soldiers, who all turned to stare at Tiamat. The two High Priests of the two most powerful gods in the land gave each other a wary hand-to-nose greeting. Master Andulli dropped a steadying hand on her shoulder as the Persian King ducked out of the shrine.

He was dressed for war, having discarded his pink-and-gold-starred robe and replaced it with a sober tunic over leg-hugging pants. His hand rested on the hilt of a sword as plain and businesslike as his men's. He looked steadily at Tiamat. She stared back coldly, determined he should realize she was doing this for her friends' sake, not his.

Master Andulli gave Kyros the formal greeting. "There isn't much time, my lord," he said.

Kyros looked down at where the Persians were loosing arrows, while the Demon's men attacked the ziqqurat from below with a frightening determination. He nodded and stepped aside to let Tiamat enter the shrine.

Inside, apart from a plain wooden bed in the centre of the floor, the shrine was similar to Babylon's House of Heaven on Earth. She couldn't see the map very well because of the bed.

"Move that thing!" snapped the High Priest of

Marduk. "Do you think the girl's come to spend a night with Nabu?"

The High Priest of Nabu pressed his lips together and motioned to the soldiers to drag the bed against the wall. Marduk's priest took Tiamat's hand and led her to the centre. "It's not a full map," he explained. "You can't open all the gates from here. This central rectangle is Borsippa. The other rectangle over there is Babylon. Ignore the rest – and remember not to look outside the Earthly Ocean!"

Tiamat couldn't help looking to see if there was a sirrush-carving like the one at Babylon. But unless the priests had put the bed over it, the sirrush wasn't there. She sighed and pressed her hand to the "Borsippa" rectangle.

The surge of power startled her, much stronger than it had been in Babylon. The golden light streaked across the floor so quickly that both High Priests jumped aside then stepped forward again, looking embarrassed. The Persian King stiffened and dropped his hand to his sword. Master Andulli whispered something in his ear and he relaxed again. The clash of blades could be heard outside. Tiamat put them out of her head and concentrated on the ghostly gate.

She pushed it open with a finger as the High Priest had shown her – and almost leapt back herself as the gateway that had not been opened in thousands of years, shining so brightly she could hardly bear to look at it, expanded to fill the shrine with its golden light. Beyond it, the shrine at Babylon could be seen like a room full of shadows glimpsed from a sunlit street.

Master Andulli touched her shoulder. "Well done! The High Priest says you'll need to keep your hand on the floor until all the soldiers are through." There was an undercurrent of unease in his words, but the pressure of his fingers was steady and comforting. "I'll stay with you – don't worry."

Tiamat missed the significance of this, she was so dizzy with the strangeness of kneeling in a gateway that should not exist. The men in the shrine stared a little longer then glanced at one another.

"I'll test it," said Marduk's priest. Without further hesitation, he stepped into the golden light. He gave a little shudder, vanished for a heartbeat, and reappeared in the shrine at Babylon. He put his head out of the door, checked around, then turned to wave at them.

"It works," Master Andulli said, sounding relieved. "But we should hurry."

At a signal from Kyros, the Persian soldiers jogged in disciplined ranks past Tiamat, were swallowed one by one by the golden light, and briefly reappeared in the shrine at Babylon before drawing their swords and heading out of the door. Tiamat turned her head away so she wouldn't have to think about them terrifying the people of the city.

The sounds of fighting on the Borsippan ziqqurat grew closer as more soldiers came into the shrine and passed through the gate. Some of their swords and spears had blood on them. Tiamat's back prickled. She shifted round so she could see the door. King Kyros cast a worried glance outside. "Can they follow us?" he said in a low tone to Master Andulli. "When we get through the gate, they'll have the advantage of attacking downhill."

"Tiamat will shut the Babylon side once we're through," Master Andulli said. He glanced at the High Priest of Nabu. "You'd best come through with us, sir."

But Nabu's priest shook his head and strode determinedly to the door. "I'm not leaving my ziqqurat in the hands of— " His protest ended in a gurgle as the first of the Demon's men burst into the shrine and swiped his sword across the High Priest's throat.

"Hurry!" roared Kyros, clashing iron with two more of the Demon's men. "Through the gate, everyone! Now!"

The last of the Persian soldiers leapt through. The King went with them. Master Andulli grabbed Tiamat's hand and dived for the golden light.

She wasn't sure what happened next.

There was a blurring of the air, as if rain had landed in her eyes, and her hand slipped out of Master Andulli's. At the same time, she saw a winged shadow cross the doorway of the shrine and a soundless cry pierced her head.

–flyhomewaitflyhome–

She froze, hardly daring to believe. But the creature had disappeared round the other side of the ziqqurat, and in the next instant she realized she was alone in the Borsippan shrine with the dying High Priest of Nabu and more than twenty out-of-breath, but heavily-armed, men. The gateway, along with Master Andulli, had vanished when her fingers lifted from the floor.

There was no time to wonder. Another of the Demon's men came staggering into the shrine, clawing at his eyes and screaming about a "monster". Then the Demon himself slithered sideways through the door and the voice she would never forget as long as she lived hissed, "Never mind the sirrush! Seize that girl!"

Tiamat's heart leapt, even as she quickly pressed her hand back to the floor. Her eyes hadn't been deceiving her. Huge wing beats could be heard outside and more screams. She wanted to run out of the shrine to make sure her sirrush, her beautiful sirrush back from the dead, was all right. But she knew she'd never get past the Demon's men.

"I'll come back for you," she promised as she plunged into the gateway. "Just don't let them catch you!"

The golden light blinded her. There was a shivery sensation, like pouring cold water over her hair on a hot day. Someone grabbed her arm. When she could see again, she found herself face to face with Master Andulli.

She sagged against the Gamesmaster in relief. "The Demon's in the shrine at Borsippa!" she gasped. "And my sirrush is outside! It's grown wings and it's attacking the Demon's men. We've got to help it—"

Someone laughed nastily.

Master Andulli thrust her behind him. "Don't you touch her!" he roared in a terrible voice. "If you do, I swear by Marduk's Name you'll answer to the whole of Babylon!"

Tiamat's breath caught as she realized her mistake. This

was still the Borsippan shrine, full of the Demon's men. Near the bed, the High Priest of Nabu lay bleeding on the floor. She supposed Master Andulli must have come back through the gate when she'd opened it again. But why hadn't she got through the other way?

"Master?" she whispered. "What happened? I don't understand."

The Demon laughed again. "Didn't you realize the Blessed of Marduk can't pass through the gateway herself, Master? You don't know your riddles, do you? *Blessed of Marduk has opened it. Ishtar's Gift comes out of it.* Why do you think it's always the princess who is blessed and not the King himself? Obvious when you think about it, though it took your little wardum to show me the error in my thinking." His tone hardened. "Stand aside, old man. This girl is under arrest."

His men converged on Master Andulli and Tiamat. They dragged them apart. Tiamat twisted and kicked and bit at them in panic, trying to get her left hand free to reopen the gate so Master Andulli, at least, could get away. But he was held between four of the Demon's men, a sword at his throat. The men who had grabbed her twisted her arms up behind her back, lifting her off the floor until she had to stop struggling because it hurt too much.

"I'm warning you, Ensi—" began Master Andulli, his eyes furious. His words cut off with a gasp as the sword pressed harder, drawing blood.

"Tiamat Nanname-daughter," said the Demon, slithering past the Gamesmaster as if he didn't exist. He regarded her struggles with amusement. "You are guilty of stealing the King's sirrush and aiding the enemies of Babylon. That gives me the power to arrest you and do anything needful to ensure your cooperation." He glanced at his men. "Blindfold her and bind her, but make sure she doesn't lose consciousness. I want her to think about her position during our journey back to Babylon. By the time we have her safely in the House of Silent Screams, I guarantee she'll be a lot more cooperative."

Tiamat's legs turned weak as one of the men unwrapped his linen sash from his waist and stepped behind her.

"Er – sir?" ventured another man. "Are you sure it's wise, holding the Egibi Gamesmaster? The Prince will want to know why he isn't at the Championships."

"So we'll tell him why." The Demon smiled and tugged Master Andulli's beard. "Fond of your little stratagems, aren't you, old man? You forget others can play the game, too. You're going to have an accident on the way down the ziqqurat. Prince Belshazzar will be told you fell while aiding the Persian King. A terrible pity you couldn't be taken back to Babylon and tried for treason, but no one's going to question my actions when they hear how guilty you are."

"No!" The pain in her shoulders was unbearable. But as the blindfold dropped across her eyes and was knotted behind her head, Tiamat heaved against her captors in fury. "Let Master Andulli go!" she cried. "You can't do this to us!"

The Demon's hand squeezed her chin. "Oh, can't I? And who are the traitors here? Tell me that."

Tiamat kicked in his direction, but he must have slithered out of range because his voice came from behind her. "We've wasted enough time. Take them away!"

They were dragged out of the shrine. Tiamat felt the heat of the sun on her exposed arms and the warm wind catch her hair. She heard Master Andulli shouting. Then brick slammed against her cheek as she was thrown face down so a rope could be wound about her wrists and ankles. She fought with the last of her strength, but it was no good. There were too many of them; she could not see... As she cried out in anguish for Master Andulli, there was a rush of wings and a great wind tore at her, knocking off the man who was tying her. He gave a single, surprised scream which tumbled away down the ziqqurat.

Tiamat staggered to her feet, clawing off the half-knotted ropes and the blindfold. The sun dazzled her. When her eyes adjusted and she could see again, there were men running everywhere. Some were pointing at the sky, others fighting the priests of Nabu, who had found some ceremonial bronze swords and were defending their god's temple with untrained but furious blows. Men were knocked off the staircases and fell, bouncing from tier to tier. Then the rush of wings came again and Tiamat stared up in joy as her sirrush swooped out of the sun, its scales glinting red and gold, wings spread wide, horn shining, claws and talons extended. As its shadow passed across the ziqqurat, everyone ducked – except the Demon, who grabbed Tiamat's hair and dragged her backwards to the edge. "Tell it to stop attacking my men!" he shouted, shaking her. "Or I'll be forced to hurt it and you."

"Don't you touch her!" yelled Master Andulli, tearing himself free of his distracted captors and launching himself at the Demon. He no longer had his dagger – the Demon's men had taken it from him when they'd seized him in the shrine – but he fastened his bare hands around the Demon's throat. "Run, Tiamat!"

The Demon let go of Tiamat's hair and plunged his sword into Master Andulli's stomach.

Tiamat stared in horror.

"Go, Tiamat!" gasped the Gamesmaster, blood spurting between his fingers as he staggered towards her, clutching the wound. "Tell Enki... it's up to him... now..."

Her horror turned to despair. The staircase was blocked by the Demon's men. Master Andulli was wounded. It was hopeless.

The Demon smiled coldly at her and brought his sword down a second time, into the Gamesmaster's back.

Tiamat could not move. More men spilled out of the shrine. The High Priest of Nabu crawled out after them and clutched the door.

"Jump, girl!" he croaked. "Marduk's creature is strong now... it'll take you home—" His words were cut off as one of the Demon's men plunged his sword into the High Priest's neck, but amidst her horror and despair Tiamat understood. The men were nearly upon her. There was only one way to go.

She shut her eyes and leapt off the edge of the golden tier into space. "Sirrush!" she cried as the wind whistled past her ears. "Sirrush! Come!"

There was a heart-stopping instant when she thought she'd made the biggest mistake of her life. Then the sirrush rose beneath her, its soft new scales rippling under her legs and its wings singing through the air as it carried her up, up into the sun.

She looked down. Far below, the Demon was standing on the top tier of the ziqqurat, staring up at her in frustration and disbelief, his sword still dripping in his hand. When he saw her look, he nudged Master Andulli's body with his toe so that it rolled over the edge and bounced down the ziqqurat like a dead fish flopping down the steps, growing smaller and smaller until Tiamat couldn't see it at all.

She pressed her face to the sirrush's mane and bit her knuckles. Tears stung her eyes, whipped away by the wind.

*–flyhom*e?– queried the sirrush inside her head.

"Yes," she whispered. "Take me back to Babylon."

EGIBI TWENTY SQUARES TEAM

16th Tashritu (afternoon)

Gamesmaster

ANDULLI (deceased)

Team

ENKI Master Andulli's son

SIMEON Jacob's son (in prison)

MUNA astrologer's daughter (in prison)

TIAMAT Nanname's adopted daughter

HILLALUM farmer's son (in prison)

Reserve

KHATAR Master Andulli's wardum (in prison)

Chapter 15

HOUSE OF SILENT SCREAMS

Thou beholdest the handiwork of creatures of the ground.

FOR THOSE FIRST few double-minutes of the sirrush's flight, Tiamat was so choked with misery, she barely registered the wonder of what she was doing. Over and over again, she saw Master Andulli's body bouncing down the tiers of the ziqqurat. She clenched her fists, wanting to go back and knock the Demon over the edge, too. But the sirrush's wings beat strongly, carrying her away from Borsippa. And as the plain opened beneath them, glittering with canals, it became impossible to ignore the fact she was flying. Peering over the sirrush's shoulder, she saw tiny black boats far below, and strings of oxen and onagers and people on foot, all heading for the city. Then – with an extra thud of her heart – she spotted a great pile of mud and stones across the river, the ground beyond churned by feet and chariot wheels.

"I saw your skin," she whispered as their shadow rippled over the Persians' dam. "I thought you were dead."

The sirrush flicked its tail.

–sheditchyskinunfurlwingsflyhome–

Tiamat clung on tighter, wondering for the first time what she was going to do when they reached Babylon. The walls were in sight already, with the blue and gold Ajiburshapu Way running through the centre of the city like a second river. When the sirrush spotted the ziqqurat glowing in the last of the sun, it gave a joyful hiss and dived for the shrine.

"Steady!" She grabbed its spiky mane, starting to think again. "The Demon might have used the gate to get back ahead of us."

They were low enough now to see details. People in their best robes thronged the streets, rubbing shoulders with those refugees who had managed to get through the gates. The sentries on Nebuchadnezzar's Wall were three deep at every lookout tower. Crowds outside the city were still trying to get in, while at every water gate men were locked in fierce, hand-to-hand fighting... Her stomach tightened as she spotted Persian helmets glinting in the alleys of the outer city. General Gobryas must have succeeded in getting under the main wall. But the gates of the inner city had been shut early, sealing off the centre. Within the high double wall, it was as if the war did not exist. Everything here was like a normal festival, with a separate party in every courtyard and parades in the wide streets. She saw enormous peacock feather fans, oxen decked in flowers, awilum dripping gold, wardum with platters of nuts and honeyed cakes, people carrying lambs to the House of Headraising to sacrifice to Marduk, others taking animals to the diviners to discover their fortunes. The temple complex and the ziqqurat appeared deserted. There was no sign of the Persian King or his men.

"He's not there. He must have already used the tunnel." Tiamat wrapped her arms around the sirrush's neck and pulled it sideways. "Take me to the Palace!"

She was afraid the creature wouldn't understand. But it banked steeply and glided over the gardens that lay between the temple and the Palace. The lawns were crowded with awilum. They had hung lamps from the branches of the trees and were feasting from tables heaped with more food than Tiamat had ever seen in one place before, laughing and dancing as they ate. They obviously thought they were secure behind their walls. But when the sirrush's shadow fell across them, they scattered in panic, pointing up at the creature and screaming.

The Palace was ahead, its sentries running towards them. Several spears flew their way. Tiamat ducked as one whistled past her ear. Then the sirrush was on the soldiers, claws and talons extended. The men yelled and jumped off the wall. Tiamat didn't have time to see if any of them survived the fall, because already the sirrush was landing in the courtyard outside the House of Silent

Screams, where the Demon had brought her at the start of everything.

She slithered from the sirrush's back and clung to its shoulder. She couldn't feel her legs. The sirrush folded its wings and crouched beside her, its horned head swinging at a group of soldiers who were crossing the courtyard with a small, plump figure in their midst. "Muna!" Tiamat whispered. The sirrush's tongue flickered. It rolled its eyes and gave a loud hiss.

The soldiers jerked their prisoner to a halt and stared at the creature in surprise. "Marduk's Teeth!" exclaimed one. "Isn't that the Demon's dragon?"

"Na, it's got wings, you fool. It can't be the same one."

"Never mind the dragon," another one shouted. "The girl's getting away!"

The soldiers whirled, undecided whether to chase their prisoner or deal with the sirrush first. None of them seemed to have noticed Tiamat, still catching her breath in the shadow of the scaled shoulder. When Muna burst across the courtyard, hair flying, and flung herself despairingly at the closed gates, Tiamat's strength returned. She pushed herself upright and ran to catch her friend.

"Muna!" she gasped. "I'm so sorry!"

The girl gave her a terrified, blank-eyed look. She started to struggle then stared at her in astonishment. "*Tia*! What are you doing here?"

"No time to explain now," Tiamat said, seeing two of

the soldiers detach themselves from the group and start towards them. "Get inside, quick!"

She dragged Muna through the only open door – into the House of Silent Screams – and slammed it behind them. It was dark inside, but a torch burned further along the passage. Tiamat found the bar and dropped it in place. Muna gave a shudder and collapsed, panting, against the wall. The soldiers could be heard trying to force open the door. There was hiss outside and a loud thump, followed by shouts of alarm in the courtyard.

"What was that monster outside?" Muna said, staring wide-eyed at the door. "How did you ever get in here? The Demon gave orders that you were to be arrested on sight."

"It's not a monster, it's my sirrush." Tiamat peered anxiously along the passage. "I thought the Persian King had killed it, but it was only its old skin that I found. It must have shed it like a snake! And now it's got wings, so we flew all the way back from Borsippa. But the Demon caught us and—" She broke off, not yet ready to tell Muna what had happened. "There's too much to explain. Where are the others? Are they all right? It was all my stupid fault, making you help me let the sirrush out. Where were they taking you just then?"

Muna was shaking her head. "Back to prison."

"*Back* to prison? But I thought—"

Her friend smiled. "It was Simeon's idea. He had it all worked out. He waited until the Demon went after you. Then he told the guards about this ancient rule of

Twenty Squares, where prisoners are allowed to play in the Championships if they've been entered. He said they had to let us into the Palace to play because we were in the Egibi Team. And Enki must have said exactly the same thing to the Prince, or whoever's in charge in there, because an officer came down to the vaults and told the Demon's men to let us out to play the first rounds. They kept us under guard the whole time, of course, but Simeon said if we won our games, we'd be in the final rounds with all the guests watching, and Master Andulli would be there, and the Demon wouldn't be able to touch any of us – at least until the Championships were over. There's this tradition, that if a prisoner wins the Garland, he gains his freedom. Simeon planned that whoever won should ask for everyone else in the Team to be freed, too. I didn't think the Demon would let us go, but it was better than being locked in the vaults. Only I couldn't concentrate with the soldiers peering over my shoulder, and I got knocked out in the very first round." She sniffed and wiped her nose with the back of her hand. "I'm sorry, Tia. Master Andulli will be so ashamed of me."

Tiamat put her arms around her friend. "Master Andulli's dead," she said gently. "The Demon killed him."

Muna stiffened. "Oh – oh, *no*."

"We'll make him pay somehow. He won't get away with it."

The thumping on the courtyard door had stopped.

Tiamat got to her feet. She reached the torch down from the wall, pushed back her shoulders and faced the darkness. "Who's still in here?"

Muna bit her lip. "Lady Nanname and Khatar."

"How many guards are there?"

"Only two. But what if more soldiers come?" Muna glanced nervously at the door behind them.

"The sirrush will keep them busy," Tiamat said, hoping they wouldn't just decide to lock the door from the outside and wait.

Muna chewed her lip again as she led the way. "Tia... there's something I haven't told you. Khatar's hurt. She got disqualified because she was too weak to play in the first round. We don't know what the Demon did to her – she wouldn't say. But we could hear her screaming... Oh, Tia! It was so horrible! We were all so scared." She shuddered and drew a quick breath. "Simeon and Hillalum are still playing the first rounds. Enki must have got through already, because he wasn't there— Oh Ishtar! Does he know about Master Andulli?"

Tiamat shook her head. "We'll have to tell him."

They'd reached the vault where the Demon had brought her that first night. She pushed open the door. It was darker and colder than before, and the smell was foul. Something dead. She took a step inside and swung the torch round, hardly daring to look through the bars.

Muna came in after her and touched her arm. "He killed the sirrush, Tia," she said softly. "He got a priest down here and made him perform some sort of ritual with the princess's seal, but whatever it was didn't work. Afterwards, he was furious and dragged Khatar off again. She must have told him what he wanted that time, because he brought her back pretty quick and rushed off to Borsippa."

Tiamat had seen enough. One thing she knew. The sirrush behind those bars would never shed its skin and grow wings like the one outside. She gripped the torch more tightly, filled with a cold, hard resolve. "Where are the guards?"

"Along here. Careful."

They crept along to the next vault. Two Babylonian soldiers lounged on a pile of reed mats in a storeroom on the other side of the passage, laughing at some coarse joke. Several large jars were stacked near the door. One of them was leaking. Lamp oil trickled across the floor.

Tiamat stared at it, the hard knot of anger still inside. "That could cause a fire, couldn't it?" she whispered.

Muna frowned. "Yes, but—" Her gaze followed Tiamat's and her eyes widened. "Tia, you can't!"

Tiamat was already moving. When she burst through the storeroom door, the guards leapt to their feet and snatched up their weapons. She thrust the torch into the spilt oil and knocked over another jar into the path of the first man. He stumbled over it and landed on his hands and knees in the burning liquid. He gave a shriek, dropped his sword and backed against the wall, beating at the flames with his hands. The second guard started warily towards Tiamat, sword raised, but Muna put her head down and butted him in the back. He staggered forward with a surprised gasp. Tiamat ducked under his arm, dragged some of the mats into the flames and darted out of the room, Muna close on her heels. They slammed the door and drew the rope-lock tightly around the handles. The trapped men yelled and beat on the other side.

"Let Nanname and Khatar out!" Tiamat said. "I'll hold them here as long as I can."

From inside the storeroom, there was a muffled boom. Flames lit the gap between the doors and scented smoke curled into the passage, making Tiamat cough. The men hammered louder. "Let us out, you maniacs! There's incense and all sorts in here. It'll go up like—"

Another boom shook the door. Tiamat staggered back, the handles too hot to hold any longer. Behind her, Muna was wrestling with the bars across the vault door. She turned to help. The door burst open. Lady Nanname limped out of the darkness and folded Tiamat in a bone-cracking hug.

"Where's Khatar?" Tiamat gasped, struggling free. "Quick, we have to get out of here."

Muna was already inside the vault helping a bruised figure out of a pile of dirty reeds. "Go!" she gasped. "We're coming."

Nanname leant heavily on Tiamat as they fled up the passage. Her leg must have been hurting her, but as they went she asked questions in breathless whispers which

Tiamat answered as best she could. By the time they staggered out into the courtyard and came face to face with the winged sirrush, Nanname was prepared enough not to scream. Muna emerged with Khatar a moment later. After a pause, the two guards they'd trapped in the storeroom staggered out of the smoke behind them, coughing and choking and yelling for someone to put out the fire before the whole Palace burnt down. The soldiers in the courtyard had already seen the smoke and were racing towards the House of Silent Screams with leather buckets, giving the sirrush a wary berth. In all the confusion, no one spared a second glance for the four escapees as they staggered to the far side of the courtyard and huddled against the wall, staring at the flames.

"I hope there's no one else down there," Nanname said.

"I hope it burns to the ground!" Muna said with uncharacteristic force.

Tiamat was hoping the Persian King would appear. Surely by now his men must have got through the tunnel Master Andulli had mentioned? Then Khatar gave a little moan and collapsed, reminding her how the Demon had discovered they were at Borsippa, and she had a horrid, cold thought.

"Hold on just a little longer, Khatar." Nanname wiped the girl's singed hair out of her eyes. "We'll get you somewhere safe and then we'll find a healer to tend you."

As the perfume-maker frowned at the closed gates

and the reinforcements running from the Palace, Tiamat seized Khatar's shoulders. "What did you tell the Demon?" she demanded. "Did you tell him Master Andulli's plans?"

The wardum's eyes flickered open and focused on her face. "Persian-Eyes!" she said with a flash of her old, cheeky grin. "He kept asking, but I didn't tell him nothin'! I knew all about the attack along the river bed and divertin' the waters and all that, of course, except I didn't breathe a word of it! He kept hurting me, but I still kept it secret. I just told him all that stupid stuff about the riddle and the ziqqurats and Ishtar's Gift and everything, and then he went off to Borsippa and—"

"You idiot!" Tiamat shook the girl. "You told him exactly where King Kyros was! It's all your fault Master Andulli got killed!"

Khatar's eyes widened. "The Master's dead...?"

"Stop it, Tia!" Muna pushed her back and cradled the wardum girl in her arms. "She didn't know. It's not her fault. Look at her! Don't you think she's been through enough?"

Tiamat shook her head, too upset to think straight. "If Khatar told him about the gate at the top of the ziqqurat and the tunnel, then that's why I couldn't see any of King Kyros's men in the temple, and why he isn't here in the Palace now. The Demon must have had men waiting for him. General Gobryas got under the wall all right, but a lot of good it's done us – he's still stuck in the outer city, and the Prince and all his fine friends are in here, safe as anything! Master Andulli died for nothing. Oh, it's all going *wrong*."

Nanname touched her shoulder. "Tia..."

Tiamat shrugged her off and eyed the sirrush, trying to think. Could it fly her deeper into the Palace? Could she get Simeon and the others out before the Demon came back? They'd have to hide, maybe out in the marshes, until things settled down...

Then Khatar whispered, "What tunnel?"

Tiamat blinked at her. "You didn't know about the tunnel from the ziqqurat into the Palace?"

Khatar shook her head.

"Then that's where they must be! Of course! I'm so stupid!" She stared round with fresh hope. "I've got to find Enki. Master Andulli said it was up to him now – that must be what he meant!"

"Steady." Nanname gripped her arm. "The first thing we have to do is find a way out of here. Do you think your sirrush can carry us all over the wall?" She gazed up at the creature's wings and swallowed.

Tiamat gave the sirrush a distracted look.

–flyonemaybetwoifsmallandlight–

"It says it can fly two of us," she reported, still looking round for a way into the Palace proper.

Nanname sighed. "Then we'll have to make two journeys. You and Muna go first—"

"No!" Tiamat said. "I have to stay and find Enki." She frowned at Nanname. "After you've got Khatar home, you can send the sirrush back for Muna."

Muna squeezed her hand. "I'm not leaving you here alone."

"Don't be silly, Muna! I won't be alone. I'll have Simeon and Hillalum and Enki to protect me."

Muna set her jaw. "I'm staying! Anyway, you need me to show you where they're playing the first rounds. It's chaos in there, believe me!"

Tiamat looked uncertainly at the Palace. The noise of the feast could be heard even out here. Revellers kept staggering into the courtyard, blinking in surprise at the sirrush and the flames and the line of soldiers passing buckets from the well to the fire, then staggering back inside again.

"All right," she said, rather relieved she wouldn't have to face Enki alone. "But we have to hurry."

Nanname clearly didn't like the idea of leaving them, but she must have seen Khatar needed her more than they did. She nodded. "I'll send the sirrush straight back. Promise me you won't take any unnecessary risks. As soon as you find the others, come over the wall. I'll see if I can find out what happened to the Persian King. At the very least, I'll tell the Egibi Family about Master Andulli and they'll do something about the Demon. Oh, girls – come here." Embarrassingly, she hugged them both.

Between them, they managed to get Nanname up on the sirrush's back with Khatar propped in front of her. The wardum girl winked down at them. "I always wondered what it was like to fly," she said. "This was almost worth gettin' arrested for!"

As the sirrush sprang into the air, Muna shook her head. "I got her all wrong," she said. "She's the bravest person I've ever met."

Tiamat sighed. "I just hope Enki knows what to do. Master Andulli didn't have time to tell me much."

"He'll know," Muna said firmly. "Inner city boys always know everything."

Chapter 16

BELSHAZZAR'S FEAST

I have poured out for thee mead, a drink from corn.

MUNA HADN'T BEEN joking. The Palace was like a huge school of unruly children without any teachers to keep order. Except in this case the "children" were grown awilum with gold in their ringlets and perfume in their beards. They were rolling on the expensive carpets, dancing on the tables, making fiery circles in the air with the torches, tearing down the curtains to wear as cloaks, having food fights, and whooping and giggling like six-year-olds. Not one of them seemed to care about the attack on the city – Tiamat wondered if they even knew about it. Amidst all this chaos, Palace guards stood stiffly to attention at doorways, trying to ignore the pistachio shells that were occasionally flicked their way.

The noise was amazing. As Muna pulled Tiamat across an inner courtyard where white and yellow roses glowed in the dusk, the shouts and laughter echoed from the walls until all she wanted to do was crouch in a corner and press her hands over her ears. The sole advantage of all this chaos was that the guards stationed inside the Palace didn't seem to think it strange that two barefoot girls with flushed faces should be running towards the Twenty Squares chamber, hand-in-hand.

"You're late!" called one of the soldiers posted at the door. "The first rounds are almost over."

Muna dragged Tiamat past the guards and leant against the wall, holding her side and wheezing from the run. Tiamat was breathing hard, too, partly from fear. They were at one end of a long room with a high, arched ceiling. A row of windows down one side looked out on yet another courtyard. These didn't have the usual grille of clay, but were screened by gold and silver wire entwined into flowers of Ishtar so that the moon shining through them set the entire wall alight. Lamps suspended from bronze chains burned brightly above rank upon rank of Twenty Squares boards. It was like a larger version of the Club room back at the Egibi Tablet House, except that here every board had its own circle of spectators – supporters in their Team's colours, and an official referee wearing the fringed, black-and-white sash that meant he was impartial to the outcome of the game.

After the chaos and noise outside, the intense concentration in the room and the ordered rattle of dice and counters were a relief.

"There's Hillalum!" Muna whispered, pointing to a

board halfway down the room, where two soldiers stood behind one of the players. "I can't see Simeon."

Tiamat's gaze darted anxiously from board to board. Muna was right. There was no sign of the Judean boy.

"Don't worry," she said, hoping she sounded more confident than she felt. "Simeon wouldn't get knocked out in the first round – he's probably through already. We should find Enki and come back for Hillalum later."

"We can't just leave him here!" Muna protested. "If he loses, they'll take him back to the House of Silent Screams!"

Even as she spoke, the farm boy threw down his counters and reached across the board to grasp his opponent by the neck of his tunic. "You cheated!" he hissed, then grunted as his guards seized his arms and pulled him back. He clenched his fists and appealed to the referee, who shook his head and turned away. The boy heaved in frustration against his guards, but it was no good. The games at the neighbouring tables paused and people looked round as he was dragged unceremoniously from the room.

Muna pulled Tiamat behind the nearest curtain as the soldiers and their prisoner approached. Meanwhile, the boy in Crown colours whom Hillalum had accused of cheating stood up and brushed off his tunic. Tiamat's stomach clenched.

"Labinsin!" she whispered.

"Forget him." Muna tugged at her sleeve. "Quick, let's follow them."

Tiamat shook her head. “We have to find Enki and Simeon first.”

“But Hillalum’s – ”

She gripped Muna’s arm fiercely, squashing an urge to leap across the room and thump Labinsin. “Don’t worry. They won’t take him back to the House of Silent Screams – it’s on fire, remember? He’ll be all right. We have to tell Enki what Master Andulli said and find out what happened to the Persians, otherwise there’s no point rescuing anyone.”

Muna watched the soldiers march Hillalum out of the room and across the moonlit court, then suddenly darted out from behind the curtain and raced after them. Tiamat cursed under her breath and gave chase. The boy seemed resigned, walking with his head down. Just in time, she caught up with Muna and put a hand over her mouth to stop her from calling out. Fortunately, at that moment, a group of giggling awilum staggered towards the guards and their prisoner and offered them mead from a golden jug. The soldiers pushed them away. Hillalum saw his chance and darted across the courtyard, his bulk sending one of the perfumed awilum men, who tried to catch him, staggering aside. The soldiers gave chase. But Hillalum had already ducked through one of the many archways on the far side of the courtyard and vanished into the maze of corridors beyond.

“Yes!” Muna cheered. “Go, Hillalum! Run!”

She still wanted to go after him, but Tiamat pulled her

back into the shadows. "He'll be fine now. Where do they play the next rounds?"

Muna reluctantly dragged her gaze from the arch where Hillalum had disappeared. "Next to the Throne Room, I think."

"Where's that?"

"I don't know."

Tiamat sighed. "Then we'll just have to follow our ears."

They turned their backs on the court and eventually, after asking everyone who looked sober enough to give them directions, found themselves in a corridor lined with blue bricks like the Ajiburshapu Way. The corridor ended in a flight of steps, leading down. More guests lounged on the steps, drinking and giggling like the awilum in the outer rooms. They pushed their way through, muttering "sorry" when they stepped on the fine robes. At the bottom of the steps was a round, windowless chamber lined with the same blue bricks, its domed ceiling done in blue and gold with an enormous flower of Ishtar in the centre. The effect made Tiamat dizzy. A single archway led into another blue corridor, thickly carpeted and guarded by two massive, black-skinned men with crossed spears.

"And where do you two think you're going?" said one of the guards as Tiamat and Muna hesitated. "Only competitors and the Prince's personal guests are allowed through here."

Muna's hand tightened on Tiamat's. "We are

competitors!" she said, lifting her chin. "We're in the Egibi Team, and we're late, so you'd better let us through!"

The spears did not move. "Where's your pass, then?" said the other guard. "Where's the evidence you got through the first rounds? Why aren't you wearing your Team's colours? Why aren't you with your Gamesmaster?"

While Tiamat was trying to think of a plausible explanation, Muna tugged her hand. "Quick, back to where they play the first rounds. I've got an idea."

By the time they got back to the Twenty Squares chamber, all but a few of the boards were empty. Most of the supporters seemed to have gone in search of food, leaving the referees to gather in one corner. The guards at the door looked bored, but when Tiamat and Muna dashed in they jerked alert and looked anxiously across the court. Seeing no immediate threat, they chuckled. "You two again! Thought you'd chickened out."

This time they didn't take refuge behind the curtain. Muna marched straight up to the huddle of referees and cleared her throat.

One of them turned and frowned at her grubby clothes. "What are you two doing in here? All children not competing must wait in the designated area in the Annexe, you know that – go on, out you go!"

"We're on the Egibi Team," Muna said, giving him the hand-to-nose gesture. "I'm sorry we're late."

"Egibi?" The referee frowned again. "The Team with

half its players in custody?" He peered closer at Muna, his mouth set in a suspicious line. "Aren't you the girl who had to play under guard earlier? How come you're back here? You can't watch the next rounds unless you've special permission." He glanced at the door and the guards.

"My friend hasn't played the first round yet," Muna said.

Finally, Tiamat understood what Muna was up to. She shook her head desperately, but Muna ignored her. The referee narrowed his eyes at Tiamat and summoned a scribe with a bucket of tablets. As the scribe searched for the appropriate entry, Muna whispered, "If you win, they'll have to let you in."

"I can't concentrate on playing *no*w! It'll be quicker to look for another way in!"

"And what if there isn't one? It's bound to be guarded, anyway."

"We can sneak past the guards somehow."

"Don't be silly, Tia. This place is a maze. How far would we get? The Prince himself watches the final, doesn't he? And all the important princes and nobles from the other cities. This is the best way, believe me. Once you've got your pass, you'll be able to get in and talk to Enki with no questions asked. I'll go and find Hillalum."

"But I mightn't win!"

Muna patted her lucky hand and smiled. "You'll win."

Tiamat almost hoped the referee would tell her she was too late to play. But after searching through his tablets, the scribe found one with the Egibi seal rolled across it. Tiamat's name had been pressed neatly into the tablet below ENKI ANDULLI-SON and above KHATAR ANDULLI-WARDUM, across which someone had stuck fresh clay stamped with the closed eye that meant "disqualified". Both names gave her a little jolt of sadness. Every time she closed her eyes, she saw Master Andulli's body falling down the tiers of the ziqqurat. She didn't know how she was going to tell Enki.

With a start, she realized the referee was speaking to her. "I said you'll have to play Crown, Green-Eyes. Have you any objections?"

Tiamat shook her head, at the same time willing silently, *Not Ikuppi, please don't let it be Ikuppi.*

But the player who settled opposite her was a thin-faced girl who kept chewing the insides of her cheeks. A few of the remaining supporters drifted across, looking rather bored. Muna stayed close by Tiamat's shoulder. The referee held out two ivory cups with the All-Seeing Eye painted on the outside and rattled the counters inside. "Since this is a Championship, no player is weaker. Traditionally, Crown picks blind." He looked expectantly at the thin-faced girl.

The girl sucked her cheeks in even further, half closed her eyes as if trying to see through the cups, and picked one. Tiamat was left with White. A good omen? She took a deep breath as she placed the first counter on White's starting square. She must clear her head of everything, concentrate on throwing with her left hand, and just hope her luck had not deserted her.

It hadn't. Eight double-minutes later, the Crown girl was losing. Impatient to end the game, Tiamat deliberately moved on to one of the Eye Symbols. An interested ring of spectators formed. The thin-faced girl relaxed slightly, scooped the out-of-play counters into her hand and smiled at Tiamat. The only time it was good strategy to land on an Eye Symbol was when there were just one or two counters out of play, giving a good chance of guessing correctly. To risk the Eye near the end of the game like this was usually fatal.

Except, of course, Tiamat wasn't guessing. "Three," she said without hesitation.

The spectators whispered among themselves. The referee shushed them. The girl's face fell. She sucked in her cheeks and lifted the cup. Three black counters gleamed on the clay.

"Egibi score doubles," said the referee. "Play on."

Two double-minutes later, he pronounced Egibi the winner.

Muna grinned in triumph. Tiamat snatched her pass from the scribe and pushed through the supporters, who were all talking about the game. "Never seen anything like it!" one exclaimed. "She wasn't wrong even once." … "And did you notice her throws? Always exactly what she needed" … "It's uncanny." …

"Other girl didn't stand a chance."

"Where are the next rounds?" she demanded of the referee, who was casting suspicious glances at Muna. "I don't want to miss them."

The referee frowned at her. "I don't know how you pulled off that trick, Green-Eyes – but I'm warning you, I'm going to be watching you very closely from now on. In fact, I think I'd better take you there myself." He turned to Muna. "You'd best come, too, my girl. I'm sure you shouldn't be wandering around the Palace unsupervised. I'm handing you both over to your Gamesmaster."

News of Tiamat's game spread fast. As they moved deeper into the Palace, they collected a tail of excited awilum, who crowded into the blue chamber at the bottom of the steps, whispering excitedly about the girl who had the luck of the ancient champions. Their sheer press of bodies broke through the guards' spears. More black-skinned guards came running up the carpeted corridor, forcing the Twenty Squares party to squash themselves against the walls. The referee who had overseen Tiamat's game shook his head. "There's going to be a riot, I knew it. I always said it was a mistake to give so much mead to the guests – in here, quick!"

The room where the final rounds were being played was small in comparison to the outer chamber. Its blue walls pressed on Tiamat until she could barely breathe. No windows. Just lamps on chains and two sets of doors: those at this end open and guarded; the ones at the far end shut and sealed with a lump of clay across a rope lock. From beyond the far doors came the faint strains of music and laughter, but the thick walls kept out most of the noise. Privileged spectators formed tight, whispering knots around the boards. Tiamat stood on tiptoe, trying to see past all the bright robes and perfumed beards, while Muna gazed anxiously back the way they'd come.

The referee was asking for the Egibi Gamesmaster. People shook their heads. Then one of the scribes pointed to a board near the far end of the room and the referee beckoned them to follow.

"ENKI!" Tiamat shouted, rushing past.

Strong hands pulled her back.

But Enki had heard her. He looked up with a frown that changed to an expression of relief as he gazed past them, searching the crowded room. Muna bit her lip. "He's looking for Master Andulli," she whispered.

Tiamat edged closer to the board, but it was impossible to get through the spectators. It looked as if they'd have to wait until the game finished. She eyed the counters. Enki was playing Black and he was losing. She looked to see who his opponent was and met a familiar, twisted smile. Her left hand tingled in memory.

"Ikuppi," she whispered, looking in surprise at his heavily-bandaged wrist. How badly had he been hurt?

Ikuppi smiled, leant across the board and whispered something to his opponent. Enki scowled. But he was still looking for Master Andulli and it was obvious he was no longer concentrating on the game. Tiamat stared at the counters, willing them to move faster. Ikuppi, in particular, seemed to be prolonging the agony, smiling whenever Enki threw badly or had a counter returned to the start. Tiamat used the wait to search the other boards for Simeon, but there were too many people in the way and she dared not leave Enki's board in case the game finished and she lost sight of him.

"See if you can find Simeon," she whispered to Muna.

But as soon as the girl started to slip away, the referee who had escorted them through the Palace grabbed her wrist. "Oh, no you don't! I'm going to clear up this custody business with your Gamesmaster first."

Muna looked helplessly at Tiamat. Tiamat bit her lip. They'd just have to find Simeon later.

"Crown wins!" came the verdict at last. Enki scraped his stool as he stood up. He glared at Tiamat. Ikuppi turned his back on his opponent. Without bothering to return Enki's hand-to-nose gesture, he pushed across the room to talk to Labinsin, who was waiting with a huddle of other Crown players. Enki's face darkened. Tiamat pushed through the remaining spectators and grabbed his elbow.

"I have to talk to you. It's urgent."

He shook her off. "Thanks to you, I'm out of the Championships! What did you have to go and distract me like that for? I should have won that game. Now all our hopes are resting on an untried Judean! Where's Father? This would never have happened if he'd been here."

Tiamat licked her lips. "Enki, I'm sorry, but he's—"

"Yes, where is the Egibi Gamesmaster?" inquired the referee who had escorted them through the Palace. "I've never known him miss a Championship."

Tiamat shook her head and grabbed Enki's arm again. "Just *listen*, will you? I've something important to tell you."

Someone had stopped the referee to ask about the first rounds. Tiamat and Muna seized the opportunity to hustle Enki through the crush to a relatively quiet spot by the far doors.

The boy frowned at them. "Do you know where Father is? He told me to play as normal until he got back. I don't know why he went off like that. We've far more important things to do here—" For the first time, he seemed to notice their ragged state. He frowned again. "What's been going on? Why are there soldiers watching Simeon? They won't even let me speak to him."

"Enki..." There was no good way to do this. "Enki, I'm really sorry, but the Demon killed your father. King Kyros and his men are somewhere in the inner city. They used the gateway at the top of the ziqqurats and I think they might be in the tunnel. Master Andulli said..." She faltered, took a deep breath and rushed on. "Your father said to tell you that it's up to you now. I hope you know what that means, because the Demon's sure to be back in Babylon by now. We set fire to the House of Silent Screams, but it won't take him long to work out where we are. I know you must be upset, but— Enki?"

The Egibi boy had backed against the doors. He was staring from one to the other of them, shaking his head. "You're lying," he whispered.

Tiamat sighed. "I wish I was. But I saw it happen. The Championships don't matter, not any more. It doesn't matter that Ikuppi beat you. We've got more important things to think about now. I know it's horrible about Master Andulli, but... oh, Enki, I'm so sorry! He was like a father to me, too."

Muna squeezed her hand.

"He cheated," Enki said in a peculiar little voice.

They glanced at each other. "Who?"

"Ikuppi. He cheated."

The referee was pushing his way through the crowds towards them with two black-skinned Palace guards in tow. The guards hesitated when they saw the expressions on the faces of the three children.

"Enki?" Muna frowned. "Did you hear what Tiamat said? She said your father's— "

"I heard."

The boy pushed himself upright, closed his eyes and opened them again. They glittered with tears, but his lips were set in a fierce line. "The Demon's not going to get away with it. Through here!"

He lowered his shoulder and made a sudden lunge at the closed doors. His momentum broke the seal across the handles. The guards leapt forwards, but Enki had already pulled the ropes free and opened the door.

The referee gave an outraged shout. "NO! Only

finalists are allowed into the Throne Room! Tiamat Nanname-daughter, if you don't come back here this double-minute, I'll disqualify you!"

A wild laugh escaped Tiamat as she followed Enki through the forbidden door. As if they cared about Twenty Squares rules *now*. All the same, she hoped Enki knew what he was doing. It wouldn't be long before they were caught.

The black-skinned guards started after them, but a horde of angry awilum poured through the doors at the other end of the finals room, demanding that they be allowed to watch "the girl with the luck of the Ancients" play. The guards were forced to turn their attention from the runaways to the riot, while the referee who'd brought Tiamat and Muna through to the inner court pressed himself against the wall, moaning about there being no respect for the rules any more.

On the other side of the forbidden door, they slithered to a halt, panting. They were at the top of a flight of wide, blue steps that led down to a carpeted hall where guests, musicians, and half-naked wardum crowded around tables heaped with fruit, honeyed nuts, whole roasted sheep, peacocks with the tail feathers still attached, boiled fish with jewels for eyes, and a thousand other dishes too exotic to take in all at once. The torchlight flashing off the golden plates and goblets dazzled; laughter and music beat at their ears; the smell of cooked meats, sweat, and heady wines made Tiamat's stomach turn. At the far end of the hall, a large dais beneath an enormous frieze of golden lions and flowers of Ishtar supported a huge golden throne. Upon this throne sat the fattest man in the world.

As the three children burst through the doors, the fat man stirred, picked some crumbs out of his beard, and yawned. Two fleshy hands embedded with rings appeared and clapped. Although they didn't make much sound, the black-skinned guards standing either side of the throne jerked alert and beat their staffs on the dais. The musicians stopped playing in mid-note. Heads turned. Every person in the hall fell silent.

"At last." The fat man's voice was thin and weedy. "Maybe now we can get this silly Twenty Squares thing over with and bring on some real entertainment."

Everyone laughed. A space cleared in front of the dais, revealing the most beautiful Twenty Squares board Tiamat had ever seen, fashioned of ivory inlaid with dark-blue lapis lazuli and blood-red carnelian. Those guests nearest the steps climbed towards the children, their faces questioning.

"Which two of you is it, then?" giggled a lady with her hair coming down from its headband. "You can't have *three* finalists."

Tiamat looked expectantly at Enki, while Muna cast nervous glances at the doors behind them.

Before any of them could speak, the Chief Referee staggered through the door at the top of the steps holding a boy's wrist in each hand. Behind him, the crossed spears of the guards struggled to keep back the clamouring supporters and two outraged soldiers who were demanding to be let through to do their duty.

"Hail, Prince Belshazzar! Governor of Babylon, Son of the Legitimate King Nabonaid, Ruler of the Four Corners of Heaven and Earth!" The Chief Referee dragged up the arms of the two boys, as determined to preserve the illusion of normality as any of the awilum outside. "I present to you the finalists of this year's Twenty Squares Championships! For the Crown Team, Ikuppi Zerim-son. And for the Egibi Team, Simeon Jacob-son. Let them play before the All-Seeing Eye of Marduk for the Garland and Immortality!"

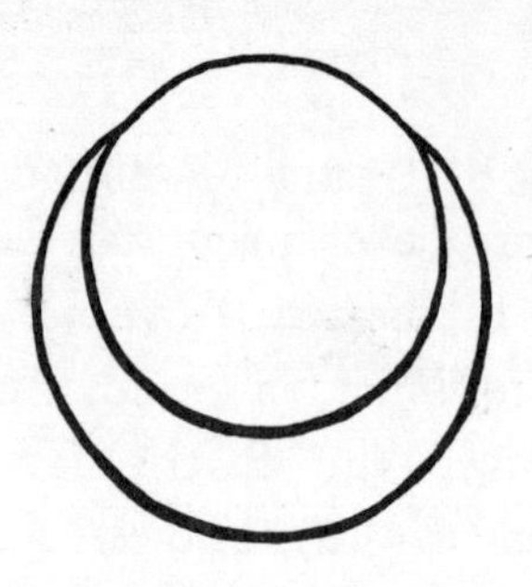

Chapter 17

WRITING ON THE WALL

I have turned towards thy power; let there be life and peace!

SILENCE FOLLOWED THE Chief Referee's announcement. Around the banqueting tables, kohl-lined eyes widened and guests tugged nervously at their gold-dusted beards. Even the rioting supporters stopped pushing at the spears that blocked their way to stare at one another in confusion.

Then the Throne Room erupted with shouts of protest. "The Egibi boy's a Judean!" ... "It's outrageous!" ... "Unthinkable!" ... "Judeans can't play in the final!" ... "Where's the Egibi Gamesmaster?"

Taking the guards by surprise, the supporters surged forwards again and this time managed to burst past the crossed spears. "We want the girl with the luck of the Ancients!" they chanted as they poured down the blue steps. "We want the girl with the green eyes!"

"Quick or they'll eat you alive!" hissed Enki,

grabbing Tiamat's elbow and dragging her off the steps into the shadows behind a row of pillars. Muna started to fight her way through the crush after them, then stopped with a joyful cry.

"Hillalum!"

Tiamat hesitated. "No, Muna!" she called. But the girl had eyes only for the broad-shouldered boy who had broken through with the supporters and was anxiously scanning the room. At the top of the steps, Simeon looked dazed, his wrist still held firmly by the Chief Referee. Some of the Prince's guests started up the steps towards him, muttering dangerously, but the supporters carried them back down again in a struggling mass. The two soldiers who had been Simeon's guard in the previous rounds unsheathed their swords and took up a protective stance in front of their charge. For the first time, Tiamat was glad they were there. On the Chief Referee's other side, Ikuppi wore a confident smile. Hillalum took a flying leap, trusting the crowd to break his fall, and caught Muna round the waist. They hugged each other tightly. Amidst the crush of perfumed bodies, they seemed oblivious to everything except each other.

Enki grunted. "How sweet!" He seized Tiamat's arm again. "Leave them. We've got to get to the wall behind the throne. Father— " He swallowed hard before continuing. "Father's original plan was for one of us to win through to the final so he could get in here officially as Gamesmaster with some of his wardum and let the Persians in while everyone else was watching the game. You'll have to help me."

"The tunnel comes out in *here*?" Tiamat said, her heart starting up again as they worked their way around the edge of the Throne Room.

"Where did you think it came out?" Enki's face was set, his fingers tight on her arm.

Suddenly nervous, Tiamat eyed the Prince of Babylon and his black-skinned bodyguards. "Enki… are you sure you know what you're doing? Nanname's gone to tell your family what happened to Master Andulli. Maybe we should wait till they get here?"

"Just hurry, will you? Why do you outer city girls have to be so difficult all the time?"

Enki dragged her past a lyre carved to look like a cow. The musician – a pretty young wardum robed in white with her hair twisted in a gold ribbon – was balancing on its curved back, trying to see what was happening in the middle of the room. Tiamat stopped, the hairs on the back of her neck prickling in response to a faint, wordless cry.

–trap–

"What's wrong now?" Enki hissed.

She shook her head, unable to explain the sudden feeling of dread that had come over her. "I don't know… But my sirrush is out in the city somewhere with Nanname and Khatar. I'm worried about them."

Enki dragged her around a final pillar and slammed her against the wall. The moulded form of a huge golden lion hung over them, its paws touching the top of her head. The blue bricks were cold against her back. She stared at the Egibi boy, breathing hard.

"Sorry," he muttered. "Didn't mean to hurt you." He took a step away from her. "Look, Tia, I know it's hard for you because you've been bonded to that creature like the princess in the King's Ritual. But it's hard for me, too. Father was supposed to be alive to do this himself… Forget your sirrush for a moment. I need your help. Afterwards, I'll help you find the creature, no matter what happens when we open that panel. Egibi honour. Agreed?"

Tiamat shivered again. Had she imagined that faint warning? They were round the back of the throne. Now the excitement on the steps was over, Prince Belshazzar had sunk back into his rolls of flesh. As the Chief Referee installed the two finalists at the Twenty Squares board and the guests and supporters crowded round to watch, a shapeless hand emerged from the throne and scooped some dates into an unseen mouth. The Prince's two bodyguards returned their spears to the upright position and turned their attention from the crowd to the board. They hadn't noticed the two children in the shadows behind the dais.

Tiamat breathed a little easier and pushed herself from the wall. "Tell me what I have to do."

Enki smiled. "Count. It's a code. We start by the seventh lion's paw. Seven bricks across, then seven down. You go one way, I go the other. We push together, when I say." He looked hard at her. "Thanks, Tia."

"For what?"

"For coming in here to tell me. That took guts."

She bit her lip. "It was my fault Master Andulli died."

Enki shook his head. "No, it wasn't. He died because of the Demon, and this is the best way we can avenge his murder." The boy's eyes were shadowed, his face older than his years. "It's up to us to finish what he began. Push hard, Tia. It might be stuck. From what Father told me, I don't think this tunnel's been opened since Nebuchadnezzar's day. I just hope the Persians are waiting on the other side as they're supposed to be."

"They'll be waiting," Tiamat said, trying not to think of the gates she'd left open at the top of the ziqqurat and what the Demon might be up to.

They counted under their breath. Seven lions. Seven bricks across. Seven down. Tiamat laid her left hand against the blue glaze and felt the brick move slightly. Her heart gave an extra thump. She looked at Enki, counting carefully in the shadows on the other side of the throne.

The room quietened as people sorted themselves out. In the interests of keeping the peace, the black-skinned guards had obviously decided to allow the invading Egibi supporters to stay and watch the game. The Gamesmasters of the beaten Teams formed a huddle in one corner, discussing strategy in whispers. The Crown Gamesmaster stood proudly behind Ikuppi. In place of the absent Egibi Gamesmaster, the Demon's two soldiers stood behind Simeon. The Chief Referee was explaining why "the girl with the luck of the Ancients" had been disqualified and why Simeon was being allowed to play. He promised that if the Judean lost, he'd be returned straight to prison. This seemed to pacify the Prince's guests, who obviously believed a Crown player would have no trouble beating an unknown Judean from the outer city. The Egibi supporters weren't so happy, but since no one could find Tiamat they didn't have much choice. "Suppose it's fair," she heard one mutter. And another said, "The Judean's good. I've seen him play."

Enki finished counting, glanced across at her and mouthed, "Ready?"

Tiamat gave him a tight smile. "Ready!"

"Then *push*!"

Tiamat leant all her weight on the seventh brick. For a horrible moment, she thought she'd counted wrongly. Then it sank suddenly into the wall, catching her off balance and tearing out the nail of her little finger. The pain made her snatch her hand back, but the brick continued to move. There was a faint grating sound deep within the wall. As if by magic, a jagged, man-sized hole appeared in the shadows between the paws of the seventh lion. A musty smell wafted out, making Tiamat cough. Prince Belshazzar stirred on his throne and two bloodshot eyes peered over one golden arm.

"What are you doing back there?" he squeaked as his eyes focused on them. "Guards! There are children playing behind my throne!"

He didn't seem to have noticed the hole. The two bodyguards, who had moved to the front of the dais to watch the game, looked round but were slow to attend their Prince.

Enki extracted a kohl pot from one of the guests' make-up boxes, which had been left behind the dais for safekeeping. He dipped a finger into the black paste and winked at Tiamat. Staring challengingly at the Prince, he started to draw black lines on the wall under the lamps, working away from the seventh lion to the edge of the room.

"Stop that!" Prince Belshazzar squeaked. "Stop it at once! Guards! The little devils are writing on my walls! Seize them! Throw them in prison! Tell my father's Demon I want them punished!"

Though her nail had been torn away from the skin by the tunnel mechanism and blood was dripping on her fine Egibi dress, Tiamat couldn't help a giggle. She cast a final look at the hole, then followed Enki's lead and worked her way in the opposite direction, smearing blood on the blue bricks and watching the guards from the corner of her eye.

When the first Persian soldier ducked out of the tunnel, ran noiselessly across the carpet, and crouched in the shadows behind the dais, no one saw him. Prince Belshazzar was pointing at the writing on his palace wall and making outraged noises. The black-skinned guards, who had finally torn themselves away from the game to deal with their Prince's demands, seemed amused. One sauntered towards Enki, trying to read what the boy had written. Tiamat slipped behind a curtain and put her bleeding finger in her mouth. She anxiously divided her attention between Enki and the soldiers coming out of the tunnel. The Persians were being very quiet and keeping their heads down behind the dais, but surely someone had to notice them soon?

There was an outbreak of excited whispers around the Twenty Squares board. The Chief Referee announced, "Egibi score doubles!" and every eye except the Prince's turned to the centre of the room.

"Play on!" instructed the Chief Referee.

"STOP!" commanded a powerful voice from the dais.

Heads turned in surprise. Tiamat looked, too. Belshazzar sat upright on his throne, eyes wide, looking quite awake. Although she'd seen the soldiers come out of the tunnel, it took her a moment to realize why. A Persian short sword lay between the folds of flesh at the Prince's throat. Holding the sword with a casual yet firm pressure was the Persian King Kyros.

For a full double-minute, no one moved. A few of the Prince's guests giggled nervously, thinking it was someone dressed up in a Persian costume as a joke.

Drops of sweat ran down Prince Belshazzar's cheeks and dripped from his beard on to Kyros's blade. Then a lady screamed, "It's the Persians! We're all going to die!" and everyone ran for the doors in a shoving, yelling mass.

The black-skinned bodyguards leapt across the dais towards their Prince. At the same time, a detachment of Babylonian soldiers came running down the blue steps at the other end of the Throne Room, shouting "Fire! Fire in the Palace!" The guests, their escape blocked by the soldiers, panicked. Some ran back into the crush around the Twenty Squares board, hampering those still trying to get out. People fell over, spilling wine and food. Amidst all the trampling feet, finely dressed awilum scratched and clawed at one another like dogs in the street.

"I SAID STOP!" shouted Kyros. "Everyone stand still or your Prince dies. I am not bluffing."

The Babylonian soldiers stopped first, staring at the Persian King in shock and disbelief. It was obvious they couldn't work out how he had got past their city's defences. They drew their swords, but seemed reluctant to endanger the life of their Prince. The civilians picked themselves up and crowded together nervously, trying to work out if the Persian King was alone. The two finalists sat frozen on their stools.

Kyros looked over his shoulder and commanded in a low voice, "Now!" The Persians who had come out of the tunnel rose from the shadows in a disciplined rustle, bronze helmets glittering in the torchlight, and rushed to surround the Babylonians. Another detachment of Kyros's men raced up the steps and secured the doors.

Tiamat clutched the curtain tighter. Enki had worked his way round the wall as far as the steps. She saw him join Muna and Hillalum and start back towards the dais, but one of the Persian soldiers intercepted them and pushed them in with the other hostages. Tiamat looked at the Persian King, then at the hole in the wall behind him.

She forced herself out from behind the curtain. Slowly, clutching her bleeding finger and shivering every time she looked at that unguarded tunnel, she worked her way back behind the throne.

"And where do you think you're going?"

She dragged her gaze from the tunnel and found herself looking at the wrong end of a Persian spear. The soldier who had stopped her shook his head in warning. "No closer. Go back and join the other civilians, girl. You will not be harmed."

"I have to talk to the King!" Tiamat said. "It's important."

"The King is busy."

"But I have to warn him about the Demon!" she insisted.

The soldier smiled. "We hold the most important princes and nobles from all the cities of the Black Head lands hostage in here. Your Demon will not risk their lives, believe me."

Tiamat clenched her fists in frustration. "You don't know him! He doesn't care about hostages. He'll kill anyone who crosses him!"

"Quiet, girl. The King is going to speak."

In the lull during which the shocked hostages began to take in their situation, King Kyros addressed the assembly.

"People of Babylon!" he said in his correct, careful Akkadian. "Please do not be afraid. I wish none of you harm. Regrettably, it has been necessary to bring my men into your Palace at this time of feasting and celebration, but I'm sure you understand I needed to get your attention. My General already holds the outer city. Some of you might be wondering how I managed to get in here without bloodshed. This is how."

There was a collective intake of breath as the High Priest of Marduk stepped out of the tunnel behind the throne. He was robed in full ceremonial regalia, his beard curled and freshly oiled. Very solemn and stern, he crossed the dais to stand beside the Persian King and looked down his nose at the Prince's frightened guests.

"As you can see," the Persian King went on, "the High Priest of your chief god Marduk has kindly allowed me to use his temple's tunnel to access the Palace. I promise you that when your great city joins the Persian Empire, there will be free passage along this tunnel as there used to be before the King of Babylon and his Demon turned their backs on the temple and tried to rule without Marduk's blessing."

The guests muttered uncomfortably. Then someone called out, "Down with the Demon! Long live King Kyros!"

There were shouts and whistles of protest. A scuffle broke out among the guests and supporters. Tiamat tried to see who had spoken in favour of the Persian King and saw Master Andulli's man, Harrim, protected by a Persian soldier.

At the other side of the room, Igmil jumped on to a table and shouted, "Give the Persian a chance! He can't do much worse than old Nabonaid. At least he won't run off to the desert to eat grass while we labour to fill his son's bottomless belly!"

There were a few wry chuckles. The protests died out as other people added their views. "We used to trade with the Persians when King Nebuchadnezzar was on the throne. They weren't so bad back then." ... "Where is the Demon, anyway?" ... "Off with Nabonaid, I bet!" ... "Saving his skin." ... "Cowards, the both of them!"

The High Priest banged his staff on the dais and called, "I should like to remind the people of Babylon and our guests that King Nabonaid and his son, Prince Belshazzar—" He gave the terrified Prince a down-the-nose look. "—have both repeatedly refused to partake in the King's Ritual at the New Year Festival and hence are responsible for the repeated famines in our countryside, and for the disease and disorder in our cities. King Kyros has agreed to restore the appropriate Rituals, which will in turn bring peace and prosperity to our land."

More muttering as the hostages digested this. "What about us?" called a prince from one of the other cities. "Can we still worship our gods, too?"

Kyros nodded. "Every city that opens their gates to me and accepts my rule will be free to worship their own gods as before. The Festivals will be reinstated. All captives wrongly imprisoned under the rule of King Nabonaid and his Ensi will be freed. You and your families will not be harmed. Your houses will be left intact. There will be Persian gold available for new building projects. I'm anxious that your land and cities become strong again so that we can open trade with the lands Beyond the River and across the Upper and Lower Seas."

The hostages glanced at each other. Some of the Babylonian soldiers surrendered their weapons and sat on the steps to listen. There was another pause. Then suddenly, it seemed, everyone was calling out questions. Kyros and the High Priest between them answered every one, but some of the awilum still had doubts. Finally, one of the Babylonian soldiers called, "What about the Judeans? Can you solve *that* one?"

An expectant silence fell. It was a test, Tiamat realized. Once, when Simeon had done something to annoy her, she'd heard Lady Nanname say that no King of Babylon had ever been able to rule the Judeans.

King Kyros smiled. "Any Judeans who wish to accept my offer will be given gold to return to their own land and rebuild their holy city beside the Salt Sea."

The Throne Room erupted for the second time that night. "That's crazy!" ... "Unheard of!" ... "Can't just let them go home." Followed by some more thoughtful observations: "Why not?" ... "Suppose it'd make space for more citizens." ... "Won't be nearly so much trouble in the outer city." ... "Certainly make our job easier." The Babylonian soldiers nodded and a few more surrendered their weapons to the Persians.

But the Prince's guests still weren't convinced. "Nobody wants to live in a Judean slum!" one shouted. "Bad enough one of them's playing in the Twenty Squares final!" Which seemed to remind everyone why they had come.

"Yes!" someone else called out. "And what about the *game*?"

Again there was a hush, more intense than before.

Tiamat stood on tiptoe to see the board, where Simeon's head and Ikuppi's could just be glimpsed in the centre of the hostages. The boys were still sitting on their stools. The counters waited on the board in mid-play. Everyone looked expectantly at the Persian King.

Kyros's green eyes glittered as he smiled. "The game must go on, of course. I understand your finalists represent the Crown Team and the Egibi Team. Perfect! Let us raise the stakes. If Crown wins, then I'll release Prince Belshazzar and he'll be allowed to govern the city as before, though under my guidance rather than

King Nabonaid's. If Egibi wins, then I select my own governor for Babylon, and Prince Belshazzar joins his father and the Ensi in prison."

Beneath Kyros's sword, the Prince's flesh was trembling – though whether from rage or fear, Tiamat didn't know. Some of the Egibi supporters laughed nervously. The Prince's guests glanced at one another then shrugged and started making whispered wagers on the outcome. Simeon and Ikuppi glared challengingly at each other as the Chief Referee picked up the die. A hush fell.

The Babylonian soldiers looked over their shoulders anxiously. "There's fire in the outer Palace!" they reminded the Persians guarding the doors. "We have to evacuate everyone. We haven't time for games."

But Kyros held up his hand and commanded, "We've time for this one. Play on!"

Tiamat returned her attention to the soldier. "I've got to talk to the King!" she said again. "Please. He knows me. I was at your camp. I'm the one who opened the gateway at the top of the ziqqurats for you! It's very important."

The soldier frowned at her. "You're the girl from Borsippa? But your priest said you couldn't get through yourself. How did you get here so quickly?"

"It'll take too long to explain!" Tiamat curled her toes in frustration. "You have to let me talk to the King. Now!"

The soldier sighed and lowered his spear. "All right,

the game's started, so I suppose he's got a few double-minutes to spare. Come with me."

He escorted her across the dais, where the Persian King still held his sword at Prince Belshazzar's throat. The High Priest gave her a startled look that turned into a frown. The soldier cleared his throat and whispered something to the King in the Persian tongue.

"Don't distract me now," Kyros replied in Akkadian, his green eyes fixed on the Twenty Squares board. "This game is important."

"So is this, sir!" Tiamat said, remembering just in time to give the King a hand-to-nose greeting. "You see, the Demon killed—"

In that instant, as the Persian King's eyes flickered to her, Prince Belshazzar moved. Startlingly quick for such an overweight man, he jerked his head away from Kyros's sword, slipped off the throne to his knees and reached up under the blade, a little dagger in his hand.

"No!" Tiamat shouted, seeing again the Demon's sword piercing Master Andulli's belly.

A fist knocked her sideways and a Persian sword plunged into Prince Belshazzar's back. She was so close, she felt the Prince shudder and heard the blade grate against bone. Blood spurted across her cheek as the soldier who had brought her to the King jerked his sword free. The Prince's dagger spun across the dais.

Tiamat backed off and stared at the dead Prince,

her hands over her mouth. Kyros was breathing hard. The whole thing was over within a few heartbeats. Most of the people watching the game hadn't even noticed. But at the back of the crowd, heads began to turn.

Kyros recovered quickly and nodded to his men, who heaved the dead Prince back on his throne and propped him up. His body with its folds of fat slouched in much the same way as when he'd been alive. Those at the back of the crowd hesitated. They must have seen the blood, but at that moment a groan passed through the guests. The Egibi supporters cheered, and their attention snapped back to the board. Kyros grimaced as he set his sword against the Prince's unresisting throat. Tiamat heard him whisper to the High Priest, "We'll just have to hope the Egibi boy wins."

The High Priest looked down his nose at the board. "Where's the Gamesmaster? I thought we'd be stuck in that tunnel for ever."

"That's what I'm trying to tell you, sir!" Tiamat interrupted, glancing at the board where Simeon seemed to be playing one of his more complicated stratagems. Ikuppi's face was as dark as the weather god in a bad mood. For the moment, Simeon seemed to be winning – though everyone knew how quickly fortunes could change in Twenty Squares. "The Demon killed Master Andulli in Borsippa!" she rushed on. "He won't care how many people he has to kill to stop you. He'll sacrifice the hostages! And it's true there's a fire –

I started it. The whole Palace could burn down!"

Now that he no longer had to concentrate on his captive, the Persian King's green gaze settled on her. He regarded her steadily and a little warily. "I'm very sorry to hear about your Gamesmaster, Tiamat. Andulli was a brave man. But we have control of the city now thanks to him – and to your magic hand, of course. Don't worry about the fire. One of my men has been to investigate and I understand it's been contained in the outer courts. Your Palace is damaged, but far from destroyed." He put his head on one side. "I know you don't trust me, Tiamat, and I'm sorry for that. But if you stay close to me, I promise I won't allow the Ensi to hurt you or any of your friends again."

Tiamat shook her head. "I know now that you didn't kill the sirrush... but you don't understand! I left the gateway open at the top of the ziqqurats! The Demon could have used it to get back. I don't know where he's hiding, but he's in the inner city somewhere, I'm sure of it."

Kyros smiled. "Wherever he's hiding, we'll find him as soon as this game is over. You play Twenty Squares, don't you? It's all a mystery to me. Perhaps you can help explain to me who's winning?"

Despite her worry over the Demon, Tiamat looked back at the board. From the dais, they had a good view over the heads of the other spectators. She could see both players' faces in profile. Simeon's guards still stood behind him, watching over his shoulder. Ikuppi was doing something with his bandaged hand under the table. Her heart gave a sudden jolt.

"He's going to cheat," she whispered. "Simeon's winning, so the little snake's going to cheat again!"

Before anyone could stop her, she ran to the edge of the dais and jumped down. The Persian soldier started after her, but Kyros called him back. She heard him question the High Priest about the game and the High Priest's arrogant reply that no boy would dare cheat during the final. Tiamat gritted her teeth and started to fight her way towards the referee. But before she got two steps from the dais, a hand grabbed her wrist and a familiar voice said, "Crown has to win, you know that."

Tiamat whirled. Her mind was spinning with so many different worries, it took her a moment to recognize the boy who had stopped her. "Labinsin!" she gasped. "Let go of me!" She pulled back, but the boy's grip was tight. He'd dragged her into the shadows near the tunnel entrance before she managed to free herself. She scowled at him. "Ikuppi's not getting away with cheating this time! That hand of his must be better by now – mine healed ages ago. He's got something hidden under his bandage, hasn't he? What is it? A loaded die? Extra counters?"

Labinsin smiled. "What if he has? I'm surprised you're worried about a silly game when your dragon is in such dreadful danger. Your lucky hand looks as if it's got hurt again. I wonder how that happened?"

Tiamat was already heading back to the crowd around the board. But Labinsin's tone made her hesitate. "What do you know about my sirrush?" She grabbed his tunic and twisted it tightly under his neck.

The boy pulled something out of his pouch. He opened his hand and thrust it under her nose. His lip curled as Tiamat stared at what he held.

A large, curved claw, bloody at one end. The type of claw that might have come from a lion, or... She turned cold and looked down at her injured finger.

Labinsin chuckled. "Thought that would get your attention. The Demon sent me to tell you he's got your dragon all nicely wrapped up in a net so it can't fly away."

"You're lying," Tiamat said. She looked at the erect backs of the Persian King and the High Priest. But they were intent on the game and hadn't noticed what was happening behind the dais.

"You know I'm not." Labinsin pulled his tunic free and dusted himself down. "Don't you recognize its claw?"

"It's a lion's," she whispered.

Labinsin touched the raw end of her finger. "Didn't you feel it happen, *Blessed of Marduk*? Why don't you come and see the creature to make sure?" He jerked his head at the tunnel.

Tiamat stared at the opening where the blue bricks had sunk into the wall. She could see dark loops inside, hanging from the tunnel roof. A net? Did the Demon have her sirrush in there? She looked at the claw again, then back at the dais. The game was hotting up. Frenzied bets were taking place among the soldiers and guests, who seemed to have accepted the Persians in their midst. The Egibi supporters were arguing the finer points of strategy. The referee kept having to silence them.

"The Demon says if you tell anyone where you're going, he'll rip out the rest of its claws, one by one." Labinsin gave her the same kind of smile he'd given her in the alley when Ikuppi's gang had attacked her and Simeon on their way home from Twenty Squares Club. "Will that hurt, do you think?"

Tiamat closed her eyes. Her finger with its missing nail was throbbing. She looked at the bloody claw again. It was the sirrush's, no question. They shared the pain. "Where is it?" she whispered.

"On the ziqqurat, of course."

She shoved Labinsin back and darted into the tunnel, fear for the sirrush driving all else from her head. She should have warned one of the Persian soldiers. She should have found Hillalum or Muna or Enki. She should have told someone, even one of the black-skinned Palace guards. But by the time she was inside the tunnel and sense returned, it was too late.

The black loops hanging from the roof were roots, pushing through from the garden above. Beyond them lay thick, musty darkness. Out of this darkness, with the silent strike of a hunting snake, darted a hand that clamped across her mouth.

"We've unfinished business, Tiamat Nanname-daughter," hissed the Demon's voice. "This time I'm taking no chances. We only need your lucky hand, not the rest of you… All right, you can knock her out now."

As she struggled wildly, trying to kick what she couldn't see, something dark blocked the light at the end of the tunnel and landed on top of her head.

EGIBI TWENTY SQUARES TEAM

16th Tashritu (evening)

Gamesmaster

ANDULLI	(deceased)

Team

ENKI	Master Andulli's son (out)
SIMEON	Jacob's son
MUNA	astrologer's daughter (out)
TIAMAT	Nanname's adopted daughter (eliminated)
HILLALUM	farmer's son (out)

Reserve

KHATAR	Master Andulli's wardum (eliminated)

Chapter 18

ISHTAR'S GIFT

Thou treadest in the bright heavens; lofty is thy place!

SHE WAS LYING face down on hard stone with something heavy on her back... a sore head... pain in her left hand... trapped... angry...

–fightmustfight–

"Must fight," Tiamat breathed, opening her eyes.

A pair of sandals and the fringed hem of a robe blurred into view. One of the sandals was firmly planted on her hand, accounting for the pain. Dirty, wrinkled toes poked out of it. The robe was so filthy she couldn't tell the colour. Purple, maybe? Beyond the dirty feet, another pair of legs paced up and down. The floor was uneven, criss-crossed by grooves filled with gold, and the far side of the room was in shadow. It had round walls lit by torches in bronze holders, though there was also a greyish light coming from behind her.

Memory rushed back as she recognized the shrine at the top of the ziqqurat. She cautiously raised her head. The second pair of legs stopped pacing as the weight on her back shifted. A hand grabbed her hair and a dagger pricked her throat.

"At last!" hissed the Demon. He came to join the man standing on her hand. "Trust your magic hand not to work when you're unconscious."

Tiamat heaved upwards. "Where's my sirrush?"

The dagger pricked harder. The weight on her back hurt with her head pulled up at such an awkward angle. "Hold still," a boy's voice said in her ear. "Or I'll cut you. Remember what happened in the alley? I've a score to settle, Green-Eyes."

She stopped struggling in confusion. She knew that voice.

"Later, Ikuppi." The Demon sounded impatient. "First she's going to open the gate for us. Then you can have her as I promised."

"H – how did you get here?" Tiamat whispered, trying to think. She abandoned the attempt to free her hand, which the stranger's foot kept pressed to the "Babylon" rectangle at the centre of the map of the Seven Islands. She couldn't see if the gate to Borsippa was still open, because the Demon was in the way. "You were playing Twenty Squares! What happened?"

Ikuppi chuckled. "What happened? I won, of course! Egibi lost. Your little Judean friend's back in prison, the Persian King lost his bet, the High Priest of Marduk has been arrested for treason, and Babylon belongs to the Crown again. There's no hope for any of you now, Green-Eyes, so you'd better do what the Demon says. He's got your dragon outside in a net. If you don't cooperate, he'll rip out another of its claws."

"No!" Again, Tiamat tried to reach the Demon, but Ikuppi and the stranger between them held her firmly to the floor. The final spark of hope, that King Kyros and his men were on their way to arrest the Demon, died. She looked at her fingers splayed beneath the dirty sandal and shuddered as she imagined the remaining nails being torn off. Ikuppi pulled her head round, the Demon stepped aside, and the golden gateway to Borsippa shimmered into view.

"It's still open," she said through gritted teeth. "You don't need me."

The Demon knelt so he could look into her eyes. He picked a stray curl off her cheek and pushed it behind her ear. "We don't need a magic gate to go to Borsippa, Tiamat. The King and I have been there plenty of times already, and I'm sure you can remember what happened last time?" He paused to let this sink in. "I thought you were a clever girl. Remember the riddle on the seal? *A gate which like a copper drum has been covered with skin, Blessed of Marduk has opened it, Ishtar's Gift comes out of it*? Andulli and Kyros had half of it right. The ancient kings did indeed travel between ziqqurats using the Earthly Gateways. But the real reason they had their princesses blessed by Marduk's creature was so they could travel beyond the Earthly Ocean and receive Ishtar's Gift. I assumed the sirrush had to die. But, of course, the real answer is so much easier, isn't it? The creature sheds its skin and transforms into something more powerful, at the same time transforming the girl it has blessed... you, Tiamat. You have the power to open the gateways. *All* the gateways."

The foot on her hand pressed harder as the stranger in the filthy robe gave a high, warbling laugh. "Ishtar's Gift is eternal life!" he shrieked. "I'll find the Tree! I'll eat its leaves! I'll be the King who lives for a thousand years, and then we'll see who dares call me mad! Open the Gate of Heaven, Blessed of Marduk. Open it now!" The foot stamped on her hand – once, twice, three times – before the man who could only be King Nabonaid lost his balance and fell over.

Tiamat thought she was going to faint from the pain. She watched Nabonaid pick himself up. He was still laughing wildly. His face was a mass of sores and peeling skin. He had blisters round his lips, and froth came from his mouth, congealing in his beard. His eyes were bloodshot and stared in two different directions. The only sign of kingship in the man who had stamped on her hand was that he wore a shining, golden crown. The crown had been knocked askew when he fell. He didn't seem to notice.

She hugged her hand to her breast and closed her eyes. "You're mad. I can't open the Gate of Heaven!"

The Demon touched her cheek again, making her

shudder. "We think you can. You managed to open the Earthly Gates for your Persian friends, didn't you? That proves you have the power." He chuckled. "Who'd have thought the blood of our late king would turn up in an outer city orphan? One of the royal brats obviously escaped – just as well, since it appears the Ritual is more accurate than I suspected. Judging from those green eyes of yours, I assume you inherited your power through Amytis, which is rather ironic considering what's happened. But it doesn't matter who was responsible, just so long as you can open the gate."

This was too much to take in at once. From outside came the sound of a scuffle and shouts of alarm. "Watch its horn!" a man yelled. "Don't let it get its wings free!"

Tiamat opened her eyes. The light coming through the door had brightened, making the torches redundant.

"Quiet out there!" roared the Demon. His shadow blocked the light a moment before he returned to crouch by Tiamat. "Seems your pet is waking up. The sun always did make them wild – that's why we never let them out in the day until you came along. We might have to extract another claw to calm it down again, unless you tell it to behave."

"Don't hurt it!" she said, her heart twisting. "Please! I'll... I'll do what you want."

The Demon smiled. "I know you will." He reached for her hand and gently placed it back on the "Babylon" rectangle. His fingertip brushed her missing nail. "Pain is a great incentive, particularly when it can be inflicted simultaneously upon two creatures who care for each other."

Tiamat stiffened, but no one trod on her hand again. Nabonaid remained crouched in the shadows at the far side of the shrine, his eyes still staring off in different directions. She shivered.

The Demon continued, "I had to hurt you. I needed to remind you who's in charge of this city. But if you're a good girl and open the gate for your rightful King, I'll order my men to release the sirrush after our safe return. That should give you an incentive to keep the gateway open for us. Ikuppi here will make sure you don't get up to any mischief while we're gone."

The boy sitting on her back chuckled again and his dagger twitched at her throat. Tiamat swallowed. She couldn't help remembering that look in Ikuppi's eyes when he'd tried to cut off her hand in the alley. But if she did what they wanted, she might get a chance to free the sirrush and find out what had happened to her friends before the King and his Ensi came back.

"Which gate do you want me to open?" she whispered, trying to sound meek, not at all sure she could open anything in this state of mind.

The Demon stroked his smooth chin. "That's a good question. Ishtar's Gift doesn't grow anywhere within the Earthly Ocean these days, so obviously it needs to be one of the gates to the Seven Islands that lie between the Earthly and Heavenly Oceans." He pointed outside the double ring and moved his finger round the circle until it reached the sirrush-carving. "I think we'll start with that one and work our way round."

Tiamat stared at the carving with a shiver of memory. "But the High Priest said that one's dangerous."

"I don't care what the High Priest said!" The Demon stood up sharply and glared down at her. "The priests like to keep their secrets to themselves. Of course they're going to say it's dangerous! But someone had to go through that gate to bring back the sirrush eggs, so it's obviously been done before. Open it!"

"I'll have to shut the other one first." She didn't know if this was true, but maybe King Kyros had escaped and retreated to Borsippa. Maybe some of her friends were still free. She wasn't going to leave the Demon a way of attacking them from behind. "I can't reach it with this lump sitting on my back," she added.

The Demon looked suspiciously at her, but nodded to Ikuppi. "Let her up."

The boy's weight lifted, though his dagger remained at her throat. Slowly, so as not to make him nervous, Tiamat reached into the golden light and shut the tiny ghostly gate on their side of the "courtyard". As it closed, the golden light faded and King Nabonaid giggled.

Tiamat looked at the sirrush-carving. She swallowed again.

"Do it!" Ikuppi hissed in her ear, giving her another prick with his dagger. "And no tricks this time, Green-Eyes!"

Tiamat pressed her left hand to "Babylon" and concentrated on the carving. As had happened last time, golden lightning licked across the floor towards the double ring that represented the Earthly Ocean. This time, there was no High Priest to break the connection. She caught her breath as the light crossed the ring and crackled like flames. The stone beneath her hand grew hot. The Demon stepped forward eagerly. Nabonaid's giggle grew louder. Drooling, he crawled towards the lines of golden fire.

"Not yet, Sire!" Tiamat called, terrified in case the King should get hurt and the Demon should blame her and decide to kill the sirrush, after all.

Nabonaid didn't seem to hear. His crawl speeded up. Quickly, she put her eye to the floor and looked along the line of fire. There was a ghostly gate as before, though this one looked more like the gate that led to the princess's garden than a city gate. Trembling a little, she pushed it open. What if there was another security measure, like the double gates to Borsippa?

–wayhomeOPEN!–

The sirrush's voice burst joyfully in her head. Light from the gateway blazed so brightly, she had to fling an arm across her face. Perfume filled the shrine as ghostly flowers and trees unfurled and sprouted from the bricks all around them. Vines curled through the roof, lilies thrust up through the lines of the map and tickled Tiamat's nose. It all happened so quickly, she had no time to wonder where they'd come from.

Ikuppi's dagger rattled to the floor as he backed against the nearest wall, eyes wide with terror. The Demon sucked in his breath and took a step backwards, too. Only the mad King Nabonaid kept crawling, his face lit by those unearthly colours, his crown gleaming in the light from beyond the Earthly Ocean. He reached the gate, pulled himself to his feet, smiled like a small child – and vanished. There was another waft of perfume and, more chillingly, a faint scream.

"So... the legends are true!" The Demon shook his head and stared at Tiamat with something like awe.

Another scream from beyond the gateway broke his trance. He snatched up Ikuppi's dagger, handed it back to the boy, and rushed to the gate. Just before he stepped through, he pointed at Tiamat. "You behave yourself, Princess! I'll be back." He drew his sword and vanished into the light after the King.

Ikuppi held the dagger loosely by his side, his eyes still wide as they took in the ghostly trees and strange-coloured flowers. Very quietly, Tiamat lifted her hand from the floor and edged towards the door. The colours, trees and gateway drifted past her out of the shrine, although now she'd broken the connection they were starting to fade.

Ikuppi jerked alert, leapt across the shrine and blocked her escape. His dagger poked her cheek. "Keep the gate open!" he yelled. "Keep your hand on the floor or I'll cut you, I swear!"

"It is still open, you idiot," Tiamat said. The perfume

from the otherworldly garden filled her head, reminding her of home and bringing a strange calm. "I don't think it's like the gate to Borsippa. I can't stop it moving. I'm only going to see if my sirrush is all right. How far am I going to get with the Demon's men all over the city?"

Ikuppi glanced uncertainly at the door. "You stay right there!" he yelled, giving her a jab with his dagger. "And bring that gate back in here! Now!"

Tiamat winced. "Please, Ikuppi! I told you I can't. Why are you doing this? The Demon won't know. He can't see us. If you've already won—"

Ikuppi poked harder. "Shut up."

She took a deep breath and tried another angle. "Why aren't you at your Garland Party? Surely you'd rather be showing off your Twenty Squares Garland than be sitting up here on your own, waiting for the King and the Demon to come back? They'll be ages if they're looking for a special plant, believe me! Some of the ones Nanname sends me to look for in the princess's garden take all day to find, and the Amytis Garden is nowhere near as big as this one." She gazed after the fading trees and flowers, dizzy with the strangeness. "Look through the gate out there! It goes on for ever."

"I said shut *up*!" Ikuppi's blade nicked her cheek. She felt blood trickle from the wound. "You're not a princess! You're just a stupid outer city orphan with a magic hand. After today, you'll be a stupid outer city orphan without a magic hand. Then I'll make you wish the dogs had eaten you when you were a baby." His giggle sounded a bit like the mad King's. "The Demon's going to smash your adoption tablet so you lose your citizenship and have to become a wardum. Then he's going to give you to me. Father says I'm almost old enough to need a slave. We'll have to train you properly, of course, and brand you so you can't run away." He giggled again and waved his dagger in front of her eyes.

Tiamat couldn't help but laugh. Ikuppi was just as scared as she was.

She jabbed her elbow backwards as hard as she could, catching him in the groin. He doubled over with a cry and dropped his dagger for the second time. Tiamat snatched it up and darted through the vanishing trees and ghostly vines, out of the door.

"Come back here!" Ikuppi yelled. "You'll be sorry if you don't!"

The sun seemed dim after the light of the otherworldly garden. Down in the streets and gardens of the inner city, people were standing with shaded eyes, staring up at the ziqqurat in amazement. In the temple courtyard itself, a fight was in progress as soldiers clashed blades on the triple staircase of the ziqqurat's first tier. She shook them from her thoughts.

On the edge of the highest tier, amidst the fading colours of the garden, crouched her sirrush. Its scales glinted red and gold in the early sun. Its wings and claws were tangled in three large nets thrown one on top of the other. The Demon's men were struggling to hold the ropes taut between them. They stared in terror at the trees and flowers floating in the air above the ziqqurat. Ghostly shapes flitted through the trees, following invisible paths across the sky. Far above the river shimmered the gateway that had left the shrine, massive and golden like a second sun. As Tiamat ran out, the sirrush's head swung round to follow the gate and it slashed at the nearest man with its horn.

–mustescape–

Tiamat ducked past the Demon's men, who dared not let go of their ropes to chase her. She sawed at the thick cords of the net with Ikuppi's dagger. The nets had been made to catch lions for the hunt and were not easily cut. Tears flowed down her cheeks as she worked. She could see the sirrush's bloody front paw, where the Demon had ripped out the claw. Its musky odour mingled with the perfume from the garden, making her dizzy. She gasped as a cord parted and the sirrush's horn jerked free.

"Stop that!" the Demon's men shouted. "Are you crazy? It'll kill us all!"

Tiamat cut another cord. The colours and the gate in the sky were fading fast now, returning to the shrine like water being sucked down a hole into a sewer. One huge wing flapped, struggled against the remaining cords, then unfurled in a flash of gold. The men on that side let go of their ropes and fled down the steps to the next tier.

"Come back, you cowards!" shouted the men they'd abandoned. "We can't hold it on our own!"

As the ropes slackened, the sirrush got another wing free, then a taloned hind foot. Its tail lashed, sweeping

four of the Demon's men over the edge into the space where the ghostly garden had been. They fell seven tiers, screaming. The gate had gone, sucked into the shrine with the trees and flowers. Tiamat stopped cutting and started to pull. The rest of the cords slipped from the sirrush's back. She pushed the net over the edge with a grunt as the freed creature half leapt, half flew towards the shrine, chasing the gateway.

Ikuppi had finally found the courage to come after Tiamat. He met the sirrush head-on as he emerged from the door. His face drained of blood. He turned and fled inside again. The shrine was too small to admit a winged sirrush. It put its head through the opening and lashed its tail, but the trees and colours had gone. The sirrush gave an anguished hiss.

–homeflyhome–

With a burst of understanding, Tiamat knew what the creature had been trying to tell her since they'd been reunited in Borsippa. She rushed to the door, gripped one of the sirrush's curly side horns and pulled its head aside so she could squeeze past. "I have to make the garden grow again so you can fly through the gate," she told it. "Get ready."

The creature sprang to the edge of the golden tier and swung its horn at the men who had retreated down the steps. Its tongue flickered. It seemed content to wait for her to reopen the gate. But suddenly it spread its wings, plunging the entire top tier of the ziqqurat into shadow, and hissed angrily at the shrine.

Tiamat whirled. Her heart missed a beat. The Demon leant against the doorway, panting. His eyes were wild and staring, his hair dishevelled, his robes torn. He'd lost a sandal and there was a great rip in his breeches. His sword dangled loosely from his hand. Glowing golden sap dripped from the blade. Behind him in the shadows, Ikuppi was pressed in terror against the far wall. There was no sign of Nabonaid.

"The King's dead," the Demon whispered. "I failed. I couldn't save him... Never thought, never guessed... so bright... so very bright..."

He staggered blindly out into the sunlight, took three wobbly steps towards the edge, then seemed to sense something and turned his head. The sirrush hissed again.

–humankilleggmates–

It sprang, a blur of red and gold. The Demon thrust blindly with his sword, but the sirrush knocked it from his hand with a casual swipe of one forepaw. Its lion-claws held the Demon down on the golden bricks while its taloned hind feet tore at his stomach. Tiamat turned her head away. The Demon's screams didn't sound human. There was a horrible crunching, followed by a disgusted cough.

–humantastebad–

Feeling sick, Tiamat ducked into the shrine, where Ikuppi was still pressed against the wall. "If you've got any sense, you'll stay there," she told him as she put her hand back on the floor.

The perfume, colours, trees and ghostly flowers

returned. They flowed out of the door and into the sky. The golden gate went with them.

"Fly home, sirrush!" she shouted. "Fly home!"

Wings beat against the sun. There was a gasp from the streets below the ziqqurat and, at the same time, an explosion of pure joy in her head.

–HOME–

The stone beneath her hand turned abruptly cold. The light, the sirrush, the colours, the ghostly garden, the Heavenly Gateway, and the half-glimpsed creatures who lived beyond it, all vanished. Only the perfume remained, lingering in the air like the memory of a dream. Tiamat lifted her hand and looked at it. Her little finger had stopped bleeding.

A scrape near the wall reminded her she wasn't alone. "Is it safe now?" Ikuppi whispered. "Has it gone?"

She only just stopped herself from laughing. "It's gone," she said in a flat voice. "Go to your Garland Party, Ikuppi. Get out of here. I never want to see you again."

Chapter 19

GARLAND

May the raising of my hand, the invocation of the great gods, give release!

FEET POUNDED UP the steps outside and men shouted, bringing Tiamat back to reality. She put her arms around herself and shivered, suddenly very weary. Let the Demon's men come for her. She'd done what she had set out to do. The sirrush was free.

A robed and bearded silhouette blocked the light at the door. "Anyone in there?" called a voice Tiamat recognized as the High Priest's. He sounded strangely nervous.

Resigned to her fate, Tiamat got to her feet and walked out into the sun. Soldiers and priests swarmed over the ziqqurat like ants over a dust mound, arguing fiercely about what they'd seen. One of the soldiers had picked up the Demon's sword and was peering at the still-glowing sap on the blade.

The High Priest snatched the sword from him, wrapped it quickly in his sash, and pushed past Tiamat to peer round the shrine. He came back out, looking more relaxed. "Has the sirrush gone?" he asked.

She nodded. She couldn't think why the High Priest wasn't in prison with the others – didn't Ikuppi say he'd been arrested? But maybe he'd been on the Demon's side all along. Maybe that was why he had abandoned her and Master Andulli at Borsippa. The unfairness of it broke through her inertia and she glared at him.

The High Priest didn't notice. He was too occupied with the sword, dipping his little finger into the sap and sniffing it. "I don't suppose the Ensi brought anything else back with him?" he said. "An egg, for example?"

Tiamat clenched her fists. "No, he didn't."

Another sigh. "A pity. That was our last sirrush. With no new egg, there can never be another Blessing, and the Gateways will be shut to us for ever."

"Good! Then maybe you won't be able to kill anyone else by leaving them on the other side! We should never have trusted you."

The High Priest gave her a startled look. "Now then, er – Tiamat, isn't it? Don't go blaming me for that. I wasn't even in the shrine when Andulli went back, otherwise I would have stopped him. His death was regrettable, but other things were more important at the time."

"You left *me* there!"

The High Priest coughed. "The legends aren't always

accurate. I thought you would probably be able to get through the Earthly Gateway all right. But it all worked out in the end, didn't it? Better than I expected, actually. A shame about losing the sirrush, but Nabonaid broke the cycle a long time ago, so I'm not surprised he was unable to secure an egg. Maybe it's for the best. We're entering a new era. A new king, new ways. I'll have to modify the rituals, but that's not a problem." He resumed his abrupt manner. "Hurry now, girl. It seems just about everyone in Babylon is looking for you. King Kyros says he won't accept the crown until he knows you're safe."

"King K – Kyros?" Tiamat stammered, thrown off her stride. "But I thought he... I thought we lost."

The High Priest frowned down his nose at her. "Whatever gave you that idea?"

"Ikuppi said—" She broke off, the dullness that had come with the closing of the gateway replaced by a fierce spark as she realized the soldiers on the ziqqurat were in Persian uniform. "Then... Egibi won?"

The High Priest chuckled, his haughty manner melting briefly. "That little Judean of Andulli's played better than anyone I've ever seen. Thrashed the Crown boy fair and square. It's almost a pity Belshazzar wasn't alive to see it."

Tiamat could feel her mouth stretching into a silly smile.

"We won," she whispered. "Simeon won the Garland!"

After that, everything happened in a blur. Somehow, she managed to descend the three thousand steps of the ziqqurat without falling over her own feet. Somebody brought her a drink, which she gulped down without tasting it. Afterwards, she realized it must have contained herbs to revive her, because the colours of the city took on a bright edge, the sun shimmered in a golden haze, and her head floated like feathers on the wind. As they left the temple complex and the High Priest thrust a way through the excited crowds, people threw flowers and cheered.

"Blessed is Marduk!" they cried. "Lord of the Rising Sun, Vanquisher of Night, Conqueror of Demons!"

Feeling dirty and scruffy amidst the priests clad in their finest robes and head-dresses, Tiamat found herself caught up in a procession along the Ajiburshapu Way. The golden lions with their white and red manes marched beside them along the blue walls, the sun beat down, and her head swam with the heat and the glare and the noise. She tried to escape into the crowd, but the priests hustled her along.

"Oh, no you don't!" they said, laughing at her protests. "King Kyros would never forgive us."

They met the Persian King and General Gobryas at the main gates of the Palace. The King rode in a chariot drawn by four black stallions decked in white and gold. He'd changed his fighting uniform for magnificent robes of purple with tiny stars picked out in beads that glittered in the sun. His beard had been oiled and perfumed until it gleamed and smelled like Nanname's laboratory, but he still wore his plain iron sword. Under the command of their General, the Persian soldiers formed a disciplined, sober escort around their King – in marked contrast to the princes and nobles Prince Belshazzar had invited to the Championships, who hiccuped and giggled as they took their places in the procession. They'd obviously made the Persian alliance into yet another excuse for a celebration. More chariots waited in the street, the horses scraping the pavement with impatient hooves. Behind them, supporters still dressed in the colours of their Twenty Squares Teams clustered under fringed parasols, pointing to the blackened walls of the outer court and exchanging greatly exaggerated stories of the danger they'd been in when the Persians had taken them hostage. The streets shimmered with clouds of incense, oiled black curls, kohl-heavy lashes, snatches of laughter, outbursts of cheering, and of course – everywhere Tiamat turned – people talking about the garden in the sky.

"It just *hung* there," exclaimed one lady. "Babylonian magic must be amazingly strong!"

"It wasn't magic, silly! They've obviously got some kind of hidden terrace, like that tunnel the Persians used to get into the Palace."

"I thought I saw trees growing on the ziqqurat."

"Trees don't grow on brick! Anyway, they're not there now."

"I saw them, too!"

"Never mind the trees. Did you see that dragon...?"

Tiamat curled her hand in memory. "Sirrush," she whispered. The priests had been brought to a halt by the chariots and people blocking the street. General Gobryas took Tiamat's arm and guided her through. He looked down at her in gruff respect and said, "The King wants to thank you personally for your part in our victory. Behave yourself." She found herself at the footplate of the King's chariot, looking up into those green eyes. He smiled at her and reached down a hand.

Feeling very self-conscious, Tiamat allowed herself to be helped into the Persian King's chariot. The platform shifted under her feet as the stallions stamped and swished their tails. More petals landed in her hair, thrown from the top of the walls, which half the population of the outer city seemed to have climbed to watch the procession. Kyros brushed them off with a gentle hand.

"I'm sorry, Tiamat," he said gravely. "I should have heeded your warning about the Demon. But he's gone now. He won't hurt you again."

"The sirrush ate him."

"Then I hope it doesn't get belly ache."

Tiamat stared at the King. He'd made a joke. She ought to laugh. Instead, she burst into tears. "I'm sorry, it's just... oh, let me down, please... I've got to find my friends..."

The King's arm went around her. His driver, struggling to hold the stallions still, gave his master a startled look then smiled to himself.

"I'll drop you off on the way," Kyros said. "They went to look for you in the garden." At her uncertain look, he gave her a squeeze and said softly in her ear, "Don't worry, not the garden we saw hanging in the sky – the earthly one your King Nebuchadnezzar built for his Persian princess, which I understand is just as wonderful. I must visit it before I leave, but I've a few things to take care of first. Your priests insist I have to visit your Akitu temple and receive Marduk's blessing. Of course, we all know it's not a true ritual any more, but I've got to go through with it for the people's sake." He looked at the cheering crowds and grimaced. "You don't know how lucky you are to escape the usual responsibilities of those with our colour eyes. Sometimes I hate being a King."

Tiamat looked sharply at him, remembering what the Demon had said in the shrine. "Did..." she swallowed. "Did Princess Amytis have green eyes, too?"

She held her breath, afraid he wouldn't know.

The Persian King smiled. "Of course she did. Very beautiful ones, by all accounts. It's been a trait in our family since the first kings came out of the hills. Now hold on tightly! I think we're finally off and my horses are as impatient to get home as you are."

It was as well he warned her. When his driver gathered up the reins, the stallions leapt forward with such eagerness that the platform jerked into the air and people scattered from their path. The driver got his horses under control again and they pranced along the Ajiburshapu Way, leading the procession towards the Ishtar Gate. Their hooves echoed in the passage, the shadow of the walls passed over them, then they were out of the inner city heading towards the river and the little temple on its bank where no King of Babylon had set foot since Nebuchadnezzar's day.

At the gate leading to the Amytis Garden, the chariot paused briefly to let Tiamat climb down. Kyros waited until she was safely down the steps at the edge of the Way before he gave the order to drive on. She watched his billowing, gold-starred robes until they were lost to sight, then thankfully slipped through the gate into the leafy shadows beyond.

Tiamat hurried up the terraces, her feet finding the way by habit. Nothing here had changed. Overgrown vines dripped into her hair, sun-warmed scents drifted from all sides, and the noise of the procession receded until it seemed part of a different world. Her shoulders relaxed for the first time since the Demon had taken her to his House of Silent Screams. When a boy broke through the bushes nearby, she turned with a smile, her only thought being whether it was Simeon, or one of the others, who had found her first.

It was Ikuppi.

He smiled back nastily. "Think you're so special, don't you, Green-Eyes? Riding in the Persian King's chariot like a little princess!"

Tiamat stiffened. The boy's eyes were wild. He'd lost his cloak, his tunic was torn, and he was barefoot. Scratches on his cheeks and arms showed where he'd fought his way through the thicket. He whistled and Labinsin pushed out of the bushes on the other side of the path, glancing nervously at the sky.

"The beast's gone, I told you!" Ikuppi snapped. "Get a hold of her."

Labinsin approached Tiamat warily. Ikuppi sighed and grabbed hold of her himself, twisting her arm behind her back. "I don't need a dagger to master you, Green-Eyes," he hissed. "Outer city scum!"

Tiamat kicked him hard on the shin. His grip loosened and she twisted free. "Leave me alone, Ikuppi!" she said. "I'm not scared of you any more."

Ikuppi rubbed his leg and glared at her. "You'll be sorry you did that. Your dragon's gone. It can't help you now."

Labinsin glanced at the sky again. "Maybe she can call it back?" he whispered.

"Don't be so silly! It's obvious she's bluffing."

Tiamat smiled at them. "Remember what my sirrush did to the Demon? It's got a taste for human meat. It can smell you."

Labinsin turned pale. "Let's go, Ikuppi – it ate the Demon, remember?"

"She won't let it eat us. She wouldn't dare."

Tiamat raised her left hand and spread the fingers.

"Try me," she said, meeting Ikuppi's gaze. "Princess Amytis had green eyes, too, you know. The King told me. Apparently, it's a Persian royal trait. And this was her garden. The power's strong here, I can feel it in my blood."

"That's nonsense!" Ikuppi stood his ground. But Labinsin was already backing away. When the bushes on the terrace above started to rustle, he gave a yell of terror and fled.

"Come back here, you coward!" Ikuppi shouted after him.

Tiamat smiled again, though she dared not take her eyes off the inner city boy to see what had caused the rustle. "Just you and me, Ikuppi," she whispered.

The boy glanced uncertainly at the terrace overhead. His face twisted as he backed down the steps. "Keep that creature away from me," he mumbled.

"I'll keep it away from you, if you stay away from me and my friends."

Another rustle, nearer this time.

"Don't worry!" Ikuppi shouted, suddenly losing his courage and racing down the steps after Labinsin. "I don't want anything more to do with you or your stupid dragon!"

When he was safely out of sight, Tiamat frowned up at the thicket. "Who's there?" she whispered.

The leaves moved and Simeon pushed his way out. He used a vine to swing down the terrace and landed lightly in front of her, grinning. "How did I do?"

She stared at him, all kinds of emotions chasing themselves around inside her. "You didn't sound anything like a sirrush."

His grin widened. "Fooled Ikuppi, though, didn't it? Thought it might hold him off until you had a chance to call the real thing. Shame he ran away so quick." He gave her a funny look. "Was that true? What you told him about being related to Princess Amytis?"

Tiamat pressed her lips together, holding her emotions on a tight rein. "Never mind that now. You won the Twenty Squares Championship, Simeon! I wish I'd been there. It must have been brilliant."

He gave a wry smile. "It was scary. Ikuppi cheated, but I just thought of all the people who would get hurt if I lost, and I got so angry I played the Eye Symbol at the end of the game, and fortunately I guessed right. Luck must have been on my side for once. I tried to find you as soon as the soldiers let me go, but no one knew where you'd gone. There was so much excitement, everyone wanting to congratulate me, and the Persian King had won the city. It was impossible to get away."

"Simeon!" Tiamat discovered she was laughing and crying at the same time. "You told me never to play the Eye at the end of the game!"

"That was before you got your lucky hand and showed us all what was possible."

"But you were never licked by a sirrush— " She stared at him in sudden fear. "Were you?"

Simeon was shaking his head. "No, no, don't worry!

I doubt Marduk would bless me, anyway – I'm a Judean, remember? We've got enough to worry about, with King Kyros telling everyone we can go back home. Grandfather wants to, of course, but Mother and Father aren't sure. Father's got a good job with the Egibi Family, and now Master Andulli's dead he'll be even more important to them—" He broke off and bit his lip. "I'm sorry, Tia. I didn't mean to remind you. It must have been horrible for you, being there."

She closed her eyes. The image of Master Andulli falling down the ziqqurat was as strong as before, but it no longer had the power to reduce her to tears. "He's gone," she said. "But he did what he wanted, and I think King Kyros will be better than old Nabonaid and the Demon."

"Yes!" Simeon brightened. "And I think I want to stay. Babylon's my home. Anyway, I'll have to stay to defend my Garland next year. Lady Nanname says that if my parents want to go back with Grandfather to see him settled in, I'll be able to stay with you until they come back, help you with the perfumes." He looked at her uncertainly. "That is, unless you have to go and live in the Palace now?"

"Whyever would I want to do that?" Tiamat said, her heart leaping as she remembered Lady Nanname flying away on the sirrush's back. "Do you know if Nanname and Khatar got home safely? Are they all right?"

Simeon smiled. "Come and see for yourself."

He led her up the remaining terraces to the fountain

where Tiamat had found the seal – so long ago, it seemed. "She wanted to come here, to see your secret place. Took ages to get her up all the steps, but Enki and Hillalum and Muna helped."

Tiamat wasn't certain whether he meant it had taken Khatar or Nanname ages to get up the steps. But they were both in the grotto. Khatar lay on the bench, her head propped on Enki's folded cloak. Nanname sat beside her, sponging the girl's forehead with a hairband soaked in what smelled like all the best perfumes she'd ever made. Around the grotto were various herbs and heaps of flower petals, and in the cracked bowl of the fountain itself was a sticky green paste. When Simeon dragged Tiamat through the vines, Khatar's eyes opened and she gave them a weak smile.

"I thought you'd never get here, Persian-Eyes! Been havin' too much fun flying on that dragon of yours, I suppose."

"Something like that." Tiamat glanced at Nanname. "Is she going to be all right?"

Nanname smiled. "The others found the herbs I needed and Simeon kindly donated his Garland. It mightn't be made from the Tree of Life these days, but it turned out the leaves have healing properties, after all." She indicated the fountain.

Tiamat stared in horror at the green paste. "That's your Twenty Squares Garland? Oh, Simeon!"

He shrugged. "It's more use to Khatar than it is to me. I don't need some silly Garland shrivelling up in a corner of my room to remind me I've won. Anyway, it was hardly a fair Championships this year."

"What do you mean, not fair? You beat Ikuppi."

"Yes, but I didn't beat the best player—"

They were interrupted by a shriek outside on the terrace. Muna burst through the vines, hair flying, and hugged Tiamat so tightly she thought her bones would break. "Tia! What happened to you? We looked everywhere! And then that snake Ikuppi and his friend disappeared, and we feared the worst. I bet they're up to something with the Demon."

"I don't think we'll have any more trouble from Ikuppi's gang," Tiamat said, exchanging a glance with Simeon. "Anyway, the Demon's dead."

"The Demon's dead?" Enki pushed past Hillalum, who was standing under the vines with a big grin on his face, and frowned at her. "Are you sure?"

"Quite sure," Tiamat said. "I watched the sirrush eat him."

The others winced. But Enki nodded. "Good," he said in a tight voice and she knew he was thinking of his father.

"That's great news!" Hillalum slid a shy arm around Muna and smiled at her. "Isn't it, Nanname?"

"Good news, yes." Nanname's gaze met Tiamat's.

Tiamat smiled. There would be questions later, she knew. But for now, it was enough to be surrounded by her friends, with the Persian King being crowned by the priests below and the Demon gone for ever.

"So," Simeon said, breaking the leaf-dripping pause. "How about a game of Twenty Squares?"

The others laughed and pushed him playfully. "So you can beat us all, you mean? No thank you! Just because you've mashed up your Garland doesn't mean we've forgotten how you thrashed Ikuppi in the Palace!"

Simeon's dark eyes rested on Tiamat. "I've still one person to play. She was eliminated unfairly."

The others went quiet. Enki curled a finger in his hair, a gesture so like his father's it sent a shiver through Tiamat. Muna and Hillalum glanced at each other. Nanname sighed and shook her head. Khatar winked. "Go for it, Persian-Eyes! Give him your lucky hand treatment, see what kind of a champ he really is!"

Tiamat bit her lip. They'd realize eventually what she'd known as soon as the Gate of Heaven closed. "No point," she told them. "The sirrush has gone home. I've lost all my luck."

Silence.

"But you told Ikuppi it would come back and eat him!" Simeon protested. "You said you were descended from Princess Amytis and you had the power to bring it back."

Tiamat laughed. "I was bluffing, silly! Ikuppi was the one who thought it would come, more fool him. The High Priest said the gateways at the top of the ziqqurats are shut for good now. The King was supposed to bring back an egg to continue the cycle, but he didn't. So now there'll be no more sirrush in Babylon, ever. Besides, I never said I was descended from Amytis, only that the princess happened to have the same colour eyes as me... that could mean anything, couldn't it, Nanname?"

Nanname considered her for a long moment, then smiled and said, "Even if we could prove you had royal blood, which we can't, no one's going to want you to live in the Palace. We're part of Kyros's Empire now, remember? As far as the rest of the world is concerned, we're all Persians. Maybe that's why the sirrush have gone."

Another silence. Simeon touched her hand, his dark eyes grave. "Tia, I'm so sorry..."

Tiamat shrugged him off. "I'm not!" she said and found to her surprise that she meant it. "I don't want to be a princess. And I'm glad my sirrush has gone home! Look at all the trouble it brought. It never belonged here, not really. And you didn't honestly think I'd want to live in the Palace, did you? All my friends are in the outer city. It's my home. Now we're both free."

Nanname hugged her. "I don't think you've lost anything," she said. "I think you'll all be surprised how much you've gained."

The others were still eyeing Tiamat, unsure – except Enki, who stared through the vines, obviously thinking of his father again.

Tiamat grinned at them. "I've told you my side of the story. What I want to know is what Enki wrote on the wall."

"Yes, Enki!" Muna said. "What *did* you write? I never got close enough to see."

The boy laughed, embarrassed. "You really want to know?"

"Yes!"

"What do you think I wrote?" He smiled mischievously and raised both arms to the sky.

"EGIBI FOR EVER!"

The Twenty Squares Board

GUIDE TO TIAMAT'S WORLD

Tiamat and her friends lived in Babylon during the reign of King Nabonaid, who ruled from approximately 555BC to 539BC. For much of that time, the city was left in the care of his son, Prince Belshazzar, while Nabonaid travelled the empire on a personal quest. In this story, the King's quest is for the Tree of Life that the Babylonians believed brought eternal life. Some of the people and places in this book appear in the Bible.

The prayers in the chapter headings are taken from a collection of magical Babylonian tablets called the "Prayers of the Lifting of the Hand", based on translations by Leonard W King.

Ajiburshapu Way	The main street of Babylon, with walls of blue-glazed brick decorated by friezes of lions and flowers in white, gold and red. Sometimes called the Processional Way, because it is used for the New Year procession of the Babylonian gods.
Akitu temple	Temple outside the city where a secret Ritual takes place during the New Year Festival.
Akkadian	Language commonly spoken in Babylon in Tiamat's time.
Amytis	Persian princess who married King Nebuchadnezzar. Because she missed the mountains of her homeland, he built her a terraced garden on the banks of the river and filled it with exotic plants.
asipu	A healer who uses magic.
astrologer	Someone skilled in star lore and astronomy.
Black Head	Someone of the Babylonian race, so called because they have black hair.

cylinder-seal A small, carved cylinder designed to be rolled across clay as someone's "signature". Cylinder-seals are made out of all sorts of materials – e.g. wood, clay, gemstones. They are often worn as jewellery. Most are carved with both pictures and text.

double-hour The Babylonian day is divided into twelve equal parts, each called a double-hour and consisting of sixty double-minutes. This accounts for the fact that Babylonian hours and minutes vary in length with the varying lengths of night and day as the seasons change – but one "light-hour" and one "dark-hour" always add up to a constant "double-hour".

Ensi The King's prime minister. He helps rule the city and has a lot of power.

evil-days The 7th, 14th, 19th, 21st, and 28th days of every month are considered evil.

Gilgamesh Legendary king of Uruk, who lived about 2000 years before Tiamat was born. He went on a famous quest for the Tree of Life.

Hanging Gardens	One of the Seven Wonders of the Ancient World. There is no evidence that the Hanging Gardens ever existed in Babylon, and scholars are still arguing about where they might have been situated!
House of Headraising	Marduk's public temple where the common people go to worship him.
House of Heaven on Earth	Marduk's temple complex, including the ziqqurat, where only his priests are permitted to go. The priests run a Temple School for the sons of important citizens on the outskirts of the complex.
Ishtar	Goddess of love and war. The most important goddess of Babylon in Tiamat's time. Her symbol is a star/flower. Her sacred creature is a lion.
Ishtar Gate	The most famous gate of Babylon, with blue-glazed bricks decorated by mouldings of bulls and sirrush.
Judeans	The people of Judea, brought to Babylon as a captive work force when King Nebuchadnezzar destroyed Jerusalem.

Khammurabi's Laws A collection of 282 laws dealing with everyday matters, inscribed on a black stone erected in the House of Headraising. Later adopted by the Persians.

King Nebuchadnezzar A famous king of Babylon who restored much of the city and built its great outer wall to enclose the outer city. He destroyed Jerusalem and brought Simeon's ancestors to Babylon.

kohl Black eye paint, worn by both men and women.

lapis lazuli A semi-precious, dark-blue stone.

Lower Sea Persian Gulf

Map of the Seven Islands Sometimes called the Babylonian "map of the world" or Mappa Mundi, this map portrays the cities of the Babylonian Empire within a central ring surrounded by the Earthly Ocean.

	Between the Earthly Ocean and the Heavenly Ocean are the Seven Islands where sirrush, demons, ghosts, etc. live. Outside the Heavenly Ocean are the stars and the signs of the zodiac. Beyond this is a place where the sun does not shine. Tiamat uses this map to open the Earthly Gateway to Borsippa, and the Heavenly Gateway to the place where the sirrush lives and the Tree of Life grows.
Marduk	The most important god of Babylon. The sirrush is his sacred creature.
onager	A locally-bred ass with striped withers, used as a beast of burden.
Persians	People from the region we now call Iran, led by King Kyros (whom the Greeks called Cyrus the Great).
River Idiklat	Tigris river.
River Purattu	Euphrates river.

shaduf A weighted lever and bucket used for raising water from one waterway to a higher level. Shadufs are still used in Iraq today.

Shamash Sun god.

Sin Moon god.

sirrush Creature sacred to Marduk, sometimes called a dragon. It is half snake, half lion, with red-gold scales, three horns (two curly, one straight), a forked tongue, lion's forepaws, eagle's talons on its hind feet, and a long, scaled tail. It is poisonous and lives in the region between the Earthly and Heavenly Oceans.

Its saliva gives humans the power to open the enchanted gateways at the top of the ziqqurats. If allowed out in the sun, the sirrush sheds its skin like a snake, emerging stronger and with wings.

Sumerian "Dead" language of Babylon, though many Sumerian tablets still exist. The language used for the riddle on Princess Amytis' seal.

tablets Babylonian "books". These are made of clay and have wedge-shaped writing (today called cuneiform) pressed into them while damp with a sharpened reed. When they dry, the writing sets hard. Sometimes they are sealed in clay envelopes with a copy of the writing on the outside.

Tashritu Seventh month of the Babylonian year – September/October.

Tree of Life A magical plant that grows beyond the Earthly Ocean and is supposed to give eternal life to whoever eats its leaves.

Twenty Squares A popular Babylonian game of chance and skill, played with seven black counters and seven white counters (and one die) on a specially-shaped board of twenty squares. Twenty Squares can be played at two skill levels, the first being a race, the second involving scoring. Only children retain the ability to use the Eye Symbol successfully. In this story, the best players from all the cities compete for the Twenty Squares Garland in Babylon each year.

Ululu Sixth month of the Babylonian year – August/September

Upper Sea Mediterranean Sea.

ziqqurat A seven-tiered tower of brick with staircases leading up the outside and a shrine on the topmost tier. Each tier is painted a different colour, the top two tiers being silver and gold. Babylon's ziqqurat is called the House of Heaven on Earth. Its shrine contains a magical map called the Map of the Seven Islands, showing the enchanted gateways between cities and between this world and the next. These gateways can be opened only by someone who has been "blessed by Marduk" – i.e. licked by a sirrush.

MAIN CLASSES OF SOCIETY

Nobles (awilum)
who live in the inner city and the palace.

Commoners (mushkenum)
who live and work in the outer city or
in the countryside.

Servants/slaves (wardum)

MAP OF THE SEVEN ISLANDS
Island 4
monsters
winged guardians
Island 5
Island 3
demons
ghosts
Island 6
Island 2
dragons (simush)
gods
Island 1
Island 7
spirits
URARTU
BITTER RIVER (Earthly Ocean)
SIPPAR
NINEVEH
AKKAD
ASSYRIA
BABYLON
BORSIPPA
ASHUR
RIVER PURATTU
DER
URUK
SUSA
SUMER
LOWER SEA
marsh
UR
HEAVENLY OCEAN (Zodiac)
Place where the sun is not seen

THE SEVEN FABULOUS WONDERS

THE GREAT PYRAMID ROBBERY

Magic, murder and mayhem spread through the Two Lands, when Senu, the son of a scribe, is forced to help build one of the largest and most magnificent pyramids ever recorded. He and his friend, Reonet, are sucked into a plot to rob the great pyramid of Khufu and an ancient curse is woken. Soon they are caught in a desperate struggle against forces from another world, and even Senu's mischievous ka, Red, finds his magical powers are dangerously tested.

000 711278 5

www.harpercollinschildrensbooks.co.uk

THE SEVEN FABULOUS WONDERS

THE AMAZON TEMPLE ·QUEST·

When King Philip of Macedon invites Lysippe's tribe of exiled Amazon warriors to join his army, they ride west eagerly, hoping to reclaim one of the Gryphon Stones of their ancestors. But others covet the power of the Stones, and the invitation is not all it seems.

Separated from her tribe and taken to Ephesos as a slave, soft-hearted Lysippe must find the Stone that can save her fatally wounded sister. Can Lysippe learn the ancient Amazon skills in time?

0007112807

THE

SEVEN FABULOUS WONDERS

THE MAUSOLEUM MURDER

Alexis has a magical gift, but it's not one he wants. It hasn't helped him find his father, who has mysteriously disappeared, or freed him from his hard-hearted stepmother. Alex's home is under seige, and he can't do anything about that either. But when Alex and his best friend meet Princess Phoebe, things start to change. Together, they must unlock the murderous secrets of Halicarnassos. Magic is the key, but there may be a high price to pay for bringing statues to life...

0 00 711281 5

Forthcoming titles...

THE STATUE OF ZEUS AT OLYMPIA

Persion terrorists, angry at Alexander the Great's invasion of their home, are targeting young athletes in this tale of treachery at the Olympic Games. Sosi has the power to save his friends, but first he must train in his brother's place and confront his own demons...

THE COLOSSUS OF RHODES

For years this titanic figure has guarded the harbour entrance on the island of Rhodes and kept watch over its people. But now a fatal prophecy foretells doom and destruction...

THE PHAROS AT ALEXANDRIA

In the days of the last Egyptian Queen, Cleopatra, the citizens of Alexandria fight for independence against the mighty Roman Empire. Their great lighthouse is the key to control of the port, but do they dare awaken the spirits of their ancestors...?

Katherine Roberts

I spent my childhood on the beaches of Devon and Cornwall, searching rock pools for weird creatures. My first stories, featuring some of these creatures with added magic, were told to my little brother at bedtime when I was eight. But it was another twenty-two years before I dared send anything to a publisher – initially short stories for adults, followed by my first children's book *Song Quest,* which won the Branford Boase Award in 2000. In the meantime, I went to university to study mathematics, worked as a computer programmer, exercised racehorses, and helped in a pet shop. I also learnt to fly a glider, morris dance, and ski down black runs... all these experiences creep into my books in fantastic ways!

The Seven Fabulous Wonders series grew out of my interest in ancient myths and legends and the creatures that inhabit them. Rather than re-tell the familiar tales, I wanted to explore what happens when legend meets history, and especially the gaps in-between that nobody knows very much about. In this series, you will meet seven extraordinary young people who lived in a time when magic and reality were closer than they are today – a time that gave birth to the fantastic fiction I so love to write.

Katherine Roberts, Ross-on-Wye
www.katherineroberts.com

The Great Pyramid Robbery

"A grand tale unravels – ancient curses, magical powers, dangerous forces and spirits make *The Great Pyramid Robbery* a wonderful fantasy-filled read! Unearth this fab book."
Funday Times

"A terrific tale of plots, curses and evil forces set in ancient Egypt."
Sunday Express

"I did nothing for the rest of the day except read it... from the first moment, it grips."
Susan Price, author of *The Sterkarm Handshake*

"Murder, magic, power struggles, spirits, adventure and a desperate race against time... all combine to make this a good choice."
School Librarian

The Babylon Game

"Katherine Roberts is a children's author of genuine skill and imagination, and *The Babylon Game* is one of her most engaging titles."
Publishing News

"Fast paced ... and starts the action straight away. Really good – recommended."
cool-reads.com

"Incredible story of adventures that twist and turn and will have you spellbound on every page."
Children's Book of the Week, South Wales Evening Post